TORMENTOR MINE

Anna Zaires

♠ Mozaika Publications ♠

Copyright © 2017 Anna Zaires and Dima Zales
http://annazaires.com/

Published by Mozaika Publications, an imprint of Mozaika LLC.
www.mozaikallc.com

Cover by Najla Qamber Designs
www.najlaqamberdesigns.com

e-ISBN: 978-1-63142-213-3
ISBN: 978-1-63142-214-0

PART 1

CHAPTER 1
PETER

5 Years Earlier, North Caucasus Mountains

"*P*apa!" The high-pitched squeal is followed by a patter of little feet as my son propels himself through the doorway, his dark waves bouncing around his glowing face.

Laughing, I catch his small, sturdy body as he launches himself at me. "Miss me, *pupsik*?"

"Yeah!" His short arms fold around my neck, and I inhale deeply, breathing in his sweet child scent. Though Pasha is almost three, he still smells like milk—like healthy baby and innocence.

I hold him tight and feel the iciness inside me melting as soft, bright warmth floods my chest. It's painful, like being submerged in hot water after freezing, but it's a good kind of pain. It makes me feel alive, fills the empty cracks inside me until I can almost believe I'm whole and deserving of my son's love.

"He did miss you," Tamila says, entering the hallway. As always, she moves quietly, almost soundlessly, her eyes downcast. She doesn't look at me directly. From childhood, she's been trained to avoid eye contact with men, so all I see are her long black lashes as she gazes at the floor. She's wearing a traditional headscarf that hides her long dark hair, and her gray dress is long and shapeless. However, she still looks beautiful—as beautiful as she did three and a half years ago, when she snuck into my bed to escape marriage to a village elder.

"And I've missed you both," I say as my son pushes at my shoulders, demanding to be free. Grinning, I lower him to the floor, and he immediately grabs my hand and tugs on it.

"Papa, do you want to see my truck? Do you, Papa?"

"I do," I say, my grin widening as he pulls me toward the living room. "What kind of truck is it?"

"A big one!"

"All right, let's see it."

Tamila trails behind us, and I realize I haven't spoken to her at all yet. Stopping, I turn around and look at my wife. "How are you?"

She peeks up at me through those eyelashes. "I'm good. I'm glad to see you."

"And I'm glad to see you." I want to kiss her, but she'll be embarrassed if I do it in front of Pasha, so I abstain. Instead, I gently touch her cheek, and then I let my son tow me to his truck, which I recognize as the one I sent him from Moscow three weeks ago.

He proudly demonstrates all the features of the toy as I crouch next to him, watching his animated face. He has Tamila's dark, exotic beauty, right down to the eyelashes, but there's something of me in him too, though I can't quite define what.

"He has your fearlessness," Tamila says quietly, kneeling next to me. "And I think he's going to be as tall as you, though it's probably too early to tell."

I glance at her. She often does this, observing me so closely it's almost as if she's reading my mind. Then again, it's not a stretch to guess what I'm thinking. I did have Pasha's paternity tested before he was born.

"Papa. Papa." My son tugs at my hand again. "Play with me."

I laugh and turn my attention back to him. For the next hour, we play with the truck and a dozen other toys, all of which happen to be some type of car. Pasha is obsessed with toy vehicles, everything from ambulances to race cars. No matter how many other toys I get him, he only plays with those that have wheels.

After playtime, we eat dinner, and Tamila bathes Pasha before bed. I notice that the bathtub is cracked and make a mental note to order a new one. The tiny village of Daryevo is high in the Caucasus Mountains and difficult to get to, so it can't be a regular delivery from a store, but I have ways of getting things here.

When I mention the idea to Tamila, her eyelashes sweep up, and she gives me a rare direct look, accompanied by a bright smile. "That would be very nice, thank you. I've had to mop up the floor almost every evening."

I smile back at her, and she finishes bathing Pasha. After she dries him and dresses him in his pajamas, I carry him off to bed and read him a story from his favorite book. He falls asleep almost immediately, and I kiss his smooth forehead, my heart squeezing with a powerful emotion.

It's love. I recognize it, even though I've never felt it before—even though a man like me has no right to feel it. None of the things I've done matter here, in this little village in Dagestan.

When I'm with my son, the blood on my hands doesn't burn my soul.

Careful not to wake Pasha, I get up and quietly exit the tiny room that serves as his bedroom. Tamila is already waiting for me in our bedroom, so I strip off my clothes and join her in bed, making love to her as tenderly as I can.

Tomorrow, I have to face the ugliness of my world, but tonight, I'm happy.

Tonight, I can love and be loved.

———————

"Don't leave, Papa." Pasha's chin quivers as he struggles not to cry. Tamila told him a few weeks ago that big boys don't cry, and he's been trying his hardest to be a big boy. "Please, Papa. Can't you stay a little longer?"

"I'll be back in a couple of weeks," I promise, crouching to be at his eye level. "I have to go to work, you see."

"You always have to go to work." His chin quivers harder, and his big brown eyes overflow with tears. "Why can't I come with you to work?"

Images of the terrorist I tortured last week invade my mind, and it's all I can do to keep my voice even as I say, "I'm sorry, Pashen'ka. My work is no place for children." Or for adults, for that matter, but I don't say that. Tamila knows some of what I do as part of a special unit of Spetsnaz, the Russian Special Forces, but even she is ignorant of the dark realities of my world.

"But I would be good." He's full-on crying now. "I promise, Papa. I would be good."

"I know you would be." I pull him against me and hug him tight, feeling his small body shaking with sobs. "You're my good boy, and you have to be good for Mama while I'm gone, okay? You have to take care of her, like the big boy you are."

Those appear to be the magic words, because he sniffles and pulls away. "I will." His nose is running and his cheeks are wet, but his little chin is firm as he meets my gaze. "I will take care of Mama, I promise."

"He's so smart," Tamila says, kneeling next to me to pull Pasha into her embrace. "It's like he's five, not almost three."

"I know." My chest swells with pride. "He's amazing."

She smiles and meets my gaze again, her big brown eyes so much like Pasha's. "Be safe, and come back to us soon, okay?"

"I will." I lean in and kiss her forehead, then ruffle Pasha's silky hair. "I'll be back before you know it."

I'm in Grozny, Chechnya, chasing down a lead on a new radical insurgency group, when I get the news. It's Ivan Polonsky, my superior in Moscow, who calls me.

"Peter." His voice is unusually grave as I pick up the phone. "There's been an incident in Daryevo."

My insides turn to ice. "What kind of incident?"

"There was an operation we weren't notified about. NATO was involved. There were… casualties."

The ice inside me expands, shredding me with its jagged edges, and it's all I can do to force the words through my closing throat. "Tamila and Pasha?"

"I'm sorry, Peter. Some villagers were killed in the crossfire, and"—he swallows audibly—"the preliminary reports are that Tamila was among them."

My fingers nearly crush the phone. "What about Pasha?"

"We don't know yet. There were several explosions, and—"

"I'm on my way."

"Peter, wait—"

I hang up and rush out the door.

Please, please, please, let him be alive. Please let him be alive. Please, I'll do anything, just let him be alive.

I've never been religious, but as the military helicopter makes its way through the mountains, I find myself praying, pleading and bargaining with whatever is up there for one small miracle, one small mercy. A child's life is meaningless in the big scheme of things, but it means everything to me.

My son is my life, my reason for existing.

The roar of the helicopter blades is deafening, but it's nothing compared to the clamor inside my head. I can't breathe, can't think through the rage and fear choking me from within. I don't know how Tamila died, but I've seen enough corpses to picture her body in my mind, to imagine with stark precision how her beautiful eyes appear blank and unseeing, her mouth slack and crusted with blood. And Pasha—

No. I can't think about it now. Not until I know for sure.

This wasn't supposed to happen. Daryevo is nowhere near the known hotspots in Dagestan. It's a small, peaceful settlement with no ties to any insurgent groups. They were supposed to be safe there, far away from my violent world.

Please let him be alive. Please let him be alive.

The ride seems to take forever, but finally, we break through the cloud cover, and I see the village. My throat closes up, cutting off my breath.

Smoke is rising from several buildings in the center, and armed soldiers are milling around.

I jump out of the helicopter the second it touches the ground.

"Peter, wait. You need clearance," the pilot shouts, but I'm already running, shoving people aside. A young soldier tries to block my path, but I rip his M16 out of his hands and point it at him.

"Take me to the bodies. Now."

I don't know if it's the weapon or the lethal edge in my voice, but the soldier obeys, hurrying toward a shed on the far end of the street. I follow him, the adrenaline like toxic sludge in my veins.

Please let him be alive. Please let him be alive.

I see the bodies behind the shed, some neatly laid out, others piled together on snow-speckled grass. There's nobody around them; the soldiers must be keeping the villagers away for now. I recognize some of the dead right away—the village elder Tamila was engaged to, the baker's wife, the man I once bought goat milk from—but others I can't identify, both because of the extent of their wounds and because I haven't spent much time in the village.

I've barely spent *any* time here, and now my wife is dead.

Steeling myself, I kneel next to a slender female body, lay the M16 on the grass, and move her headscarf off her face. A chunk of her head has been blown off by a bullet, but I can make out enough of her features to know it's not Tamila.

I move on to the next woman's body, this one with several bullet wounds through her chest. It's Tamila's aunt, a shy woman in her fifties who'd spoken less than five words to me in the last three years. To her and the rest of Tamila's family, I've always been a foreigner, a frightening stranger from a different world. They didn't understand Tamila's decision to marry me, condemned it even, but Tamila didn't care.

She'd always been independent like that.

Another female body draws my attention. The woman is lying on her side, but the gentle curve of her shoulder is achingly familiar. My hand shakes as I turn her over, and white-hot pain pierces me as I see her face.

Tamila's mouth is just as slack as I imagined, but her eyes aren't vacant. They're closed, her long eyelashes singed and her eyelids glued together with blood. More blood covers her chest and arms, turning her gray dress nearly black.

My wife, the beautiful young woman who had the courage to choose her own fate, is dead. She died without ever leaving her village, without seeing Moscow like she dreamed. Her life was snuffed out before she had a chance to live, and it's all my fault. I should've been here, should've protected her and Pasha. Hell, I should've known about this fucking operation; nobody should've been here without informing my team.

Rage rises inside me, mixing with agonizing grief and guilt, but I shove it aside and force myself to keep looking. There are only adult bodies laid out in the rows, but there's still that pile.

Please let him be alive. I'll do anything as long as he's alive.

My legs feel like burned matches as I approach the pile. There are detached limbs there, and bodies damaged beyond recognition. These must've been the victims of the explosions. I move each body part aside, sorting through them. The smell of stale blood and charred flesh is thick in the air. A normal man would've thrown up by now, but I've never been normal.

Please let him be alive.

"Peter, wait. There's a special task force on the way, and they don't want us touching the bodies." It's the pilot, Anton Rezov, approaching from behind the shed. We've worked together for years and he's a close friend, but if he tries to stop me, I will kill him.

Without replying, I continue my gruesome task, methodically looking over each limb and burned torso before laying it aside. Most of the body parts seem to belong to adults, though I come across some child-sized ones too. They're too big to be Pasha's, though, and I'm selfish enough to feel relief over that.

Then I see it.

"Peter, did you hear me? You can't do this yet." Anton reaches for my arm, but before he can touch me, I spin around, my hand curling automatically. My fist crashes into his jaw, and he reels back from the blow, his eyes rolling back in his head. I don't watch him fall; I'm already moving, tearing through the remaining pile of bodies to reach the little hand I saw earlier.

A little hand that's curled around a broken toy car.

Please, please, please. Please let there be a mistake. Please let him be alive. Please let him be alive.

I work like a man possessed, all my being focused on one goal: to get to that hand. Some of the bodies on top of the pile are nearly whole, but I don't feel their weight as I throw them aside. I don't feel the burn of exertion in my muscles or smell the sickening stench of violent death. I just bend and lift and throw until body parts are strewn all around me, and I'm drenched in blood.

I don't stop until the small body is uncovered in its entirety, and there's no longer any doubt.

Trembling, I sink to my knees, my legs unable to hold me.

By some miracle, the right half of Pasha's face is undamaged, his smooth baby skin unmarred by so much as a scratch. One of his eyes is closed, his little mouth parted, and if he were lying on his side like Tamila was, he could've been mistaken for a sleeping child. But he's not lying on his side, and I see the gaping hole where the explosion ripped away half of his skull. His left arm is missing too, as is his left leg below the knee. His right arm, however, is unscathed, its fingers curled convulsively around the toy car.

In the distance, I hear a howl, a mad, broken sound of inhuman rage. It's only when I find myself clutching the little body to my chest that I realize the sound is coming from me. I fall silent then, but I can't stop rocking back and forth.

I can't stop hugging him.

I don't know how long I stay like that, holding my son's remains, but it's dark by the time the task force soldiers come. I don't fight them. There's no point. My son is gone, his bright light extinguished before it had a chance to shine.

"I'm sorry," I whisper as they drag me away. With each meter of distance between us, the cold inside me grows, the remnants of my humanity bleeding out of my soul. There's no more pleading, no more bargaining with anyone or anything. I'm empty of hope, devoid of warmth and love. I can't turn back the clock and hold my son longer, can't stay behind like he asked me to. Can't take Tamila to Moscow next year, like I promised her I would.

There's only one thing I can do for my wife and son, and that's the reason I'll keep on living.

I will make their killers pay.

Each and every single one of them.

They will answer for this massacre with their lives.

CHAPTER 2
SARA

United States, Present Day

"Are you sure you don't want to come out for drinks with me and the girls?" Marsha asks, approaching my locker. She's already changed out of her nurse's scrubs and put on a sexy dress. With her bright red lipstick and flamboyant blond curls, she looks like an older version of Marilyn Monroe and likes to party just as much.

"No, thank you. I can't." I soften my refusal with a smile. "It's been a long day, and I'm exhausted."

She rolls her eyes. "Of course you are. You're always exhausted these days."

"Work will do that to you."

"Yeah, if you work ninety hours a week. If I didn't know better, I'd say you're trying to work yourself to death. You're no longer a resident, you know? You don't have to put up with this bullshit."

I sigh and pick up my bag. "Someone has to be on call."

"Yes, but it doesn't have to be you all the time. It's Friday night, and you've worked every weekend for the past month, plus all those nightshifts. I know you're the newest doctor in your practice and all that, but—"

"I don't mind the nightshifts," I interrupt, walking over to the mirror. The mascara I put on this morning has left dark smudges under my eyes, and I use a wet paper towel to wipe them away. It doesn't improve my haggard appearance much, but I suppose it doesn't matter, since I'm heading straight home.

"Right, because you don't sleep," Marsha says, coming to stand behind me, and I brace myself, knowing she's about to get on her favorite topic. Though she has a good fifteen years on me, Marsha is my best friend at the hospital, and she's been increasingly vocal about her concerns.

"Marsha, please. I'm too tired for this," I say, pulling my unruly waves into a ponytail. I don't need a lecture to know I'm running myself ragged. My hazel eyes look red and bleary in the mirror, and I feel like I'm sixty instead of twenty-eight.

"Yeah, because you're overworked and sleep-deprived." She folds her arms across her chest. "I know you need a distraction after George and all, but—"

"But nothing." Spinning around, I glare at her. "I don't want to talk about George."

"Sara…" Her forehead furrows. "You have to stop punishing yourself for that. It wasn't your fault. He *chose* to get behind the wheel; it was *his* decision."

My throat closes, and my eyes prickle. To my horror, I realize I'm on the verge of crying, and I turn away in an effort to control myself. Only there's nowhere to turn; the mirror is in front of me, and it reflects everything I'm feeling.

"I'm sorry, hon. I'm an insensitive ass. I shouldn't have said that." Marsha looks genuinely regretful as she reaches over and squeezes my arm lightly.

I take a deep breath and turn around to face her again. I *am* exhausted, which doesn't help the emotions threatening to overwhelm me.

"It's all right." I force a smile to my lips. "It's no big deal. You should get going; the girls are probably waiting for you." And I have to get home before I break down and cry in public, which would be the height of humiliation.

"All right, hon." Marsha smiles back at me, but I see the pity lurking in her gaze. "You just get some sleep this weekend, okay? Promise me you'll do that."

"Yes, I will—*Mom.*"

She rolls her eyes. "Yeah, yeah, I get the hint. I'll see you Monday." She walks out of the locker room, and I wait a minute before following her to avoid running into her group of girlfriends in the elevators.

I've had about as much pity as I can handle.

As I enter the hospital parking lot, I check my phone out of habit, and my heart skips a beat when I see a text from a blocked number.

Stopping, I swipe across the screen with an unsteady finger.

All is well, but have to postpone this weekend's visit, the message says. *Scheduling conflict.*

My breath whooshes out in relief, and right away, the familiar guilt bites at me. I shouldn't feel relieved. These visits should be something I want to do, instead of an unpleasant obligation. Only I can't help the way I feel. Every time I visit George, it brings back memories of that night, and I don't sleep for days afterward.

If Marsha thinks I'm sleep-deprived now, she should see me after one of those visits.

Slipping the phone back into my bag, I approach my car. It's a Toyota Camry, the same one I've had for the past five years. Now that I've paid off my med school loans and accumulated some savings, I can afford better, but I don't see the point.

George was the one into cars, not me.

The pain grabs at me, familiar and sharp, and I know it's because of that text. Well, that and the conversation with Marsha. Lately, I've had days when I don't think about the accident at all, going about my routine without the crushing pressure of guilt, but today is not one of those days.

He was an adult, I remind myself, repeating what everyone always says. *It was his decision to get behind the wheel that day.*

Rationally, I know the truth of those words, but no matter how often I hear them, they don't sink in. My mind is stuck on a loop, replaying that evening over and over again, and as hard as I try, I can't stop the ugly reel from spinning.

Enough, Sara. Concentrate on the road.

Taking a steadying breath, I pull out of the parking lot and head toward my house. It's about a forty-minute drive from the hospital, which is about forty minutes too long right now. My stomach is beginning to cramp, and I realize part of the reason I'm so emotional today is that I'm about to start my period. As an OB-GYN, I know better than anyone how powerful the effect of hormones can be, and when PMS is combined with long hours and reminders about George... Well, it's a miracle I'm not a blubbering mess already.

Yes, that's it. I'm just hormonal and tired. I need to get home, and all will be well.

Determined to get a handle on myself, I turn on the radio, tune in to a late-nineties pop station, and begin singing along with Britney Spears. It might not be the most serious music, but it's upbeat, and that's exactly what I need.

I won't let myself fall apart. Tonight, I *will* sleep, even if I have to take an Ambien to make that happen.

My house is on a tree-lined cul-de-sac, just off a two-lane road that winds through farmland. Like many others in the upscale area of Homer Glen, Illinois, it's huge—five bedrooms and four baths, plus a fully finished basement. There's an enormous back yard, and so many oaks surround the house it's as if it's sitting in the middle of a forest.

It's perfect for that big family George wanted and horribly lonely for me.

After the accident, I considered selling the house and moving closer to the hospital, but I couldn't bring myself to do it. I still can't. George and I renovated the house together, modernizing the kitchen and the bathrooms, painstakingly decorating each room to give it a cozy, welcoming vibe. A *family* vibe. I know the odds of us having that family are nonexistent now, but a part of me clings to the old dream, to the perfect life we were supposed to have.

"Three kids, at least," George told me on our fifth date. "Two boys and a girl."

"Why not two girls and a boy?" I asked, grinning. "What happened to gender equality and all that?"

"How is two against one equal? Everybody knows girls twist you around their pretty little fingers, and when you have two of them..." He shuddered theatrically. "No, we need two boys, so there's balance in the family. Otherwise, Daddy is screwed."

I laughed and punched him in the shoulder, but secretly, I liked the idea of two boys running around raising hell and protecting their little sister. I'm an only child, but I've always wanted a big brother, and it was easy to adopt George's dream as my own.

No. Don't go there. With effort, I push away the memories, because good or bad, they lead to that evening, and I can't cope with that now. The cramps have gotten worse, and it's all I can do to keep my hands on the wheel as I pull into my three-car garage. I need Advil, a heating pad, and my bed, in that order, and if I'm really lucky, I'll pass out right away, no Ambien required.

Holding back a groan, I close the garage door, punch in the code for the alarm, and drag myself into the house. The cramps are so bad I can't walk without bending, so

I head straight for the medicine cabinet in the kitchen. I don't even bother turning on the lights; the light switch is inconveniently far from the garage entrance, plus I know the kitchen well enough to navigate around it in the dark.

Opening the cabinet, I find the Advil bottle by feel, extract two pills, and throw them in my mouth. Then I go to the sink, fill my hand with water, and swallow the pills. Panting, I grip the kitchen counter and wait for the medicine to kick in a little before I attempt to do something as ambitious as going to the master bedroom on the second floor.

I feel him only a second before it happens. It's subtle, just a displacement of air behind me, a whiff of something foreign... a sense of sudden danger.

The hairs on the back of my neck rise, but it's too late. One moment, I'm standing by the sink, and the next, a big hand is covering my mouth as a large, hard body traps me against the counter from the back.

"Don't scream," a deep male voice whispers in my ear, and something cold and sharp presses against my throat. "You don't want my blade to slip."

CHAPTER 3

SARA

I don't scream. Not because it's the smart thing to do, but because I can't make a sound. I'm frozen by terror, utterly and completely paralyzed. All my muscles have locked up, including my vocal cords, and my lungs have ceased functioning.

"I'm going to remove my hand from your mouth," he murmurs into my ear, his breath warm on my clammy skin. "And you're going to stay silent. Got it?"

I can't so much as whimper, but I somehow manage a faint nod.

He lowers his hand, his arm looping around my ribcage instead, and my lungs choose that moment to resume working. Without meaning to, I pull in a wheezing breath. Immediately, the blade presses deeper into my skin, and I freeze again as I feel hot blood trickling down my neck.

I'm going to die. Oh God, I'm going to die here, in my own kitchen. The terror is a monstrous thing inside me, piercing me with icy needles. I've never been so close to death before. Just an inch to the right and—

"I need you to listen to me, Sara." The intruder's voice is soft, belying the knife digging into my throat. "If you cooperate, you'll walk out of here alive. If you don't, you'll leave in a body bag. It's your choice."

Alive? A spark of hope cuts through the haze of panic in my brain, and I realize he has a faint accent. It's something exotic. Middle Eastern, maybe, or Eastern European.

Oddly, that detail centers me a little, provides something concrete for my mind to latch on to. "W-what do you want?" The words come out in a quaking whisper, but it's a miracle I can speak at all. I feel like a deer in the headlights, stunned and overwhelmed, my thought processes bizarrely slow.

"Just a few answers," he says, and the knife retreats slightly. Without the cold steel cutting into my skin, some of my panic subsides, and other details register, like the fact that my assailant is at least a head taller than me and packed with muscle. The arm around my ribcage is like a steel band, and there's no give in the large body pressing against my back, no hint of softness anywhere. I'm of average height for a woman, but I'm slim and small-boned, and if he's as muscular as I suspect, he must be almost double my weight.

Even if he didn't have the knife, I wouldn't be able to get away.

"What kind of answers?" My voice is a little steadier this time. Maybe he's just here to rob me and all he needs is the combination to the safe. He smells clean, like laundry detergent and healthy male skin, so this is not some meth addict or bum off the streets. A professional burglar, maybe? If so, I'll gladly give up my jewelry and the emergency cash George stashed in the house.

"I want you to tell me about your husband. Specifically, I need to know his location."

"George?" My mind goes blank as a new fear bites at me. "W-what... why?"

The blade presses in. "I'm the one asking questions."

"P-please," I choke out. I can't think, can't focus on anything but the knife. Hot tears slide down my face, and I'm shaking all over. "Please, I don't—"

"Just answer my question. Where is your husband?"

"I—" Oh God, what do I tell him? He must be one of *them*, the reason for all the precautions. My heart is beating so fast I'm hyperventilating. "Please, I don't... I haven't—"

"Don't lie to me, Sara. I need his location. Now."

"I don't know it, I swear. Please, we're—" My voice cracks. "We're separated."

The arm around my ribcage tightens, and the knife digs in a fraction deeper. "Do you want to die?"

"No. No, I don't. Please..." I'm shaking harder, the tears streaming down my face uncontrollably. After the accident, there were days when I thought I wanted to die, when the guilt and pain of regrets were overwhelming, but now that the blade is at my throat, I want to live. I want it so badly.

"Then tell me where he is."

"I don't know!" My knees are threatening to buckle, but I can't betray George like this. I can't expose him to this monster.

"You're lying." My assailant's voice is pure ice. "I've read your messages. You know exactly where he is."

"No, I—" I try to think of a plausible lie, but I can't come up with one. Panic is acrid on my tongue as frantic questions pop into my mind. How could he have read my messages? When? How long has he been stalking me? Is he one of *them*? "I—I don't know what you're talking about."

The knife presses in a hair deeper, and I squeeze my eyes shut, my breath coming in sobbing gasps. Death is so close I can taste it, smell it… feel it with every fiber of my being. It's the metallic tang of my blood and the cold sweat running down my back, the roar of my pulse in my temples and the tension in my quivering muscles. In another second, he'll nick my jugular, and I'll bleed out, right here on my kitchen floor.

Is this what I deserve? Is this how I atone for my sins?

I clench my teeth to prevent them from chattering. *Please forgive me, George. If this is what you need…*

I hear my attacker sigh, and in the next instant, the knife is gone and I'm flipped over onto the counter. My back hits the hard granite, and my head flops backward into the sink, my neck muscles screaming from the strain. Gasping, I kick out and try to punch him, but he's too strong and fast. In a flash, he leaps onto the counter and straddles me, pinning me in place with his weight. He secures my wrists with something hard and unbreakable before gripping them with one hand, and no matter how hard

I struggle, I can't do anything to get free. My heels slide uselessly on the sleek counter, and my neck muscles burn from holding up my head. I'm helpless, pinned down, and a new kind of panic washes over me.

Please, God, no. Anything but rape.

"We're going to try something different," he says, and a piece of cloth drops over my face. "See if you're truly willing to die for that bastard."

Panting, I twist my head from side to side, trying to throw off the cloth, but it's too long and I can barely breathe underneath it. Is he trying to suffocate me? Is that the plan?

Then the faucet handle squeaks, and everything becomes clear.

"No!" I struggle harder, but he grips my hair with his free hand, holding me under the faucet with my head arched back.

The initial shock of wetness isn't so bad, but within seconds, the water travels up my nose. My throat clenches, my lungs seize, and my whole body heaves up as I gag and choke. The panic is instinctive, uncontrollable. The rag is like a wet paw clamped over my nose and mouth, squeezing them shut. The water is in my nose, in my throat. I'm suffocating, drowning. I can't breathe, can't breathe...

The faucet turns off, and the cloth is yanked off my face. Coughing, I suck in air, sobbing and wheezing. My whole body is a heaving, trembling mess, and white spots dance in my vision. Before I can recover, the cloth is slapped over my face again, and the water is turned back on.

This time, it's even worse. My nasal passages burn from the water, and my lungs scream for air. I'm heaving and gagging, choking and crying. I can't breathe. *Oh, God, I'm dying; I can't breathe*—

In the next instant, the cloth is gone, and I'm convulsively dragging in air.

"Tell me where he is, and I'll stop." His voice is a dark whisper above me.

"I don't know! Please!" I can taste the vomit in my throat, and the knowledge that he'll do it again turns my blood into acid. It was easy to be brave with the knife, but not this. I can't handle dying like this.

"Last chance," my tormentor says softly, and the wet cloth drops over my face.

The faucet begins to squeak.

"Stop! Please!" The scream is wrenched out of me. "I'll tell you! I'll tell you."

The water turns off, and the cloth is pulled off my face. "Speak."

I'm sobbing and coughing too hard to form a coherent sentence, so he pulls me off the counter to the floor and crouches to encircle me in his arms. To someone looking in, it might've seemed like a consoling embrace or a lover's protective hold. Adding to the illusion, my torturer's voice is soft and gentle as he croons in my ear, "Tell me, Sara. Tell me what I want to know, and I'll leave."

"He's—" I stop a second from blurting out the truth. The panicked animal inside me demands survival at all costs, but I can't do this. I can't lead this monster to George. "He's in Advocate Christ Hospital," I choke out. "The long-term care unit."

It's a lie, and apparently not a good one, because the arms around me tighten, nearly crushing my bones. "Don't fucking bullshit me." The soft croon in his voice is gone, replaced by biting rage. "He's gone from there—has been gone for months. Where is he hiding?"

I'm sobbing harder. "I... I don't—"

My assailant rises to his feet, pulling me up with him, and I scream and struggle as he drags me toward the sink. "No! Please, no!" I'm hysterical as he lifts me onto the counter, my bound hands swinging as I try to claw at his face. My heels drum on the granite as he straddles me, pinning me in place again, and bile rises in my throat as he grips my hair, arching my head back into the sink. "Stop!"

"Tell me the truth, and I'll stop."

"I—I can't. Please, I can't!" I can't do this to George, not after everything. "Stop, please!"

The wet cloth slaps over my face, and my throat seizes in panic. The water is still off, but I'm already drowning; I can't breathe, can't breathe...

"Fuck!"

I'm abruptly yanked off the counter and onto the floor, where I collapse in a sobbing, shaking heap. Only this time, there are no arms to restrain me, and I dimly realize he stepped away.

I should get up and run, but my hands are tied and I can't make my legs function. All I can manage is a pathetic roll to the side, followed by an attempt at a crawl. The fear is blinding, disorienting, and I can't see anything in the darkness.

I can't see *him*.

Run, I will my limp, shaking muscles. *Get up and run.*

Sucking in air, I grab at something—a countertop corner—and pull myself up to my feet. Only it's too late; he's already on me, the hard band of his arm wrapping around my ribcage as he grabs me from behind.

"Let's see if this works better," he whispers, and something cold and sharp stabs me in the neck.

A needle, I realize with a jolt of terror, and my consciousness fades away.

A face swims in front of my eyes. It's a handsome face, beautiful even, despite the scar that bisects the left eyebrow. High, slanted cheekbones, steel-gray eyes framed by black lashes, a strong jaw darkened by five-o'clock shadow—a man's face, my mind supplies fuzzily. His hair is thick and dark, longer on the top than the sides. Not an old man, then, but not a teenager either. A man in his prime.

The face is wearing a frown, its features set in harsh, grim lines. "George Cobakis," the hard, sculpted mouth says. It's a sexy mouth, well shaped, but I hear the words as though from a megaphone in the distance. "Do you know where he is?"

I nod, or at least I attempt to. My head feels heavy, my neck strangely sore. "Yes, I know where he is. I thought I knew him too, but I didn't, not really. Do you ever really know someone? I don't think so, or at least I didn't know *him*. I thought I knew, but I didn't. All those years together, and everyone thought we were so perfect. The perfect couple, they called us. Can you believe it? The perfect couple.

We were the cream of the crop, the young doctor and the rising star journalist. They said he'd win a Pulitzer prize one day." I'm vaguely aware I'm babbling, but I can't stop. The words pour out of me, all the pent-up bitterness and pain. "My parents were so proud, so happy on our wedding day. They had no idea, no idea at all about what was come, what would happen—"

"Sara. Focus on me," the megaphone voice says, and I catch a hint of a foreign accent. It pleases me, that accent, makes me want to reach over and press my hand to those sculpted lips, then run my fingers over that hard jaw to see if it's bristly. I like bristly. George would often come home from his trips abroad, and he'd be all bristly and I liked it. I liked it, though I'd tell him to shave. He looked better clean-shaven, but I liked feeling the bristle sometimes, liked feeling that roughness on my thighs when he'd—

"Sara, stop," the voice cuts in, and the frown on the exotically handsome face deepens.

I was speaking out loud, I realize, but I don't feel embarrassed, not at all. The words don't belong to me; they just come of their own accord. My hands act of their own accord too, attempting to reach over to that face, but something stops them, and when I lower my heavy head to look down, I see a plastic zip tie around my wrists, with a man's big hand over my palms. It's warm, that hand, and it's holding my hands pinned down on my lap. Why is it doing that? Where did the hand come from? When I look up in confusion, the face is closer, its gray eyes peering into mine.

"I need you to tell me where your husband is," the mouth says, and the megaphone moves closer. It sounds like it's right next to my ear. I cringe, but at the same time, that mouth intrigues me. Those lips make me want to touch them, lick them, feel them on my—wait. They're asking something.

"Where my husband is?" My voice sounds like it's bouncing off the walls.

"Yes, George Cobakis, your husband." The lips look tempting as they form the words, and the accent caresses my insides despite the persistent megaphone effect. "Tell me where he is."

"He's safe. He's in a safe house," I say. "They could come for him. They didn't want him to run that story, but he did. He was brave like that, or stupid—probably stupid, right?—and then the accident happened, but they could still come for him, because they do that. The mafia doesn't care that he's a vegetable now, a cucumber, a tomato, a zucchini. Well, tomato is a fruit, but he's a vegetable. A broccoli, maybe? I don't know. It's not important, anyway. It's just that they want to make an example of him, threaten other journalists who'd stand up to them. That's what they do; that's how they operate. It's all about greasing palms and bribing, and when you shed light on that—"

"Where is the safe house?" There is a dark light in those steely eyes. "Tell me the address of the safe house."

"I don't know the address, but it's on the corner near Ricky's Laundromat in Evanston," I say to those eyes. "They always bring me there in a car, so I don't know the exact address, but I saw that building from a window. There are at least two men in that car, and they drive around forever, switch cars sometimes too. It's because of the mafia, because they might be watching. They always send a car for me, and they couldn't this weekend. Scheduling conflict, they said. It happens sometimes; the guards' shifts don't align and—"

"How many guards are there?"

"Three, sometimes four. They're these big military guys. Or ex-military, I don't know. They just have that look. I don't know why, but they all have that look. It's like witness protection, but not, because he needs special care and I can't leave my job. I don't want to leave my job. They said they could move me, have me disappear, but I don't want to disappear. My patients need me, plus my parents. What would I do with my parents? Never see or call them again? No, that's crazy. So they disappeared the vegetable, the cucumber, the broccoli—"

"Sara, hush." Fingers press against my mouth, stopping the stream of words, and the face moves even closer. "You can stop now. It's over," the sexy mouth murmurs, and I open my lips, sucking in those fingers. I can taste salt and skin, and I want more, so I swirl my tongue around the fingers, feeling the roughness of the calluses and the blunt edges of the short nails. It's been so long since I've touched someone, and my body heats from this small taste, from the look in those silver eyes.

"Sara…" The accented voice is lower now, deeper and softer. It's less of a megaphone and more of a sensual echo, like music done on a synthesizer. "You don't want to go there, *ptichka*."

Oh, but I do. I want to go there badly. I keep swirling my tongue around the fingers, and I watch the gray eyes

31

darken, the pupils visibly expanding. It's a sign of arousal, I know, and it makes me want to do more. It makes me want to kiss those sculpted lips, rub my cheek against that bristly jaw. And the hair, that thick dark hair. Would it feel soft or springy? I want to know, but I can't move my hands, so I just take the fingers deeper into my mouth, making love to them with my lips and tongue, sucking on them like they're candy.

"Sara." The voice is thick and husky, the face tight with barely restrained hunger. "You have to stop, ptichka. You'll regret this tomorrow."

Regret? Yes, I probably will. I regret everything, so many things, and I release the fingers to say so. But before I can utter a word, the fingers pull away from my lips, and the face moves farther away.

"Don't leave me." The cry is plaintive, like that of a clingy child. I want more of that human touch, that connection. My head feels like a bag of rocks, and I ache all over, especially near my neck and shoulders. My belly is cramping too. I want someone to brush my hair and massage my neck, to hold me and rock me like a baby. "Please, don't leave."

Something resembling pain crosses the man's face, and I feel the cold prick of the needle in my neck again.

"Goodbye, Sara," the voice murmurs, and I'm gone, my mind floating away like a fallen leaf.

CHAPTER 4
SARA

The headache. I first become aware of the headache. My skull feels like it's splitting into pieces, the waves of pain a drumbeat in my brain.

"Dr. Cobakis... Sara, can you hear me?" The female voice is soft and gentle, but it fills me with dread. There's worry in that voice, mixed with restrained urgency. I hear that tone in the hospital all the time, and it's never good.

Trying not to move my throbbing skull, I pry my eyelids open and blink spasmodically at the bright light. "What... where..." My tongue is thick and unwieldy, my mouth painfully dry.

"Here, sip this." A straw is placed near my mouth, and I latch on to it, greedily sucking in the water. My eyes are starting to adjust to the light, and I can make out the room. It's a hospital, but not my hospital, judging from the unfamiliar decor. Also, I'm not where I usually am. I'm not standing by someone's hospital bed; I'm lying in one.

"What happened?" I ask hoarsely. As my mind clears, I become aware of nausea and an array of aches and pains. My back feels like one giant bruise, and my neck is stiff and sore. My throat feels raw too, as though I've been screaming or vomiting, and when I lift my hand to touch it, I find a thick bandage on the right side of my neck.

"You were attacked, Dr. Cobakis," a middle-aged black woman says softly, and I recognize her voice as the one who spoke earlier. She's dressed in nursing scrubs, but somehow she doesn't look like a nurse. When I stare at her blankly, she clarifies, "In your house. There was a man. Do you remember anything about that?"

I blink, straining to make sense of that confusing statement. I feel like a giant cotton ball has been stuffed into my brain, alongside the beating drum. "My house? Attacked?"

"Yes, Dr. Cobakis," a male voice answers, and I flinch instinctively, my pulse jumping before I recognize the voice. "But you're safe now. It's over. This is a private facility where we treat our agents; you're safe here."

Carefully turning my aching head, I gaze at Agent Ryson, and my stomach hollows at the expression on his pale, weathered face. Bits and pieces of my ordeal are filtering in, and with the memories comes a surge of terror.

"George, is he—"

"I'm sorry." The creases in Ryson's forehead deepen. "There was an attack on the safe house last night as well. George... He didn't make it. Neither did the three guards."

"What?" It's as if a scalpel punctured my lungs. I can't take in his words, can't process the enormity of them. "He's... he's gone?" Then the rest of his statement sinks in. "And the three guards? What... how—"

"Dr. Cobakis—Sara." Ryson steps closer. "I need to know exactly what happened last night, so we can apprehend him."

"Him? Who's *him*?" It's always been *them*, the mafia, and I'm too dazed for the sudden change in pronoun. George is gone. George and three guards. I can't wrap my mind around that, so I don't try. Not yet, at least. Before I let the grief and pain in, I need to recover more of those memories, piece together the horrifying puzzle.

"She might not remember. The cocktail in her blood was pretty potent," the nurse says, and I realize she must be with Agent Ryson. That would explain why he's speaking so freely in front of her when he's usually discreet to the point of paranoia.

As I process that, the woman steps closer. I'm hooked up to a vital signs monitor, and she checks the blood pressure cuff around my arm, then gives my forearm a light squeeze. I look at my arm, and a cold fist grips my chest when I see a thin red line around my wrist. The other wrist has it too.

Zip tie. The recollection comes to me with sudden clarity. There was a zip tie around my wrists.

"He waterboarded me. When I wouldn't tell him where George was, he stuck a needle in my neck."

I don't realize I spoke out loud until I see the horror on the nurse's face. Agent Ryson's expression is more re-strained, but I can tell I shocked him too.

"I'm so sorry about that." His voice is tight. "We should've foreseen this, but he hadn't gone after the fami-lies of the others, and you didn't want to move away... Still, we should've known he wouldn't stop at anything—"

"What others? Who is he?" My voice rises as more memories assault my mind. *Knife at my throat, wet cloth over my face, needle in my neck, can't breathe, can't breathe...*

"Karen, she's having a panic attack! Do something." Ryson's voice is frantic as the monitors start to beep. I'm hyperventilating and shaking, yet I somehow find the strength to glance at those monitors. My blood pressure is spiking, and my pulse is dangerously fast, but seeing those numbers steadies me. I'm a doctor. This is my environ-ment, my comfort zone.

I can do this. *Suck in air. Let it out.* I'm not weak. *Suck in air. Let it out.*

"That's good, Sara. Just breathe." Karen's voice is soft and soothing as she strokes my arm. "You're getting the hang of it. Just take another deep breath. There you go. Good job. Now another. And one more..."

I follow her gentle instructions as I watch the numbers on the monitors, and slowly, the suffocating sensation re-cedes and my vitals normalize. More dark memories are edging in, but I'm not ready to face them yet, so I shove them aside, slam a mental door on them as tightly as I can.

"Who is he?" I ask when I can speak again. "What do you mean by 'the others?' George wrote that article by himself. Why is the mafia after someone else?"

Agent Ryson exchanges looks with Karen, then turns to me. "Dr. Cobakis, I'm afraid we weren't entirely truthful with you. We didn't disclose the real situation to protect you, but clearly, we failed in that." He takes a breath. "It wasn't the local mafia who was after your husband. It was an international fugitive, a dangerous criminal your husband encountered on an assignment abroad."

"What?" My head throbs painfully, the revelations almost too much to take in. George started off as a foreign correspondent, but in the last five years, he'd been taking on more and more domestic stories. I'd wondered about that, given his passion for foreign affairs, but when I asked, he told me he wanted to spend more time home with me, and I let it drop.

"This man, he has a list of people who have crossed him—or who he thinks have crossed him," Ryson says. "I'm afraid George was on that list. The exact circumstances around that and the identity of the fugitive are classified, but given what happened, you deserve to know the truth—at least as much of it as I'm allowed to disclose."

I stare at him. "It was one man? A fugitive?" A face pops into my mind, a harshly beautiful male face. It's hazy, like an image from a dream, but somehow I know it's him, the man who invaded my home and did those terrible things to me.

Ryson nods. "Yes. He's highly trained and has vast resources, which is why he's been able to stay ahead of us for so long. He has connections everywhere, from Eastern Europe to South America to the Middle East. When we learned that your husband's name was on his list, we took George to the safe house, and we should've done the same with you. We just thought that—" He stops and shakes his head. "I suppose it doesn't matter what we thought. We underestimated him, and now four men are dead."

Dead. Four men are dead. It hits me then, the knowledge that George is gone. I hadn't registered it before, not really. My eyes begin to burn, and my chest feels like it's being squeezed in a vise. In a burst of clarity, the puzzle pieces click into place.

"It's me, isn't it?" I sit up, ignoring the wave of dizziness and pain. "I did this. I somehow gave away the safe house location."

Ryson exchanges another look with the nurse, and my heart drops. They're not answering my question, but their body language speaks volumes.

I'm responsible for George's death. For all four deaths.

"It's not your fault, Dr. Cobakis." Karen touches my arm again, her brown eyes filled with sympathy. "The drug he gave you would've broken anyone. Are you familiar with sodium thiopental?"

"The barbiturate anesthetic?" I blink at her. "Of course. It was widely used to induce anesthesia until propofol became the standard. What does—oh."

"Yes," Agent Ryson says. "I see you know about its other use. It's rarely utilized that way, at least outside the intelligence community, but it's quite effective as a truth serum. Lowers the higher cortical brain functions and makes the subjects chatty and cooperative. And this was a designer version, thiopental mixed with compounds we haven't seen before."

"He drugged me to make me talk?" My stomach churns with bile. This explains the headache and the brain fog, and the knowledge that this was done to me—that I was violated like that—makes me want to scrub inside my skull with bleach. That man didn't just invade my home; he invaded my mind, broke into it like a thief.

"That's our best guess, yes," Ryson says. "You had a lot of this drug in your system when our agents found you tied up in your living room. There was also blood on your neck and thighs, and they initially thought that—"

"Blood on my thighs?" I brace myself for a new horror. "Did he—"

"No, don't worry, he didn't hurt you that way," Karen says, shooting Ryson a dark look. "We did a full-body examination when you were brought in, and it was your menstrual blood, nothing more. There were no signs of sexual trauma. Other than a few bruises and the shallow cuts on your neck, you're fine—or you will be, once the drugs wear off."

Fine. Hysterical laughter bubbles up my throat, and it takes all my strength not to let it escape. My husband and three other men are dead because of me. My home was broken into; my *mind* was broken into. And she thinks I'm going to be fine?

"Why did you make up that lie about the mafia?" I ask, struggling to contain the expanding ball of pain in my chest. "How would that protect me?"

"Because in the past, this fugitive hadn't gone after the innocent—the wives and children of the people on his list who weren't involved in any way," Ryson says. "But he did kill one man's sister because that man confided in her and involved her in the cover-up. The less you knew, the safer you were, especially since you didn't want to relocate and disappear alongside your husband."

"Ryson, please," Karen says sharply, but it's too late. I'm already reeling from this new blow. Even if I could be forgiven for my drug-induced blabbing, my refusal to leave is solely on me. I'd been selfish, thinking of my parents and my career instead of the danger I could pose to my husband. I believed *my* safety was on the line, not his, but that's no excuse.

George's death is on my conscience, just as much as the accident that damaged his brain.

"Did he—" I swallow thickly. "Did he suffer? I mean… how did it happen?"

"A bullet to the head," Ryson answers in a subdued tone. "Same as the three men guarding him. I think it happened too quickly for any of them to suffer."

"Oh God." My stomach heaves with sudden violence, and vomit rushes up my throat.

Karen must've seen my face leach of color, because she acts fast, grabbing a metal tray off a nearby table and shoving it in my hands. It's just in time too, because the contents of my stomach spill out, the acid burning my esophagus as I hold the tray with shaking hands.

"It's okay. It's okay. Here, let's get you cleaned up." Karen is all brisk efficiency, just like a real nurse. Whatever her role with the FBI is, she knows what to do in a medical setting. "Come, let me help you to the bathroom. You'll feel better in a second."

Setting the tray on the bedside table, she loops an arm around my back to help me off the bed and leads me to the bathroom. My legs are shaking so hard I can barely walk; if it weren't for her support, I wouldn't have made it.

Still, I need a moment of privacy, so I tell Karen, "Can you please step out for a moment? I'm okay for now."

I must sound convincing enough because Karen says, "I'll be right outside if you need me," and closes the door behind her.

I'm sweating and shaking, but I manage to rinse out my mouth and brush my teeth. Then I take care of other urgent business, wash my hands, and splash cold water on my face. By the time Karen knocks on the door, I'm feeling a tiny bit more human.

I'm also keeping my mind blank. If I think about the way George and the others died, I'll throw up again. I've seen a number of gunshot wounds during my residency stint in the ER, and I know the devastating damage bullets inflict.

Don't think about it. Not yet.

"Have my parents been notified?" I ask after Karen helps me return to the bed. She's already removed the tray, and Agent Ryson is sitting in a chair next to the bed, his craggy face lined with weary tension.

"No," Karen says softly. "Not yet. We wanted to discuss that with you, actually."

I look at her, then at Ryson. "Discuss what?"

"Dr. Cobakis—Sara—we think it might be best if the exact circumstances of your husband's demise, as well as the attack on you, were kept confidential," Ryson says. "It would save you a lot of unpleasant media attention, as well as—"

"You mean, it would save *you* a lot of unpleasant media attention." A spurt of anger chases away some of the haze in my mind. "That's why I'm here, instead of a regular hospital. You want to cover this up, pretend it never happened."

"We want to keep you safe and help you move past this," Karen says, her brown gaze earnest on my face. "Nothing good can come of blasting this story to all the papers. What happened was a terrible tragedy, but your husband was already on life support. You know better than anyone that it was only a matter of time before—"

"What about the other three men?" I cut in sharply. "Were they on life support too?"

"They died in the line of duty," Ryson says. "Their families have already been informed, so you don't have to worry about that. With George, you were his only family, so…"

"So now I've been informed too." My mouth twists. "Your conscience is appeased, and now it's cleanup time. Or should I say 'cover your ass' time?"

His face tightens. "This is still largely classified, Dr. Cobakis. If you go to the media, you'll be stirring up a hornet's nest, and trust me, you don't want that. Neither would your husband, if he were alive. He didn't want anyone to know about this matter, not even you."

"What?" I stare at the agent. "George knew? But—"

"He didn't know he was on the list, and neither did we," Karen says, laying her hand on the back of Ryson's chair. "We learned about that after the accident, and at that point, we did what we could to protect him."

My head is throbbing, but I push the pain away and try to concentrate on what they're telling me. "I don't understand. What happened on that assignment abroad? How did George get involved with this fugitive? And when?"

"That's the classified part," Ryson says. "I'm sorry, but it's really best if you leave it alone. We're searching for your husband's killer now, and we're trying to protect the remaining people on his list. Given his resources, that's not an easy task. If the media is on our heels, we won't be able to do our job as effectively, and more people may die. Do you understand what I'm saying, Dr. Cobakis? For your safety, and that of other people, you have to let it drop."

I tense, recalling what the agent said about the others. "How many has he already killed?"

"Too many, I'm afraid," Karen says somberly. "We didn't find out about the list until he got to several people in Europe, and by the time we were able to put the proper safeguards in place, there were only a few individuals left."

I draw in a shaky breath, my head spinning. I'd known what George did as a foreign correspondent, of course, and I'd read many of his articles and exposés, but those stories hadn't felt entirely real to me. Even when Agent Ryson approached me nine months ago about the supposed mafia threat to George's life, the fear I experienced was more academic than visceral. Outside of George's accident and the painful years leading up to it, I'd led a charmed life, one filled with the typical suburban concerns about school, work, and family. International fugitives who torture and kill people on some mysterious list are so far outside my realm of experience I feel like I've been dropped into someone else's life.

"We know it's a lot to take in," Karen says gently, and I realize some of what I'm feeling must be written on my face. "You're still in shock from the attack, and to learn about all this on top of that…" She inhales. "If you need someone to talk to, I know a good therapist who's worked with soldiers with PTSD and such."

"No, I…" I want to refuse, tell her I don't need anyone, but I can't make my mouth form the lie. The ball of pain inside my chest is choking me from within, and despite my mental wall, more horrible memories are filtering in, flashes of darkness and helplessness and terror.

"I'll just leave you his card," Karen says, stepping up to the bed, and I see her give the beeping monitors a worried glance. I don't need to look at them to know that my heart rate is spiking again, my body going into an unnecessary fight-or-flight mode.

My lizard brain doesn't know that the memories can't hurt me, that the worst has already happened. Unless—

"Will I have to disappear?" I gasp out through a tightening throat. "Do you think he'll—"

"No," Ryson says, immediately understanding my fear. "He won't come for you again. He got what he wanted from you; there's no reason for him to return. If you'd like, we can still look into relocating you, but—"

"Shut it, Ryson. Can't you see she's hyperventilating?" Karen says sharply, gripping my arm. "Breathe, Sara," she tells me in a soothing tone. "Come on, honey, just take that deep breath. And one more. There you go…"

I follow along with her voice until my heart rate steadies again, and the worst of the memories are locked behind the mental wall. I'm still trembling, however, so Karen wraps a blanket around me and sits next to me on the bed, hugging me tight.

"It'll be okay, Sara," she murmurs as the pain over-flows and I begin to cry, the tears like streaks of lava on my cheeks. "It's over. You'll be okay. He's gone, and he will never hurt you again."

CHAPTER 5
PETER

"*Ashes to ashes, dust to dust...*"

The priest's droning voice reaches my ears, and I tune him out as I scan the crowd of mourners. There are over two hundred people here, all wearing dark clothes and somber expressions. Under the sea of black umbrellas, many eyes are red-rimmed and swollen, and some women are audibly crying.

George Cobakis was popular during his lifetime.

The thought should anger me, but it doesn't. I don't feel anything when I think of him, not even the satisfaction that he's dead. The rage that's consumed me for years has quieted for the moment, leaving me strangely empty.

I stand at the back of the crowd, my black coat and umbrella like those of the other mourners. A light brown wig and a thin mustache disguise my appearance, as do my slouched posture and the flat pillow padding my midsection.

I don't know why I'm here. I've never attended any of the funerals before. Once a name is crossed off my list, my team and I move on to the next one, coldly and methodically. I'm a wanted man; it makes no sense to linger here, in this little suburban town, yet I can't make myself leave.

Not without seeing her again.

My gaze travels from person to person, searching for a slender figure, and finally I see her, all the way at the front as befits the wife of the deceased. She's standing next to an elderly couple, holding a big umbrella over the three of them, and even in a crowd, she manages to look remote, somehow distant from everyone.

It's like she exists on a different plane, like me.

I recognize her by the chestnut waves visible under her small black hat. She left her hair down today, and despite the grayness of the rainy sky, I see the reddish glints in the dark brown mass that falls a few centimeters past her shoulders. I can't see much else—there are too many people and umbrellas between us—but I watch her anyway, like I've been watching her for the past month. Only my interest in her is different now, infinitely more personal.

Collateral damage. That's how I thought of her initially. She wasn't a person to me, but an extension of her husband. A smart and pretty extension, sure, but that didn't matter to me. I didn't particularly want to kill her, but I would've done what was necessary to achieve my goal.

I *did* do what was necessary.

She froze in terror when I grabbed her, her reaction the response of the untrained, the primitive instinct of incapacitated prey. It should've been easy at that point—a couple of shallow cuts and done. That she didn't crack instantly under my blade was both impressive and annoying; I'd had seasoned killers piss themselves and start singing with less incentive.

I could've done more to her at that point, worked her over with my knife for real, but instead, I went with a less damaging interrogation technique.

I put her under the faucet.

It worked like a charm—and that's when I made a mistake. She was shaking and sobbing so hard after the first session that I took her down to the floor and wrapped my arms around her, restraining her and calming her at the same time. I did it so she'd be able to talk, but I didn't count on my response to her.

She felt small and breakable, utterly helpless as she coughed and sobbed in my embrace, and for some reason, I remembered holding my son that way, comforting him when he cried. Only Sara is not a child, and my body reacted to her slim curves with startling hunger, with a desire as primitive as it was irrational.

I wanted the woman I'd come to interrogate, the one whose husband I intended to kill.

I tried to ignore my inconvenient reaction, to continue as before, but when I had her on the counter again, I found myself unable to turn on the water. I was too aware of her; she'd become a person to me, a living, breathing woman instead of a tool to be used.

That left the drug as the only option. I hadn't planned to use it on her, both because of the time it required to work properly and because it was our final batch. The chemist who made it was recently killed, and Anton warned me it would take time to find another supplier. I'd been saving that batch in case of emergencies, but I had no choice.

I, who had tortured and killed hundreds, couldn't bring myself to hurt this woman more.

"He was a kind and generous man, a talented journalist. His death is a loss beyond measure, both for his family and his profession..."

I tear my eyes away from Sara to focus on the speaker. It's a middle-aged woman, her thin face streaked with tears. I recognize her as one of Cobakis's colleagues from the newspaper. I investigated all of them to determine their complicity, but luckily for them, Cobakis was the only one involved.

She continues going through all of Cobakis's outstanding qualities, but I tune her out again, my gaze drawn to the slender figure under the giant umbrella. All I can see of Sara is her back, but I can easily picture her pale, heart-shaped face. Its features are imprinted on my mind, everything from her wide-set hazel eyes and small straight nose to her soft, plush lips. There's something about Sara Cobakis that makes me think of Audrey Hepburn, a kind of old-fashioned prettiness reminiscent of the movie stars of the forties and fifties. It adds to the sense that she doesn't belong here, that she's somehow different from the people surrounding her.

That she's somehow above them.

I wonder if she's crying, if she's grieving for the man she admitted she hadn't really known. When Sara first told me she and her husband were separated, I didn't believe her, but some of the things she said under the drug's influence made me rethink that conclusion. Something had gone very wrong in her supposedly perfect marriage, something that left an indelible trace on her.

She's known pain; she's lived with it. I could see it in her eyes, in the soft, trembling curve of her mouth. It intrigued me, that glimpse into her mind, made me want to delve deeper into her secrets, and when she closed her lips around my fingers and started sucking on them, the hunger I'd been trying to suppress returned, my cock hardening uncontrollably.

I could've taken her then, and she would've let me. Fuck, she would've welcomed me with open arms. The drug had lowered her inhibitions, stripped away all her defenses. She'd been open and vulnerable, needy in a way that called to the deepest parts of me.

Don't leave me. Please, don't leave.

Even now, I can hear her pleas, so much like Pasha's the last time I saw him. She didn't know what she was asking, didn't know who I was or what I was about to do, but her words shook me to the core, making me long for something utterly impossible. It had taken all my willpower to walk away and leave her tied in that chair for the FBI to find.

It had taken everything I had to leave and continue with my mission.

My attention returns to the present when Cobakis's colleague stops speaking, and Sara approaches the podium. Her slim, dark-clothed figure moves with unconscious grace, and anticipation coils in my gut as she turns and faces the crowd.

A black scarf is wrapped around her neck, shielding her from the chilly October wind and hiding the bandage that must be there. Above the scarf, her heart-shaped face is ghost pale, but her eyes are dry—at least as far as I can tell from this distance. I'd love to stand closer, but that's too risky. I'm already taking a chance by being here. There are at least two FBI agents among the attendees, and a couple more are sitting unobtrusively in government-issue cars on the street. They're not expecting me to be here—security would be much tighter if they were—but that doesn't mean I can let my guard down. As it is, Anton and the others think I'm crazy for showing up here.

We normally leave town within hours of a successful hit.

"As you all know, George and I met in college," Sara says into the microphone, and my spine tingles at the sound of her soft, melodious voice. I've been watching her long enough to know that she can sing. She often sings along to popular music when she's alone in her car or while doing chores around the house.

Most of the time, she sounds better than the actual singer.

"We met in a chemistry lab," she continues, "because believe it or not, George was thinking about going to med school at the time." I hear a few chuckles in the crowd, and

Sara's lips curve in a faint smile as she says, "Yes, George, who couldn't stand the sight of blood, actually considered becoming a doctor. Fortunately, he quickly discovered his true passion—journalism—and the rest is history."

She goes on to talk about her husband's various habits and quirks, including his love for cheese sandwiches drizzled with honey, then moves on to his achievements and good deeds, detailing his unwavering support for the veterans and the homeless. As she speaks, I notice that everything she says has to do with *him*, rather than the two of them. Other than the initial mention of how they first met, Sara's speech could've been made by a roommate or a friend—anyone who knew Cobakis, really. Even her voice is steady and calm, with no hint of the pain I glimpsed in her eyes that night.

It's only when she gets to the accident that I see some real emotion on her face. "George was many wonderful things," she says, gazing out over the crowd. "But all those things ended eighteen months ago, when his car hit that guardrail and went over. Everything he was died that day. What remained was not George. It was a shell of him, a body without a mind. When death came for him early Saturday morning, it didn't get my husband. It got only that shell. George himself was long gone by then, and nothing could make him suffer."

Her chin lifts as she says this last part, and I stare at her intently. She doesn't know I'm here—the FBI would be all over me if she did—but I feel like she's speaking directly to me, telling me that I failed. Does she sense me on some level? Feel me watching her?

Does she know that when I stood over her husband's bedside two nights ago, for a brief moment I considered not pulling the trigger?

She finishes her speech with the traditional words about how much George will be missed, and then she steps off the podium, letting the priest have his final say. I watch her walk back to the elderly couple, and when the crowd starts to disperse, I quietly follow the other mourners out of the cemetery.

The funeral is over, and my fascination with Sara must be too.

There are more people on my list, and fortunately for her, Sara is not one of them.

PART II

CHAPTER 6
SARA

"Darling, are you not eating again?" Mom asks with a worried frown. Though she was vacuuming when I dropped by, her makeup is as perfect as always, her short white hair is prettily curled, and her earrings match her stylish necklace. "You've been looking so thin lately."

"Most people would consider that a good thing," I say dryly, but to appease her, I reach for a second serving of her homemade apple pie.

"Not when you look like a chihuahua could drag you away," Mom says and pushes more pie toward me. "You have to take care of yourself; otherwise, you won't be able to help those patients of yours."

"I know that, Mom," I say between bites of the pie. "Don't worry, okay? It's been a busy winter, but things should slow down soon."

"Sara, darling…" The worry lines on her face deepen. "It's been six months since George—" She stops and takes a breath. "Look, what I'm saying is you can't keep working yourself to death. It's too much for you, your regular workload, plus all this new volunteering. Are you sleeping at all?"

"Of course, Mom. I sleep like the dead." It's not a lie; I pass out the moment my head hits the pillow and don't wake up until my alarm goes off. Or at least that's what happens if I'm completely worn out. On the days when I have something approaching a normal schedule, I wake up shaking and sweating from nightmares, so I do my best to exhaust myself every day.

"How's the house sale going? Any offers yet?" Dad asks, shuffling into the dining room. He's using a walker again, so his arthritis must be acting up, but I'm pleased to see that his posture is a bit straighter. He's actually following his physical therapist's orders this time and swimming in the gym every day.

"The realtor is having an Open House next week," I answer, suppressing the urge to praise Dad for doing the right thing. He doesn't like to be reminded of his age, so anything having to do with his or my mom's health is off limits as far as dinnertime conversation. It drives me crazy, but at the same time, I can't help but admire his resolve.

At almost eighty-seven years of age, my dad is as tough as ever.

"Oh, good," Mom says. "I hope you'll get some offers from that. Be sure to bake cookies that morning; they make the house smell nice."

"I might ask my realtor to buy some and microwave them before the first visitors arrive," I say, smiling at her. "I don't think I'll have time to bake."

"Of course she won't, Lorna." Dad takes a seat next to Mom and reaches for a slice of pie. Glancing up at me, he says gruffly, "You probably won't be home at all, right?"

I nod. "I'm supposed to go to the clinic straight from the hospital that day."

He frowns. "You're still doing that?"

"Those women need me, Dad." I try to keep the exasperation out of my voice. "You have no idea what it's like in that neighborhood."

"But, darling, that neighborhood is precisely why we don't want you going there," Mom interjects. "Can't you volunteer elsewhere? And going there at night, after you've already put in one of your long shifts..."

"Mom, I never carry cash or valuables with me, and I'm only there for a couple of hours in the evenings," I say, hanging on to my patience by a thread. We've had this argument at least five times in the last three months, and each time, my parents pretend like we've never discussed this before. "I park right in front of the building, and go straight in. It's as safe as can be."

Mom sighs and shakes her head, but doesn't argue further. Dad, however, keeps frowning at me over his slice of pie. To distract him, I get up and say, "Would anyone like some coffee or tea?"

"Decaf coffee for your dad," Mom says. "And chamomile tea for me, please."

"One decaf coffee and one chamomile tea coming up," I say, walking over to the fancy coffee machine I got for them last Christmas. After I make the requested drinks and bring them to the table, I go back and make a cup of real java for myself.

After this dinner, I'm going to be on call and could use the caffeine.

"So guess what, darling?" Mom says when I rejoin them at the table. "We're going to have the Levinsons over for dinner on Saturday."

I take a sip of my coffee. It's hot and strong, just like I like it. "That's nice."

"They've been asking about you," Dad says, stirring sugar into his coffee.

"Uh-huh." I keep my expression neutral. "Please tell them hello for me."

"Why don't you come over too, darling?" Mom says, as though the idea just occurred to her. "I know they would love to see you, and I'll make your favorite—"

"Mom, I'm not interested in dating Joe—or anyone—right now," I say, softening my refusal with a smile. "I'm sorry, but I'm not there yet. I know you love Joe's parents, and he's a wonderful lawyer and a very nice man, but I'm just not ready."

"You won't know if you're ready until you get out there and try," Dad says while Mom sighs and looks down into her tea cup. "You can't let yourself die alongside George, Sara. You're stronger than that."

I gulp down my coffee instead of replying. He's wrong. I'm not strong. It's all I can do to sit here and pretend that

I'm okay, that I'm still whole and functional and sane. My parents, like everyone else, don't know what happened that Friday night. They think George passed away in his sleep, his death the belated result of the car accident that put him in a coma eighteen months earlier. I explained away the closed-casket funeral as a way for me to cope with my grief, and nobody questioned it. If my parents knew the truth, they'd be devastated, and I'll never do that to them.

Nobody except the FBI and my therapist know about the fugitive and my role in George's death.

"Just think about it," Mom says when I remain silent. "You don't have to commit to anything or do anything that you don't want to do. Just please, consider coming over this Saturday."

I look at her, and for the first time, I notice the strain hidden under her perfect makeup and stylish accessories. My mom is nine years younger than my dad, and she's so trim and energetic that sometimes I forget that age is taking a toll on her too, that all this worry about me can't be good for her health.

"I'll think about it, Mom," I promise and get up to clear the dishes off the table. "If I don't have to work on Saturday, I'll try to come over."

CHAPTER 7
SARA

*M*y on-call shift is a blur of emergencies, everything from a five-months-pregnant woman coming in with severe bleeding to one of my patients going into labor seven weeks early. I end up performing a C-section on her, but luckily, the baby—a tiny but perfectly formed boy—is able to breathe and suckle on his own. The woman and her husband sob in happiness and thank me profusely, and by the time I head into the locker room to change out of my scrubs, I'm physically and emotionally drained. However, I'm also deeply satisfied.

Every child I bring into this world, every woman whose body I help heal, makes me feel a tiny bit better, alleviating the guilt that smothers me like a wet rag.

No, don't go there. Stop. Only it's too late, and the memories flood in, dark and toxic. Gasping, I sink down on the bench next to my locker, my hands clutching at the hard wooden board.

A hand over my mouth. A knife at my throat. A wet cloth over my face. Water in my nose, in my lungs—

"Hey, Sara." Soft hands grip my arms. "Sara, what's happening? Are you okay?"

I'm wheezing, my throat impossibly tight, but I manage a small nod. Closing my eyes, I concentrate on slowing my breathing as the therapist taught me, and after a few moments, the worst of the suffocating sensation recedes.

Opening my eyes, I look at Marsha, who's staring at me with concern.

"I'm fine," I say shakily, standing up to open my locker. My skin is cold and clammy, and my knees feel like they're about to buckle, but I don't want anyone at the hospital knowing about my panic attacks. "I forgot to eat again, so it's probably just low blood sugar."

Marsha's blue eyes widen. "You're not pregnant, are you?"

"What?" Despite my still-uneven breathing, I'm startled into a laugh. "No, of course not."

"Oh, okay." She grins at me. "And here I thought you were finally living it up."

I give her a *get real* look. "Even if I were, you think I don't know how to prevent pregnancy?"

"Hey, you never know. Accidents happen." She opens her locker and starts changing out of her scrubs. "Seriously, though, you should grab a bite with me and the girls. We're heading out to Patty's right now."

I raise my eyebrows. "A bar at five in the morning?"

"Yeah, so what? We're not going to be boozing it up. They have breakfast twenty-four-seven, and it's way better than the cafeteria. You should try it."

I'm about to refuse, but then I remember I have next to nothing in my refrigerator. I didn't lie about not eating today; the dinner at my parents' house was over ten hours ago, and I'm starving.

"Okay," I say, surprising Marsha almost as much as I surprise myself. "I'll come."

And ignoring my friend's excited squeals, I put on my street clothes and walk over to the sink to freshen up.

———

When we get to Patty's, I'm not surprised to see many familiar faces there. A lot of the hospital staff go to this bar to unwind and socialize after work. I didn't expect the place to be this full at this time of night—or morning, depending on one's perspective—but if they serve breakfast as well as alcohol, it makes sense.

Marsha, myself, and two nurses from the ER make our way to a table in the corner, where a harried-looking waitress takes our orders. The moment she's gone, Marsha launches into a story about her crazy weekend at a club in downtown Chicago, and the two nurses—Andy and Tonya—laugh and tease her about the guy she almost picked up. Afterward, Andy tells everyone about her boyfriend's insistence on using purple condoms, and by the time our food comes out, the three of them are laughing so hard the waitress gives us all dirty looks.

I'm laughing too, because the story *is* funny, but I don't feel the joy that normally comes with laughter. I haven't felt it in a long time. It's as if something inside me is frozen, dulling all emotions and sensations. My therapist says it's another way my PTSD manifests itself, but I don't know if he's right. Long before the stranger invaded my home—before the accident, even—I've been feeling like there is a barrier between me and the rest of the world, a wall of false appearances and lies.

For years, I've been wearing a mask, and now it feels like I've become that mask, like there's nothing real underneath it.

"What about you, Sara?" Tonya asks, and I realize I zoned out, chowing down my eggs on autopilot. "How was your weekend?"

"It was good, thanks." Putting down my fork, I attempt a smile. "Nothing exciting. I'm selling my house, so I had to clean out my garage and do some other boring stuff." I was also on call for eighteen hours and volunteered at the clinic for five more, but I don't tell Tonya that. Marsha already thinks I'm a workaholic; if she heard I'm subbing in for some of the other doctors at my hospital-owned practice and helping at the clinic on top of my usual workload, I'd never hear the end of it.

"You should come out with us next Friday," Tonya says, extending a slim brown arm to pick up a salt shaker. At twenty-four, she's one of the youngest nurses on staff, and from what Marsha's told me, she's even more of a party girl than my friend, driving guys of all ages wild with her dimpled smile and tight body. "We're going to grab some drinks at Patty's, then head into the city. I know a promoter at that hot new club downtown, so we won't even have to wait in line."

I blink at the unexpected offer. "Oh, I don't know… I'm not sure if—"

"You're not working Friday night," Marsha says. "I know, I checked the schedule."

"Yes, but you know how it is." I spear eggs with my fork. "Babies don't always arrive on a schedule."

"Come on, Marsha, let her be," Andy says, tucking a red curl behind her ear. "Can't you see the poor girl is tired right now? If she wants to go, she'll go. No need to drag her anywhere."

She winks at me, and I give her a grateful smile. This is my first time interacting with Andy outside the hospital hallways, and I'm discovering that I genuinely like her. Like me, she's in her late twenties, and according to Marsha, she's had a steady boyfriend for the last five years. The boyfriend—he of the purple condoms—is apparently a self-absorbed douchebag, but Andy loves him anyway.

"You moved here from Michigan, right?" I ask her, and Andy nods, grinning, then tells me all about how Larry, her boyfriend, got a job in the area, forcing the two of them to move. Listening to her, I decide that Marsha is not far off in her assessment of Andy's boyfriend.

Larry does seem like a selfish douche.

The rest of the meal flies by in casual, friendly conversation, and by the time we pay the bill and head out of the bar, I'm feeling lighter than I have in months. Maybe my dad is right; getting out and socializing could be good for me.

Maybe I *will* go to that dinner with the Levinsons, and even to the club with Tonya.

My improved mood continues as I say goodbye to the three women and walk the two blocks to the hospital parking lot to get my car. Lady Gaga is singing in my headphones, and the sky is just beginning to lighten. It feels like the early dawn is speaking to me, promising me that at some point in the not-too-distant future, the darkness may dissipate for me too.

It feels good, that tiny ray of hope. It feels like a step forward.

I'm already in the parking lot when it happens again.

It starts off as a light prickle across my skin… a quiet pinging in my nerves. The blast of adrenaline is next, accompanied by a surge of debilitating terror. My heart rate spikes, and my body tenses for an attack. Gasping, I spin around, tearing off my headphones as I rummage in my bag for a canister of pepper spray, but there's no one there.

There's just that sense of danger, a feeling of being watched. Panting, I turn in a circle, clutching the pepper spray, but I don't see anyone.

I never see anyone when my brain misfires like this.

Shaking, I make my way to my car and get inside. It takes several minutes of breathing exercises before I'm calm enough to drive, and I know that despite my tiredness, I won't be able to sleep today.

Pulling out of the parking lot, I turn left instead of right.

I might as well go to the clinic. They're not expecting me until tomorrow, but they're always grateful for the help.

CHAPTER 8
SARA

"Tell me about this latest episode, Sara," Dr. Evans says, crossing his long legs. "What made you think someone was watching you?"

"I don't know. It was just..." I inhale, trying to find the right words, then shake my head. "It was nothing concrete. I honestly don't know."

"Okay, let's backtrack for a second." His tone is both warm and professional. That's part of what makes him a good therapist, that ability to project caring while remaining detached at the same time. "You said you went out for breakfast with some coworkers; then you were walking back to your car, right?"

"Right."

"Did you hear anything? Or see anything? Anything that might've triggered you? A car door slamming, leaves blowing... a bird, perhaps?"

"No, nothing specific that I can recall. I was just walking, listening to music, and then I felt it. I don't know how to explain it. It was like—" I swallow, my heart rate quickening at the memories. "It was like that time in my kitchen, when I sensed him a second before he grabbed me. That same kind of feeling."

The therapist's thin, intelligent face takes on an expression of concern. "How frequently is this happening now?"

"It was the third time this week," I admit, embarrassment heating my cheeks as he jots down something in his notepad. I hate this out-of-control feeling, the knowledge that my brain is playing tricks on me. "The first time was in a grocery store, then as I was entering the clinic, and now in the hospital parking lot. I don't know why this is happening. I thought I was getting better; I really did. I only had one small panic attack in the last two weeks, and I felt genuinely hopeful after that breakfast yesterday. It just doesn't make sense."

"Our minds take time to heal, Sara, just like our bodies. Sometimes you have a relapse, and sometimes the illness takes a different course. You know that as well as I do." He makes another note in his notepad, then looks up. "Have you considered speaking to the FBI again?"

"No, they will think I've gone crazy."

I talked to Agent Ryson after the first paranoid episode a month ago, and he told me that at that very moment, Interpol was tracking my husband's killer somewhere in South Africa. Just in case, though, he put a protective detail on me. After following me around for several days, they determined there was no threat of any kind, and Agent

Ryson pulled them off with mumbled apologies about limited funds and manpower. He didn't accuse me of being paranoid, but I know he secretly thought it.

"Because the man you fear is far away," Dr. Evans says, and I nod.

"Yes. He's gone, and he has no reason to return."

"Good. Rationally, you know that. We'll work on convincing your subconscious of that, too. First, though, you need to figure out what triggers your paranoia, so you can learn to spot the triggers and manage your response to them. The next time it happens, pay attention to what you were doing and how you were feeling when you first got that sensation. Are you in a public place or by yourself? Is it noisy or quiet? Are you indoors or outdoors?"

"Okay, I'll make sure to note all that as I'm freaking out and clutching my pepper spray."

Dr. Evans smiles. "I have faith in you, Sara. You've already made tremendous progress. You can go near your kitchen sink again, right?"

"Yes, but I still can't touch the faucet," I say, my hands tightening on my lap. "It's kind of useless without that."

The sink in my kitchen is one of the many reasons I'm selling the house. At first, I couldn't even go into the kitchen, but after months of intensive therapy, I'm at the point where I can approach the sink without a panic attack—though not yet turn on the water.

"Baby steps," Dr. Evans says. "You'll turn on the water someday too. Unless you sell the house first, of course. Are you still planning to do that?"

"Yes, my realtor is having an Open House in a few days, in fact."

"Okay, good." He smiles again and puts his notepad away. "Our session is over for today, and I'm away on vacation for the next week and a half, but I'll see you later this month. In the meantime, please keep doing what you're doing and take detailed notes if you have any more paranoid episodes. We'll discuss that and tackle your feelings about the house sale in the next session, okay?"

"Sounds good." I get up and shake the doctor's hand. "I'll see you then. Enjoy your vacation."

And walking out of his office, I head to my car, forcing my hand to be at my side and not inside my bag, curled around the pepper spray.

———

I sleep well that night, and the night after. It's because I work so much that I literally pass out. When I'm that tired, I can sleep anywhere, even in my big, oak-shielded house. The Feds couldn't figure out how the fugitive got in without setting off the alarm or breaking any locks, so even though I've upgraded my security system, I feel about as safe in my home as I would sleeping out on the street.

It's on the third night that the nightmares find me. I don't know if it's because I had another paranoid episode earlier that day—this time, on a busy street next to a cof-feeshop—or because I only worked twelve hours, but that night, I dream of *him*.

As usual, his face is vague in my mind; I can only make out his gray eyes and the scar bisecting his left eyebrow.

Those eyes pin me in place as he holds a knife against my throat, his gaze as sharp and cruel as his blade. Then George is there too, his brown eyes vacant as he comes toward me.

"Don't," I whisper, but George keeps coming, and I see the blood trickling from his forehead. It's a small, neat wound, nothing like the gaping hole the real bullet left in his head, and some part of me knows I'm dreaming, but I still sob and shake as the gray-eyed man picks me up and carries me to the sink.

"Don't, please," I beg the man, but he's relentless, holding my head over the sink as George continues shuffling toward me, his dead face twisted with hatred.

"For what you did to me," my husband says, turning on the water. "For everything you did."

I wake up screaming and wheezing, my sheets soaked with sweat. When I calm down a little, I go downstairs and make myself a cup of decaffeinated tea, using the water from the refrigerator filter. As I drink my tea, the microwave clock stares at me, the blinking green numbers informing me that it's not even three in the morning—far too early for me to get up if I'm to have any hope of making it through the upcoming day's extra-long shift. I have a surgery in the afternoon, and I need to be sharp for that; anything less would endanger my patient.

After a few moments of internal debate, I get up and get Ambien from the medicine cabinet. Cutting a pill in half, I swallow it with the remnants of my tea and go back upstairs.

As much as I hate drugging myself, there's no other choice today. I only hope that I won't dream of the fugitive again. Not because I'm afraid of the waterboarding night-mare—it never comes twice on the same night—but be-cause in my dreams, he's not always torturing me.

Sometimes, he's fucking me, and I'm fucking him back.

CHAPTER 9
PETER

I stand over her bedside, watching her sleep. I'm taking a risk by being here in person instead of watching her through the cameras my men installed throughout her house, but the Ambien should keep her from waking up. Still, I'm careful not to make a sound. Sara is sensitive to my presence, attuned to me in some strange way. That's why she's taken to carrying that pepper spray, and why she looks like a hunted doe each time I get near.

Subconsciously, she knows I'm back. She senses I'm coming for her.

I still don't know why I'm doing this, but I've given up trying to analyze my madness. I've tried to stay away, to remain focused on my mission, but even as I tracked down and eliminated all but one name on my list, I kept thinking about Sara, picturing how she looked that day at the funeral and recalling the pain in her soft hazel eyes.

Remembering how she wrapped her lips around my fingers and begged me to stay.

There's nothing normal about my infatuation with her. I'm sane enough to admit that. She's the wife of a man I killed, a woman I tortured like I'd once tortured suspected terrorists. I should feel nothing for her, just like I've felt nothing for my other victims, but I can't get her out of my mind.

I want her. It's completely irrational, and wrong on so many levels, but I want her. I want to taste those soft lips and feel the smoothness of her pale skin, to bury my fingers in her thick chestnut hair and breathe in her scent. I want to hear her beg me to fuck her, and then I want to hold her down and do exactly that, over and over again.

I want to heal the wounds I inflicted and make her crave me the way I crave her.

She continues to sleep as I watch her, and my fingers itch to touch her, to feel her skin, if only for a moment. But if I do that, she might wake up, and I'm not ready for that.

When Sara sees me again, I want it to be different.

I want her to know me as something other than her assailant.

CHAPTER 10
SARA

*O*ver the next several days, my paranoia intensifies. I constantly feel like I'm being watched. Even when I'm alone at home, with all the shades drawn and doors locked, I sense invisible eyes on me. I've taken to sleeping with the pepper spray under my pillow, and I even bring it with me to the bathroom, but it's not enough.

I don't feel safe anywhere.

On Tuesday, I finally break down and call Agent Ryson.

"Dr. Cobakis." He sounds both wary and surprised. "How may I help you?"

"I'd like to talk to you," I say. "In person, if possible."

"Oh? What about?"

"I'd rather not discuss it over the phone."

"I see." There are a couple of beats of silence. "All right. I suppose I can meet you for a quick coffee this afternoon. Would that work for you?"

I glance at my schedule on my laptop. "Yes. Could you meet me at Snacktime Cafe by the hospital? Around three?"

"I'll be there."

———————

I end up getting held up with a patient, and it's ten minutes after three by the time I rush into the cafe.

"I was just about to leave," Ryson says, standing up from a small table in the corner.

"So sorry about that." Breathless, I slide into the seat across from him. "I promise to make this quick."

Ryson sits down again. The server comes by, and we place our orders: a shot of espresso for him and a cup of decaf coffee for me. My jitters don't need the added caffeine today.

"All right," he says when the server is gone. "Go ahead."

"I need to know more about this fugitive," I say without preamble. "Who is he? Why was he after George?"

Ryson's bushy eyebrows pull together. "You know that's classified."

"I do, but I also know that this man waterboarded me, drugged me, and killed my husband," I say evenly. "And that you knew he was coming and never bothered to inform me. Those are the things I know—the only things I know, really. If I knew more—say, his name and motivation—it might help me understand and get over what happened. Otherwise, it's like an open sore, or maybe a blister that hasn't been lanced. It just festers, you see, and it's constantly on my mind. Someday, I might not be able to hold it in, and the blister might pop on its own. Do you see my dilemma?"

Ryson's jaw tightens. "Don't threaten us, Sara. You won't like the results."

"It's Dr. Cobakis to you, Agent Ryson." I match his hard stare. "And I already don't like the results. George's colleagues at the paper wouldn't like them either—if they were to catch wind of them. That's why you told me about the fugitive, right? So I'd keep my mouth shut and go along with the whole 'he died peacefully in his sleep' bullshit? You knew George's colleagues would've investigated the hell out of the supposed mafia hit, and you didn't need that. You still don't, am I right?"

He glares at me, and I see his internal debate. Share classified information and potentially get in trouble, or not share it and definitely get in trouble? Self-preservation must win out, because he says grimly, "All right. What do you want to know?"

"Let's start with his name and nationality."

Ryson glances around, then leans in closer. "He goes by many aliases, but we believe his real name is Peter Sokolov." He pitches his voice low even though the tables around us are empty. "According to our files, he's originally from a small town near Moscow, Russia."

That explains the accent. "What is his background? Why is he a fugitive?"

Ryson leans back. "I don't know the answer to that last question. I don't have sufficient security clearance." He falls silent as the server approaches with our drinks. After the server leaves, he says, "What I can tell you is that prior to him becoming a fugitive, he was Spetsnaz, part of the Russian Special Forces. His job was tracking down and interrogating anyone deemed a threat to Russian security—terrorists, insurgents from the former Soviet Union republics, spies, and so on. He was reportedly very good at it. Then, about five years ago, he switched sides and started working for the worst of the criminal underworld—dictators convicted of war crimes, Mexican cartels, illegal arms dealers... In the process, he came up with a list of names—people he believes have harmed him somehow—and he's been systematically eliminating them ever since."

My hand is unsteady as I reach for my coffee cup. "And George was on that list?"

Ryson nods and knocks back his espresso in one big gulp. Putting down the cup, he says, "I'm sorry, Dr. Cobakis. This is all I can tell you, because this is all I know. I have no idea what your husband or any of the others did to end up on that list. I understand you'd like more answers, and believe me, so would we, but a lot of Sokolov's file is redacted." He stops to let the server pass by again, then adds quietly, "You need to forget about this man, Dr. Cobakis, both for your safety and ours. You don't want to attract his attention again, believe me."

I nod, my stomach knotted tight. I don't know why I thought that knowing a few details about the man who haunts my dreams would be better than remaining in the dark. If anything, I'm more anxious now, my hands and feet icy with anxiety.

"Are you sure he's gone?" I ask as the agent gets to his feet. "Are you certain he's nowhere near here?"

"Nobody can be certain of anything when it comes to this psychopath, but for what it's worth, a little over six weeks ago, he killed another person on his list—this one in South Africa," Ryson says bleakly. "And before that, he took out two more in Canada despite our best attempts to safeguard them. So yes, as far as we know, he's far from US soil."

I stare at him, rendered mute by horror. Three more victims in the last six months. Three more lives lost while I've been battling nightmares and paranoia.

"Good luck, Dr. Cobakis," Ryson says, not unkindly, and places a few dollar bills on the table. "Time really does heal, and one day, you'll move past this too. I'm sure of that."

"Thank you," I say in a choked voice, but he's already walking away, his stocky figure disappearing through the glass doors of the cafe.

That night, I dream of Peter Sokolov's attack again, and the nightmare takes the turn I dread the most. Instead of him holding me under the faucet, he has me pinned under him on a bed, his steely fingers shackling my wrists. I feel him moving inside me, his cock long and thick as he invades my body, and heat thrums under my skin, my nipples taut and aching as they rub against his muscled chest.

"Please," I beg, wrapping my legs around his hips as his metallic eyes stare into mine. "Harder, please. I need you."

I'm slick with that need; it burns inside me, hot and dark, and he knows it. He feels it. I can see it in the coldness of his silver gaze, in the cruel set of his sensuous mouth. His fingers tighten around my wrists, cutting into my skin like a zip tie, and his cock turns into a blade, slicing me open, making me bleed.

"Harder," I plead, my hips rising up to meet his knife-like thrusts. "Don't leave me. Take me harder."

He does exactly that, each stroke ripping me open, and I scream with pain and twisted pleasure, with relief and sweet agony.

I scream as I die in his arms, and it's the best death I can imagine.

———————

I wake up with my sex slick and throbbing and my stomach churning with nausea. Out of all the tricks my brain's been playing on me, these perverted dreams are the worst. I can understand the panic attacks and the paranoia—they're a natural result of what I've been through—but there's nothing natural about the sexual slant of these nightmares. Just thinking about them makes me physically ill with shame.

Getting up, I pull on a robe over my pajamas and go down to the kitchen. My breathing is unsteady and my heart is racing, but this time, it's not from fear. I feel flushed and agitated, my body aching with frustrated arousal.

I almost came during that dream. Another few seconds, and I would've orgasmed—like I've orgasmed during these dreams twice before.

Self-disgust is a heavy brick in my stomach as I make my decaf tea. What kind of twisted person has sexual dreams about her husband's killer? How messed up does one have to be to enjoy dying in said killer's arms?

I've considered discussing this with Dr. Evans, but whenever I try to bring up the topic in our sessions, I shut down. I simply can't bring myself to form the words. Verbalizing the dreams would give them substance, transforming them from a nebulous product of my sleeping subconscious to something I think and talk about when I'm awake, and I can't have that.

In any case, I know what the therapist would tell me. He'd say that I'm a young, healthy woman who hasn't had sex in a long time, and that it's normal to feel those types of urges. That it's my guilt and self-loathing that are transforming my sexual fantasies into something dark and twisted, and the dreams don't mean I'm actually attracted to the man who tortured me and killed George.

Dr. Evans would try to alleviate my guilt and shame, and that's not something I deserve.

When the tea is ready, I carry it over to the kitchen table and sit down. I'm about to take my first sip when I get the watched feeling again. Rationally, I know I'm alone, but my heart rate speeds up, and my palms dampen with sweat.

My pepper spray container is upstairs, so I get up and, as calmly as I can, make my way to the knife rack on the counter. I select the biggest, sharpest knife and bring it back to the table with me. I know it would be useless against someone like Peter Sokolov, but it's better than nothing. After a few deep breaths, I calm down enough to drink my tea, but the unsettling sensation of invisible eyes persists.

If the house doesn't sell soon, I'll just move out, I decide as I go back to bed.

I can afford a second residence, and even a crappy studio would be preferable to this.

CHAPTER 11
SARA

"So how did your Open House go yesterday?" Marsha shouts over the music as we wait for our fourth round of drinks at the bar.

"The realtor says it was good," I shout back, trying not to slur my words. I haven't done this in forever, and the alcohol is hitting me hard. "We'll see if any offers come of it."

"I can't believe you own a house and are selling it," Tonya says as the next song comes on and the music volume drops from deafening to merely loud. "I'd love to buy a house someday, but it'll take forever to save up."

"Yeah, if you spend half your paycheck on clothes and shoes," Andy says with a grin, her red curls dancing as she sways her curvy hips in tune with the music. "Besides, Sara here is a doctor. She makes the big bucks, even if she doesn't act as stuck up as the rest of them."

Tonya giggles, her long earrings jiggling. "Oh, yeah, that's right. You look so young, Sara, I keep forgetting you're a real MD."

"She is young," Marsha says before I can respond. "She's our own little Doogie Howser."

"Oh, shut up." I elbow Marsha, my cheeks flaming with embarrassment as I see the tattooed bartender grinning at me. He's making our Lemon Drops with practiced motions, his brown gaze trained on me with unmistakable interest.

"Here you go, ladies," he says, sliding our drinks over, and Andy winks at me as she hands me one of the glasses.

"Bottoms up," she says, and we knock back the shots before going back to the dance floor, where the next song is already beginning to blast through the speakers.

I wasn't going to come out this Friday after the shitty week I had, but at the last minute, I decided that going out and getting drunk would be preferable to passing out early and risking another twisted sex dream. Luckily, I keep a pair of cute silver flats in my locker at work, and Tonya lent me a short black dress that fit surprisingly well.

"H&M, baby," she said proudly when I asked her where she got it, and I made a mental note to stop by the trendy store and get something similar for myself—in case I'm ever tempted to repeat this insanity.

We started off with a couple of drinks at Patty's, then got a car to take us to the club Tonya talked about. True to her word, the promoter was able to get us in without a line, and we've been dancing nonstop for the past two hours. I'm sweating, my feet hurt, and I'll probably have the mother of all hangovers tomorrow, but this is the most fun I've had in... well, years.

Maybe longer than five years.

The crowd at the club ranges from college kids to hot forty-somethings like Marsha, but the majority look to be in their late twenties, like myself. The DJ is outstanding, mixing the latest hits with hip-hop classics, and I sing along as we dance, belting out my favorite songs with abandon. I've always loved music and dancing—I did ballet all through elementary and middle school and took salsa classes in college—and with the buzz of alcohol in my veins, I feel sexy and carefree, for once like any other young woman at the club. Tonight, I'm not the serious student, the overworked doctor, the dutiful daughter, or the perfect wife. I'm not even the widow with paranoia and messed-up dreams.

Tonight, I'm just me.

The four of us dance by ourselves for a while; then a couple of guys join us, dancing up to Tonya and Marsha. Andy drags me away to the bathroom with her, and by the time we return, Tonya and Marsha are full-on flirting with the guys.

"You want to get another drink?" Andy yells over the music, and I nod, following her to the bar. The room is spinning around me, so I figure I'll just get some water.

The club has become more crowded in the last hour, the dance floor spilling over to the bar and lounge area, and when a group of laughing women cuts in front of me, I lose sight of Andy. I'm not particularly worried—I can catch up to her at the bar—so I go around the group to avoid the most dense parts of the crowd.

I'm within a few feet of the bar when strong fingers wrap around my upper arm, and a deep male voice murmurs into my ear, "Dance with me, Sara."

I freeze, my blood solidifying in my veins.

I know that voice, that subtle Russian accent.

Slowly, I turn my head and meet the metallic gaze that stalks my dreams.

Peter Sokolov is in front of me, his sculpted mouth curved in a faint smile.

CHAPTER 12
PETER

She sways on her feet, her face chalk white, and I grip her other arm to steady her. She clearly knows who I am; she recognizes me.

"Don't scream," I say. "I'm not here to hurt you."

Her hazel eyes look wild, and I know she's not really processing what I'm saying. All she sees is a mortal threat, and she's reacting accordingly. In another few seconds, she'll either faint or become hysterical, and neither would be a good thing.

"Sara." I make my voice hard. "I'm not here to hurt anyone, but I will if I have to. Do you understand? If you do anything to attract attention to us, people will die."

The mindless panic in her gaze abates slightly, replaced by a fear that's more rational, if not any less intense. I'm getting through to her.

It helps that I'm not bluffing.

"W-what do you want?" Even with the layer of lipgloss over them, her trembling lips are pale. "Why are you here?"

"I wanted to see you," I say, pulling her with me through the crowd as I maneuver away from the cameras positioned around the bar. Sara's bare arms are tense in my grasp, her skin chilly to the touch, but as expected, she doesn't scream.

From everything I know about her, the little doctor would sooner die than endanger a bunch of strangers.

"Dance with me," I say again when I have her where I want her—next to a wall in a dimly lit part of the dance floor, where the crowd forms a human shield around us. To facilitate her compliance with my request, I release her arms and clasp her waist, being careful to keep my grip gentle.

Her body is as stiff as a block of ice as I hold her close, but to everyone around us, we look like any other couple swaying to the music. The illusion is only strengthened when her hands come up and her palms splay against my chest. She's trying to push me away, but she's too shocked to put much strength behind it. Not that it would help if she put *all* her strength behind it.

I can overpower most men with minimal effort, much less a woman as slight as her.

"Don't be afraid," I murmur, holding her gaze. Even on a crowded dance floor, I can smell her scent, something delicate and flowery, and my body reacts to her proximity, my cock hardening at the feel of her slender waist between my palms. I want to pull her closer, feel her body against mine, but I force myself to keep a small distance. I don't want to scare her with the intensity of my need. As it is, the look in Sara's eyes is that of a small animal caught in a trap, all blind fear and desperation. It makes me want to pick her up and cuddle her against my chest, but that would just terrify her more. There's no action of mine that wouldn't terrify her at this point; I could invite her to sing karaoke, and she'd have a panic attack.

"What do you want from me?" Her breathing is fast and shallow as she stares up at me. "I don't know anything—"

"I know." I keep my voice gentle. "Don't worry, Sara. That part is over."

Confusion edges out some of the terror in her eyes. "But then why…"

"Why am I here?"

She nods warily.

"I'm not really sure," I say, and it's the absolute truth.

Over the past five and a half years, vengeance ruled my life. Everything I did was in pursuit of that goal, but now that I'm almost through with my list, the future lies dull and empty in front of me, the path ahead shrouded in a bleak fog. Once I kill the last person responsible for my family's deaths, I won't have a purpose. My reason for existing will be well and truly gone.

Or so I thought until I met her and saw the pain in her doe-like eyes. Now *she* consumes my dreams and haunts my waking moments. When I think of Sara, I don't see my son's torn body and Tamila's bloodied face.

I only see her.

"Are you going to kill me?"

She's trying—and failing—to keep her voice steady. Still, I admire her attempt at composure. I approached her in public to make her feel safer, but she's too smart to fall for that. If they've told her anything about my background, she must realize I can snap her neck faster than she can scream for help.

"No," I answer, leaning closer as a louder song comes on. "I'm not going to kill you."

"Then what do you want from me?"

She's shaking in my hold, and something about that both intrigues and disturbs me. I don't want her to be afraid of me, but at the same time, I like having her at my mercy. Her fear calls to the predator within me, turning my desire for her into something darker.

She's captured prey, soft and sweet and mine to devour.

Bending my head, I bury my nose in her fragrant hair and murmur into her ear, "Meet me at the Starbucks near your house at noon tomorrow, and we'll talk there. I'll tell you whatever you want to know."

I pull back, and she stares at me, her eyes huge in her heart-shaped face. I know what she's thinking, so I lean in again, dipping my head so my mouth is next to her ear.

"If you contact the FBI, they'll try to hide you from me. Just like they tried to hide your husband and the others on my list. They'll uproot you, take you away from your parents and career, and it will all be for nothing. I'll find you, no matter where you go, Sara... no matter what they do to keep you from me." My lips brush against the rim of her ear, and I feel her breath hitch. "Alternatively, they might want to use you as bait. If that's the case—if they set a trap for me—I'll know, and our next meeting won't be over coffee."

She shudders, and I drag in a deep breath, inhaling her delicate scent one last time before releasing her.

Stepping back, I melt into the crowd and message Anton to get the crew into position.

I have to make sure she gets home safe and sound, un-molested by anyone but me.

CHAPTER 13

SARA

I don't know how I make it home, but somehow I find myself in my shower, naked and shivering under the hot spray. I have only a vague recollection of making some awkward excuse to Andy and stumbling out of the club to catch a cab; the rest of the trip is a blur of shock-induced numbness and alcoholic haze.

Peter Sokolov spoke to me. He *held* me.

My husband's killer, the man who tortured me and ripped apart my life, danced with me.

My knees fold under me, and I sink to the floor, panting. A wave of dizziness makes the shower stall rotate around me, and all the drinks I consumed threaten to come up.

Peter Sokolov was in the club with me. It wasn't my mind playing tricks; he was actually there.

I swallow convulsively as my nausea worsens. The water beats down on me, the spray almost painfully hot, but I can't stop shivering.

The monster from my nightmares is real.

He's coming after me.

My dizziness intensifies, and I lie down, curling into a fetal ball on the tile floor. My hair is all over my face, wet and thick, and my throat constricts as memories of that night press in. For the first few days after the attack, I avoided washing my hair because I couldn't take the feeling of water streaming over my head, but eventually, the need to be clean won out over the phobia.

One breath in. One breath out. Slow and steady.

Slowly, the suffocating sensation recedes, leaving only misery behind. I feel drunk and sick, and it takes all my strength to struggle to my feet and turn off the shower.

Why is he here? What made him come back? What does he want from me?

The questions streak through my mind as I towel off, but I'm no closer to answers than I was back at the club. My mind feels like a swamp, all my thoughts sluggish and slow.

Wrapping the towel around my wet hair, I stumble to the bedroom and fall onto my king-size bed. The ceiling rocks back and forth, as though I'm on a ship, and I know I'm in for a brutal hangover tomorrow. I haven't been this drunk since college, and my body doesn't know how to handle it.

Taking small, shallow breaths, I curl up on my side, hugging the blanket to my chest. The alcohol is dragging me under, but for once, I'm fighting the lure of sleep. I need to think, to understand what happened and figure out what to do.

The killer who waterboarded me wants to meet for coffee tomorrow.

It would be comical if it weren't so terrifying. I don't understand what he's after. Why come up to me in the club? Why ask me to meet him in public again? He's wanted by just about every law enforcement agency out there; surely he has to know that. Why take that kind of risk?

Unless... unless he feels it's not a risk.

Maybe he's arrogant enough to think he can evade justice forever.

Anger ignites inside me, clearing some of the haze from my brain. I sit up, fighting a wave of dizziness, and reach for the corded phone on my nightstand. It's a dinosaur, clunky and unnecessary in the age of cellphones, but George insisted on having a landline in the house.

"You never know," he said in response to my objections. "Cell phones aren't always reliable. If power goes out during a winter storm, what are you going to do?"

My eyes sting at the recollection, and I pick up the phone with an unsteady hand. I have a knack for remembering numbers, so I dial Agent Ryson's from memory, pushing one button after another.

I have most of the number keyed in when a sudden thought freezes me in place.

Could Peter have bugged my phone? Is that what he meant when he said he'll know if they set a trap for him?

My mind leaps to another possibility.

Could he be watching me right now?

My breathing quickens, my skin prickling with adrenaline. Before the club, I would've dismissed the idea as a manifestation of my paranoia, but it's not paranoia if it's real.

I'm not insane if it's truly happening.

Peter has resources, Ryson said. Could he have access to high-tech spyware?

Are there cameras and listening devices inside my house?

My heart hammering, I drop the phone back on its cradle and grab the blanket, pulling it up to cover my naked breasts. I rarely bother putting on a robe in my bedroom; even in the winter, I sleep in the buff, covered only by my blanket. I've never been self-conscious about my body— George loved it when I walked around naked—but the thought that his killer might've seen me nude makes me feel violated and painfully exposed.

It also makes me recall my twisted dreams.

No. No, no, no. Panting, I wrap the blanket around me and stumble to the closet to grab a T-shirt and a pair of underwear. I can't think of those dreams. I refuse to. I'm drunk; that's the only reason my mind went there in connection with that monster.

Except he doesn't look like a monster. Even with the scar cutting through his eyebrow, he's a stunningly good-looking man, the kind that women salivate over. If I'd met him at the club without knowing who he is, I would've danced with him.

I would've wanted his strong arms around me, his hard body grinding against mine.

My hands shake as I pull on the underwear, and I feel a spot of dampness where my sex touches the cotton fabric.

No. This isn't happening. I'm not turned on.

Putting on the first T-shirt I find, I stagger back to bed and collapse on it, wrapping myself in the blanket. The room is doing cartwheels around me, and my stomach roils along with it. I pant through the nausea and realize my lids are growing heavy as my thoughts start to drift.

Clenching my teeth, I force my eyes to open. I can't pass out until I decide what to do about tomorrow.

Staring at the spinning ceiling, I mentally go over my options.

The sane thing to do would be to tell Ryson about this and hope they can protect me. Except if my suspicions are right and Peter Sokolov is indeed watching me, he'll know that I contacted the FBI, and I might not survive long enough for the agents to reach me.

Of course, if he decides to kill me, I might not survive even with the FBI protection. The people on his list certainly didn't, and he said he'd come after me.

He promised to find me no matter where I go.

Still, it's probably worth the risk, because the alternative is going along with whatever cruel game Peter is playing. I don't know what he wants from me, but whatever it is, it can't be good. Maybe he hated George enough to want to torment his widow, or maybe, despite what he said, he thinks I know something—like the sister of that poor man he killed.

At this very moment, he might be devising some new, exotic torture for me, something spectacularly horrible that somehow involves coffee.

My eyelids droop again, and I rub my hands over my face, trying to keep my eyes open. I know I'm not thinking straight, but I can't go to sleep without making this decision.

Do I call the FBI or not? And if not, do I actually go to that Starbucks?

A violent shudder ripples through me as I try to picture meeting my husband's murderer for coffee. I don't think I can do it. Just the idea of it makes my insides somersault. But what would I do instead? Hide in bed all day and then go to my parents' house for dinner with the Levinsons as promised? Pretend the monster who destroyed my life isn't after me?

It's the thought of my parents that decides it. If I were on my own, I might chance the FBI's dubious protection, but I can't endanger my parents that way. I can't force them to leave their house and everyone they know on the un-likely possibility that Ryson and his colleagues would be able to protect us better than they've protected the others. And leaving my parents behind is out of the question; even if their age wasn't an issue, I can't risk Peter interrogating them like he interrogated me about George.

There's only one thing I can do.

I have to meet my tormentor tomorrow and hope that whatever he does to me won't extend to the rest of my family.

When I finally close my eyes and pass out, I dream of him again. Only this time, he's neither torturing nor fucking me.

He's sitting on my bed and watching me, his gaze warm and strangely possessive on my face.

CHAPTER 14
SARA

By the time I pull up to the Starbucks at noon, the stabbing pain in my skull has quieted to a dull throb, and my stomach doesn't threaten to revolt every second. However, my palms are damp with anxiety, and my hands shake so much I almost drop my keys when I come out of the car.

I cross the parking lot, feeling like I'm going to my execution. Fear pulses through me with every rapid heartbeat. He could kill me at this very moment, just take me out with a sniper rifle. Maybe that's why he lured me here: to murder me in a public place and leave my body to terrorize everyone.

But no bullet finds me, and when I come into the coffeeshop, I see him right away. He's sitting at one of the empty tables in the corner, his big hand wrapped around a paper cup.

I meet his gaze, and everything inside me jolts, as though I got shocked with a defibrillator. For the first time, I see him in the light of day without alcohol or drugs in my system.

For the first time, I fully comprehend how dangerous he is.

He's leaning back in his chair, his long, jean-clad legs stretched out and crossed at the ankles under the small round table. It's a casual pose, but there's nothing casual about the dark power that rolls off him in waves. He's not just dangerous; he's lethal. I see it in the metallic ice of his gaze and the coiled readiness of his large body, in the arrogant set of his jaw and the cruel curve of his lips.

This is a man who lives and breathes violence, an apex predator for whom rules of society don't exist.

A monster who's tortured and killed countless people.

The surge of anger and hatred that comes with the thought cuts through my fear, and I take a step forward, then another and another until I'm walking toward him on almost steady legs. If he wanted to kill me, he could've already done it in a million different ways, so whatever he wants today must be something different.

Something even more evil.

"Hello, Sara," he says, rising to his feet as I approach. "It's good to see you again."

His deep voice wraps around me, his soft Russian accent caressing my ears. It should sound ugly, that voice from my nightmares, but like everything else about him, it's deceptively appealing.

"What do you want?" I'm being rude, but I don't care. We're long past politeness and good manners. There's no use pretending this is a normal get-together.

The only reason I'm here is because not showing up could endanger my parents.

"Please, sit." He motions to the chair across from him and sits down. "I took the liberty of ordering a cup of coffee for you. Black, no sugar... and decaf, since you're not working today."

I glance at the second cup—prepared exactly the way I would've ordered it—then meet his gaze again. My heart drums in my throat, but my voice is even as I say, "You *have* been watching me."

"Yes, of course. But you figured that out last night, didn't you?"

I flinch. I can't help it. If he saw me try to make that call, then he saw me stagger drunkenly into the bathroom and come out naked.

If he's been watching me for a while, he's seen me in all sorts of private moments.

"Sit, Sara." He gestures at the chair again, and this time, I obey—if only to give myself a chance to calm down. Rage and fear are a tangle of live wires in my chest, and I feel like I'm one deep breath away from exploding.

I've never been a violent person, but if I had a gun on me, I'd shoot him. I'd blow his brains all over the trendy Starbucks wall.

"You hate me." He says it calmly, as a statement of fact rather than a question, and I stare at him, caught off-guard.

Does he read minds, or am I that transparent?

"It's okay," he says, and I catch a glimmer of amusement in his eyes. "You can admit it. I promise not to hurt you today."

Today? What about tomorrow and the day after? My hands form into fists under the table, my nails digging into my skin. "Of course I hate you," I say as steadily as I can manage. "Is that a surprise?"

"No, of course not." He smiles, and my lungs tighten, preventing me from breathing. It's not a perfect smile—his teeth are white, but one is slightly crooked on the bottom, and his lower lip has a tiny scar that wasn't visible until now—but it's magnetic nonetheless.

It's a smile nature designed for one purpose only: to lure in unwary women and make them forget the monster underneath.

My nails dig deeper into my palms, the bite of pain centering me as he says, "You have every right to hate me for what I did."

I gape at him. "Are you trying to *apologize?* Do you seriously think that—"

"You misunderstand." The smile disappears, and his silver eyes flash with sudden fury. "Your husband deserved it. If he weren't brain dead, I would've made him suffer so much more."

I recoil instinctively, pushing my chair back, but before I can jump to my feet, his hand catches my wrist, shackling it to the table.

"I didn't say you could go, Sara." His voice is dark ice. "We're not done here yet."

His fingers are like a molten iron cuff around my wrist, his grip burning hot and unbreakable. I remain sitting and instinctively glance around. The nearest patrons are a good dozen feet away, and nobody is paying attention to us. Panic beats in my chest, but I remind myself the lack of attention is a good thing. I haven't forgotten how he threatened the others at the club.

Pushing my fear aside, I focus on slowing my breathing. "What do you want from me?"

"I'm trying to decide that," he says, his face smoothing out. Releasing my wrist, he picks up his coffee cup and takes a sip. "You see, Sara, I don't hate *you*."

I blink, caught off-guard again. "You don't?"

"No." He puts the cup down and regards me with cool gray eyes. "It probably seems that way, given what I've done to you, but I hold no ill will toward you. Just the opposite, in fact."

My pulse lurches before settling into a new frantic rhythm. "What do you mean?"

The corners of his mouth turn up. "What do you think it means, Sara? You intrigue me. You fascinate me, in fact." He leans in, his gaze pinning me in place. "You don't remember what you said to me when you were drugged, do you?"

A hot flush crawls up my neck and spreads over my face. I don't remember everything from that night, but I remember enough. Bits and pieces from my drugged confession surface in my mind at random times when I'm awake and pop into my dreams at night.

Into my most twisted dreams, the ones I try not to think about.

"I see you do remember." His voice turns low and husky, his lids lowering halfway as his large, warm hand settles over my trembling palm. "I've been wondering what would've happened if I'd stayed that night... if I'd taken you up on your offer."

His touch burns through me before I yank my hand away, clenching it into a fist under the table. "There was no offer." My heart is pounding in my ears, my voice tight with mortification. "I was high. I didn't know what I was saying."

"I know. Drugs that lower inhibitions tend to have that effect." He leans back, freeing me from the potent effect of his nearness, and my lungs drag in a full breath for the first time in two minutes. "You didn't know who I was or what I was doing. You would've reacted similarly to any other reasonably attractive man who had you in that position."

"That's... that's right." My face is still blazing hot, but the rational explanation steadies me a little. "You could've been anyone. It wasn't directed at you."

"Yes. But you see, Sara"—he leans in again, his gaze filled with dark intensity—"my reaction was directed at you. I wasn't drugged, and when you came on to me, I wanted you. I still want you."

Horror ices my blood even as my sex clenches in response. He can't be saying what I think he's saying. "You're—you're insane." I feel like I've been dropped from a plane with no parachute. "I'm not... This is just sick." I want to jump up and run, but I press on, pushing through the panic. I have to make this clear to him, put a stop to this insanity once and for all. "I don't care what you want, or what your reaction was. I'm not going to sleep with you after you killed my husband and God knows how many others. After you tortured me and—"

"I know, Sara." His hand finds my knee under the table and rests on it. "I wish I could go back, because I would've found a different way."

Startled, I push my chair to the side, scooting out of his reach. "You wouldn't have killed George?"

"I wouldn't have tortured you," he clarifies, placing his hand back on the table. "I could've located that sookin syn some other way. It would've taken longer, but it would've been worth it not to hurt you."

My freefall from the plane resumes, the air whooshing past my ears. What planet is this man from? "You think torturing me is a problem, but killing my husband would've been okay?"

"The husband who lied to you? The one you said you didn't really know?" Rage ignites in his eyes again. "You can tell yourself whatever you want, Sara, but I did you a favor. I did the whole fucking world a favor by getting rid of him."

"A favor?" An answering fury blazes to life inside me, burning away all caution. "He was a good man, you... you psycho! I don't know what you think he did, but—"

"He massacred my wife and son."

Shock paralyzes my vocal cords. "What?" I gasp out when I can finally speak.

A muscle pulses in Peter's jaw. "Do you know what your husband did for a living, Sara? What he really did?"

A sick sensation spreads through me. "He was a… a foreign correspondent."

"That was his cover, yes." The Russian's upper lip curls as he straightens in his seat. "I figured you didn't know. The spouses rarely know, even when they sense the lies."

My world tilts off its axis. "What do you mean, cover? He was a journalist. He wrote stories for—"

"Yes, he did. And in the process of getting those stories, he gathered information for the CIA and carried out covert missions for them."

"What? No." I frantically shake my head. "You're wrong. You made a mistake. You had the wrong man. I knew you must've had the wrong man. George wasn't a spy. That's impossible. He didn't even know how to change a tire. He—"

"He was recruited in college," Peter says flatly. "University of Chicago, which you both attended. They often do that, hit up college campuses to round up the best and the brightest. They look for certain things: few family ties, a patriotic bent, smart and ambitious but lacking focus… Any of that sound like your husband?"

I stare at him, my chest squeezing tighter and tighter. George's mother died in a car accident during his last year of high school, and his father, a Marine, had been killed in Afghanistan when George was just a baby. His elderly uncle helped put him through college, but he died too, several years back, leaving only distant cousins to attend George's funeral six months ago.

No. It couldn't be true. I would've known.

"Only if he told you," Peter says, and I realize I spoke my last thought out loud. "They teach them how to conceal their real job from everyone, even their own families. Didn't you find it suspicious how Cobakis discovered his passion for journalism overnight? How one day he was a biology major, and then he was interning at magazines abroad?"

"No, I—" My chest is so tight I can barely take a breath. "That's just college. You're supposed to discover yourself, find your passion."

"And he did: working for your government." There's no mercy in the Russian's silver gaze. "They trained him, gave him the focus he was lacking. Taught him how to lie to you and everyone else. When he graduated, they got him a job at the paper, and he had an excuse to go to every hotspot in the world."

I jump to my feet, unable to listen further. "You're wrong. You don't know what you're talking about."

He stands up too, his large frame towering over me. "Don't I? Think back, Sara. Think back to the man you married, to the life you really had together. Not the perfect one you showed to the world, but the one you led behind closed doors. Who was he, this husband of yours? How well did you really know him?"

My insides feel like lead as I take a step back, my head shaking in nonstop denial. "You're wrong," I repeat in a choked voice, and spinning around, I run out of the coffeeshop, heading blindly for my car.

It's only when I stop at a red light near my house that I realize Peter Sokolov didn't do anything to stop me.

He just stood there and watched me go.

CHAPTER 15
PETER

I watch through the binoculars as Sara enters her parents' house; then I open my laptop and bring up the camera feed from inside the hallway.

Sara's parents live in a small, neat house that could use a few upgrades but is otherwise warm and cozy. Even I can tell it's a home, not just a place to live. For some bizarre reason, it reminds me of Tamila's house in Daryevo, though this suburban American home is nothing like a mountain village hut.

Sara kisses both of her parents in the hallway, then follows them to the dining room. I switch to the camera feed there, zooming in on her face as she greets the other guests—an older couple and a tall, lean man in his mid-thirties.

It's the Levinsons and their son Joe, the lawyer Sara's parents want her to date.

Something ugly stirs inside me as Sara shakes the lawyer's hand with a polite smile. I don't want to see her with him; just the idea of it makes me want to plunge my blade between his ribs. Yesterday, when the bartender was smiling at her, I wanted to smash my fist into his grinning mug, and the violent urge is even stronger today.

I might not have claimed her yet, but she's going to be mine.

Sara helps her parents bring out the appetizers and sits down next to the lawyer. I crank up the audio feed and listen as the two of them make small talk. For someone who just found out about her husband's double life, the little doctor is remarkably composed, her smiling mask firmly in place. Nobody looking at her would know that before coming here, she hid in her closet for hours and emerged less than forty minutes ago with her eyes red and swollen.

Nobody would suspect she's terrified because I want her.

It took everything I had to let her stay in that closet and cry on her own. She went in there to escape my cameras, and I let her have this time to herself. She would've been even more upset if I'd gone in and embraced her—if I'd tried to comfort her the way I wanted.

I need to give her more time to get used to the idea of us—and to trust I won't hurt her.

The dinner lasts a couple of hours; then Sara helps her mother clear off the table and makes an excuse to leave. The lawyer asks for her phone number, and she gives it, but I can see it's mostly out of politeness. Her cheeks are perfectly pale—there isn't even a hint of the color that floods her face in my presence—and her body language speaks of indifference. Joe Levinson doesn't excite her, and that's a good thing.

It means he gets to go home alive.

I follow Sara at a distance as she drives to the clinic, and then I wait in my car until she emerges, entertaining myself by watching her through the cameras I installed inside the clinic. I know what I'm doing is stalker behavior at best, but I can't stop myself.

I have to know where she is and what she's doing.

I have to make sure she's safe.

I could entrust the physical guard duty to Anton and my other guys—they already watch her when I can't—but I want to be here in person. I want to see her with my own eyes. With each day that passes, my need for her intensifies, and now that I've held an actual conversation with her, my fascination is quickly morphing into an obsession.

I have to have her. Soon.

She comes out of the clinic some three hours later, and I follow her as she drives to a hotel. She probably thinks she'll be safer there than at her house with all the cameras, but she's wrong.

I wait until she checks into the hotel and goes up to her room, and then I get out of the car and go in.

CHAPTER 16
SARA

The clinic shift was particularly rough today. I had a fourteen-year-old patient who asked for morning-after pills because her brother raped her and another patient barely out of her teens who came in with her third miscarriage. I did what I could, but I know it's not enough.

Nothing I do for those girls will ever be enough.

I'm so emotionally drained it takes all my energy to shower and brush my teeth with the little toothbrush the front desk gave me. Coming here for the night was an impulse decision, so I don't even have a change of underwear with me. I'll have to stop by my house tomorrow morning before going to work, but it's better than being home and knowing that my deadly stalker might be watching me at that very moment.

Watching me and wanting me. Maybe even jacking off at the sight of my naked body.

It's sick, but heat licks between my legs at the thought.

Exiting the shower, I wrap a towel around my chest and stare at myself in the mirror. Visine eye drops did a good job of removing the redness from my eyes, but my lids still look swollen from my crying jag earlier today, and my face is reddened from the hot shower. I also have a tension headache that makes me disinclined to think, which is just as well.

I did too much thinking earlier as is.

George as a spy. George leading a double life. It seems impossible, yet it would explain so much. The FBI agents' protection that came out of nowhere. His long absences when he supposedly chased a story yet often came home without one. The moods that started shortly after our marriage six years earlier. Did something go wrong on one of his covert assignments?

Could his real job be the reason he changed so much in the years leading up to the accident?

My headache intensifies, and I realize I'm doing it again. I'm thinking about George, obsessing about the past I can't change rather than focusing on the future that's still within my control. I should be trying to figure out what to do about the killer who's stalking me, but my mind simply refuses to go there.

I'll think about him later, when I've had some sleep and my brain isn't so fried.

Wrapping a second towel around my dripping hair, I open the bathroom door, step out, and jump up with a startled scream.

Peter Sokolov is sitting on the bed, his hooded gaze trained on my face.

CHAPTER 17
SARA

"Don't scream, Sara." He rises fluidly to his feet. "No need to involve the other guests in this."

I gasp for air, needles of adrenaline piercing my skin as he comes toward me, his large body moving with predatory ease.

"You… you followed me here." My knees knock together as I instinctively back away, clutching the flimsy towel covering my body.

"Yes." He stops a couple of feet from me, his gray eyes gleaming. "You shouldn't have come here. Your alarm system at home poses at least a small challenge. Here, I can walk right in."

"Why are you here?" My heart feels like it's about to jump out of my throat. "What do you want?"

His lips twitch in dark amusement. "You're a doctor who deals with the effects of this activity. You can probably guess what I want."

Oh God. My skin feels both hot and icy, and my pulse jacks up even more. "Get out. I—I will scream, I swear."

He tilts his head quizzically. "Will you? Why haven't you done so yet?"

I take another step back, my gaze flicking to the room door for a fraction of a second. *Would I make it before he catches me?*

"Don't try it, Sara. If you run, I will chase you."

I continue backing away. "I told you, I'm not sleeping with you."

"No? We'll see about that."

He comes toward me, and I back up more, my stomach twisting. I know what sexual assault does to women; I've seen the aftermath, the physical and emotional wreckage left behind. I don't know if I can survive that on top of everything else.

I don't know if I can survive it from *him.*

My trembling hand touches the door, but before I can twist the knob, his palms slap against the door on each side of me, caging me between his powerful arms.

"You can't escape me, ptichka," he says softly, gazing down at me. "Not now, and not ever. You might as well get used to that."

He's not touching me, but he's so close I can feel the heat coming off his large body and see a couple more tiny scars on his symmetrical face. The imperfections add a deadly edge to his magnetism, intensifying its impact on my senses. My heartbeat is a panicked roar in my ears, yet my body tightens in a way that has nothing to do with fear. I should be screaming my head off, or at least trying to fight him, but I can't move. I can't do anything but stare at the lethally beautiful killer holding me captive.

"Come, Sara." His hand slides down to lock around my wrist in a familiar iron shackle. "I won't hurt you."

I inhale shakily. "You won't?" Maybe he'll be gentle. *Please, let him at least be gentle.* I've experienced violence at his hands, and it terrifies me even more than the specter of rape.

"No. Now come."

He pushes away from the door, but instead of leading me to the bed, he takes me to the chair in front of the vanity mirror.

"Sit." He presses down on my shoulders, and I sink into the chair, trying to steady my ragged breathing. What is he doing? Why isn't he just attacking me? My face in the mirror is deathly pale, my eyes wide as he steps behind me and pulls something from the inner pocket of his jacket.

It's a small hairbrush wrapped in plastic—one of those cheap ones they sometimes give out in hotels and upscale airlines.

"This is all they had at the gift shop downstairs," he says, removing the plastic wrap before meeting my gaze in the mirror. "I figured it's better than nothing."

Better than nothing for what? Some weird kinky game? My throat constricts, but before the panic can overtake me, he unwraps the towel on my head and drops it on the floor. His strong, sun-browned hands look huge next to my skull as he gathers my hair into a wet ponytail and begins working through the knots with the brush.

Shock steals all air from my lungs. My husband's killer—the man who's been stalking me—is *brushing my hair.*

His touch is gentle but sure, lacking any trace of hesitation. It's as if he's done this a dozen times before. He runs the brush through the ends first, getting them smooth and tangle-free; then he systematically moves up until the small brush can run through the entire length of my hair without snagging. And throughout the process, there's no pain— just the opposite, in fact. The plastic bristles massage my skull with every stroke, and prickles of pleasure run down my spine whenever his warm fingers brush against the sensitive skin of my nape.

Fear or not, it's the most sensuous experience of my life.

A strange sense of unreality seizes me as I sit there, watching him brush my hair in the mirror. In each of our prior encounters, I'd been so focused on the danger he poses I didn't pay attention to less important things, like his clothes. So now, for the first time, I notice that he's wearing a distressed gray leather jacket over a black thermal shirt and a pair of dark jeans paired with black boots. The clothes are casual, something any man might wear during early spring in Illinois, but there's no mistaking my tormentor for a regular guy on the street.

Peter Sokolov is nothing less than a force of nature, ruthless and completely unstoppable.

He brushes my hair for several long minutes while I sit as still as I can, not daring to twitch a muscle lest I do something to make him stop. Each stroke of the brush feels like a caress, each touch of his rough hands soothing and thrilling at the same time. More importantly, while he's brushing my hair, he's not doing other things to me—things I'm dreading.

All too soon, however, he puts the brush down on the vanity table, and his eyes catch mine in the mirror. "Up," he orders, his hands curling around my bare shoulders and propelling me to my feet.

Swallowing thickly, I turn around to face him when he releases me, but he's already stepped away and is removing his jacket.

My heart sinking, I watch as he hangs the jacket on the chair and reaches for the bottom of his long-sleeved thermal shirt. In one smooth move, he pulls the shirt off over his head, and my breath hitches in my throat as he hangs it over the jacket.

His shoulders are wide, his arms roped with thick, clearly defined layers of muscle. More muscle covers his lean, V-shaped torso, and his flat, ridged abdomen lacks even a hint of fat. Like his hands, his chest and shoulders are tanned, as if he's spent a lot of time in the sun, and his left arm is almost completely covered by tattoos that extend from the top of his shoulder to his wrist. Amidst a dusting of dark hair on his chest, I see several more faded scars, and I catch myself staring at the sexy trail of hair that starts at his navel and disappears into the waistband of his low-slung jeans.

He reaches for the jeans next, unzipping the fly, and I force myself to look away. Despite his primal male beauty, a layer of cold sweat covers my body, and my pulse is sickeningly fast. He might be a gorgeous beast, but that's all he is: a beast, a cold-hearted monster. It doesn't matter that under different circumstances, I would've been wildly attracted to him. I don't want what's about to happen. It would devastate me.

Out of the corner of my eye, I see him step out of his boots and push his jeans down his legs, revealing a pair of navy briefs stretched over a thick, long bulge, and powerful legs dusted with dark hair. He bends to remove the jeans completely, and my terror reaches a new peak.

Forgetting his warnings, I bolt for the door.

This time, I don't even get near my goal. He catches me two feet from the door, one strong arm looping around my ribcage and lifting me off my feet while his other hand slaps over my mouth, muffling my instinctive scream.

I claw at his forearms, my feet kicking at his shins as he carries me to the bed, but it's useless. All I achieve is having the towel unwrap in the back. His arm around my ribcage keeps it from falling to the floor, but my back, buttocks, and the right side of my body are completely exposed. I can feel his bare chest rubbing against my back, smell the clean male musk of his skin, and the unwanted intimacy intensifies my panic, making me struggle even harder.

"Fuck," he growls as my heel connects with his knee, and I feel a small flare of triumph.

It doesn't last long. A second later, he falls backward on the bed, dragging me with him, and before I can react, he rolls over, pinning me underneath him. I end up facedown on the blanket, my hands scratching uselessly at the soft surface and my legs weighed down by his heavily muscled calves. With his palm over my mouth, I can't do anything except make muffled noises, and tears of panic burn my eyes as I feel the hard log of his erection against the curve of my ass. Only his briefs separate us now, and I double my struggles despite the futility of it all.

It takes a couple of minutes for me to wear myself out—and to realize he's not moving.

He's restraining me, but he's making no attempts to take me.

"Are you done now?" he murmurs when I go limp, my muscles shaking from exertion and my lungs screaming for air. "Or do you want to wrestle some more? I can do this all night long."

I believe him. He's so much bigger than me that all he has to do is lie on top, and I can neither hurt him nor get away. The effort expended on his part is minimal, while I'm using all my strength with zero success.

"Will you behave if I remove my hand?" His lips hover just above my ear, his breath heating my skin.

My shoulders bunch up to protect my neck from those encroaching lips, and he lets out an audible sigh. "All right, I guess I'll gag you and get my handcuffs."

I make a muffled noise behind his palm, and he chuckles. "No? Will you behave then?"

I manage a small nod. Defeat is an acrid burn in my throat, but I don't want to be gagged and cuffed.

"Good girl." He shifts off me and removes his hand from my mouth, enabling me to drag air into my oxygen-starved lungs. "Now that you got that out of your system, how about we go to sleep? I know you have a long day tomorrow, and so do I."

"What?" I'm so startled I roll over onto my back, forgetting my nudity.

A slow, wicked smile curves his mouth as his gaze travels over my body before returning to my face. "Sleep, ptichka. We both need it."

I sit up and grab a pillow, holding it pressed against my chest as I scoot toward the headboard—as far away from him as the bed allows. What he's saying makes no sense. He clearly wants me; his huge erection is all but tearing through his briefs. "You... you want to *sleep* with me? *Just* sleep?"

The smile leaves his face, and his eyes gleam with dark heat. "Obviously, I want more, but tonight, I'll settle for sleep. I told you, Sara—I won't hurt you again. I'll wait until you're ready... until you want me as much as I want you."

Want him? I want to scream that he's insane, that I will never voluntarily have sex with him, but I swallow the retort. I'm too vulnerable right now, and he's too unpredictable. Besides, when he's asleep, I'll have a chance to get away—maybe even smack him over the head and call the cops.

"All right." I try to look even more helpless than I truly am. "If you promise not to hurt me..."

His lips quirk. "I promise." Getting off the bed, he pulls the blanket from under me with one strong tug and turns it down before fluffing up the remaining pillows. Patting the exposed sheets, he says, "Come here."

I scoot a few inches toward him, hugging my pillow to my chest.

"Closer."

I repeat the maneuver, my heart thudding with anxiety. I don't trust him one bit. He could be toying with me, lying about his intentions for some bizarre purpose.

"Get under the blanket," he says, and I obey, glad to have something other than a pillow to cover me. Unfortunately, my relief is short-lived. As soon as I lie down, he turns off the overhead light and gets under the blanket next to me, his long, muscular body stretching out beside me like he belongs there.

"Roll over onto your right side," he says and does so himself after turning off the bedside lamp—our last remaining source of illumination.

My ribcage tightens as I understands what he intends.

My husband's killer wants to spoon with me.

Ignoring the disorienting darkness and the choking feeling in my throat, I turn onto my side and try to breathe evenly as one muscular arm stretches out under the pillow below me and the other one wraps possessively around my ribcage, pulling me into the curve of his big body. However, breathing evenly is impossible. My naked butt nestles against the hard length of his cock, his warm, minty breath fans the fine hair at my temple, and his legs mold against mine from the back. I'm surrounded, completely overtaken by his size and strength. And heat. God, his body generates so much heat. Wherever his bare flesh presses against mine, I feel burned, as if he runs hotter than a regular human being. Except it's not him—it's me. I'm so frozen I'm shivering, the cold sweat having evaporated on my skin.

I don't know how long we lie there like that, but eventually, his warmth seeps into me and transforms into a different kind of heat, the treacherous one that invades my dreams and makes me burn with shame. Now that I'm not so terrified, I'm aware of his powerful body as something more than a threat... of his hard cock as something other than a tool of violation. His warm male scent surrounds me, and my breasts feel heavy and sensitive above the thick band of his arm, my nipples tight and my sex aching with slick, throbbing emptiness. How long has it been since I've been held like this? Two years? Three? I can't recall the last time George and I had sex, much less lay together like lovers, and despite the wrongness of the situation, the animal part of me enjoys being held like this, feeling the warmth of a man's body and the pulsing hum of arousal in my core.

It's a good thing I'm not planning to sleep, because there's no way I'd be able to like this—not with my heart racing a mile a minute and my mind outpacing it with a scramble of thoughts. Fear and anger, arousal and shame—it all blends together, spiking my heart rate and souring my stomach. What does Peter really want? What does he get out of this bizarre cuddling? That massive erection must be uncomfortable, if not downright painful, but he seems content to lie there, doing nothing more than holding me. Why? What's his deal? Why did he latch on to me?

And could it possibly be true, what he said about George? Could my husband have somehow harmed his family?

It's the worst idea in the world, but I can't stop myself. My mouth seems to operate independently of my brain as I whisper, "Um, Peter... can you tell me something about yourself?"

I can feel his surprise in the minute tightening of his muscles and the change in his breathing. I've never addressed him by his name before, but it would be strange to call him anything else when I'm lying naked in his arms. Also, a little emotional intimacy might make him more inclined to answer my questions—and less likely to hurt me for asking them.

"What do you want to know?" he murmurs after a second, shifting to fit me more comfortably against him.

Why do you think my husband massacred your family? That's what I'm dying to ask, but I'm not stupid enough to go there directly. I remember his rage the last time we touched on this topic. Instead, I say softly, "They told me you were born in Russia. Is that true?"

"Yes." His deep voice takes on a note of amusement. "You can't tell by the accent?"

"It's very mild, so no. You could be from pretty much anywhere in Europe or the Middle East. In general, your English is excellent." I'm speaking too fast from nervousness, so I make myself take a breath and slow down. "Did you learn it in school?"

"No, at my job."

The job where he tracked down and interrogated supposed threats to Russia? I suppress a shudder and try not to think about those interrogation methods. *Keep it light, I tell myself. Work up to the heavy stuff.* In an upbeat tone, I say, "As an adult? That's impressive. Usually, you have to learn a language as a child to be able to speak it as well as you do."

There, that's good. A little flattery, a little genuine admiration. That's what you're supposed to do when you're in a vulnerable position: establish a rapport with your attacker, make him see you as someone he can empathize with. Of course, that strategy hinges on said attacker's ability to empathize—something I suspect the psychopath wrapped around me is missing.

"Well, I did learn a few English words and phrases as a child," he says. "I suppose that helped."

"Oh? Where did you learn them? In school, or from your parents?"

He chuckles, his muscular chest expanding against my back. "Neither. Just from American movies. They're your main export, you know—that and hamburgers."

"Right." I inhale, trying to ignore the heavy arm slung across my ribcage and the hard evidence of his arousal throbbing against my ass. It bothers me in ways I don't care to think about. "So what made you decide to go into your... um, profession?"

He buries his nose in my hair and inhales deeply, as if breathing me in. "What exactly did Ryson tell you?"

I tense at his casual use of the agent's last name, then force myself to relax. Of course he'd know who Ryson is;

he likely saw us talk at the cafe. "He said you were Russian Special Forces. Is that right?"

"Yes." His voice sounds husky as he shifts behind me again, his cock like a steel pole pressed against me. "I headed a small off-the-books unit specializing in counter-terrorism and counterinsurgency."

"That's... unusual." Talking to him—and thus keeping him awake in this aroused state—is probably not such a great idea, but I can't make myself shut up. "How does one get into something like that? Did you join the army and get recruited there?"

"No." He continues to nuzzle his face against my hair. "They found me in what you would call juvie."

"A prison for juvenile delinquents?"

"It was more of a labor camp, but yes."

"What—" I swallow, trying to concentrate on his words rather than the effect his obvious desire for me is having on my body. "What did you do to end up there?"

This has nothing to do with George, but I can't suppress my curiosity. I suspect that whatever I learn will only frighten me more, but I want to know what makes my enemy tick.

I want to know his weaknesses, so I can use them against him.

"I killed the headmaster of the orphanage where I was raised." There's no trace of regret or apology in Peter's words, no emotion beyond the lust thickening his voice. He could just as well have been relaying what he had for dinner. "I guess you could say I started on my career path early."

"I see." My skin crawls, but I do my best to sound calm. "How old were you?"

"Eleven, almost twelve."

"What did he do to you?"

He sighs and pulls back slightly. "Does it really matter, ptichka? You've made up your mind about me, and no sob story from my past is likely to change it. Right now, you hate me too much to feel anything other than joy at whatever misfortune I might've endured."

So much for building that emotional rapport. "Well, what did you expect?" I ask bitterly, dropping all pretense of sympathetic listening. "That you could torture me and kill my husband, and we'd be pals?"

"No, ptichka. Despite what you may think, I'm not delusional. Your negative feelings toward me are rational and expected. I'm just hoping to change them over time."

He is delusional if he thinks I'll ever feel anything but hatred toward him, but I don't bother arguing. "What is that word you keep calling me? Ptee-something?"

"Ptichka." He resumes nuzzling my hair, or smelling it, or whatever the hell he's doing. "It means *little bird* in Russian."

My hands fist in the blanket in front of me. "A bird?"

"Hmm. A small songbird, pretty and graceful like you." He pauses, then adds softly, "Also caged, like you."

The asshole. I clench my teeth and try to shift away from him as much as the restraining arm around my waist would allow. "That's a temporary situation."

"Oh, I don't mean caged by me." I can hear the smile in his voice as he tightens his grip on me, preventing me from squirming away. "I might be holding you at the moment, but you were imprisoned long before I entered your life."

I freeze in surprise. "What?"

"Oh, yes. Don't pretend you don't know what I'm talking about, Sara. I know you've felt it: all the expectations from society, from your parents and your husband and your friends... The pressure to succeed because you were born smart and pretty, the desire to be perfect, the need to be everything to everyone at all times..." His voice is soft and dark, wrapping me in a silky, seductive web. "I saw it in the club yesterday: your longing for freedom, your desire to live without the restraints placed on you. For a few moments on that dance floor, you let the shackles fall away, and I saw the pretty bird exit her golden cage and fly free. I saw *you*, Sara, and it was beautiful."

For a couple of seconds, all I can do is lie unmoving, my chest aching and my eyes burning in the darkness. I want to laugh and deny his words, but I'm afraid that if I try to speak, I'll break down and scream. How could this man, this violent stranger, know something so private— something I've just begun to understand about myself?

How could he know that my nice, comfortable life no longer makes me happy... that maybe it never did?

Forcing down the swelling bubble in my throat, I let out a derisive snort and say, "So you're going to... what? Liberate me from my restrictive life? Set me free and watch me fly?"

"No, ptichka." His voice is filled with gentle mockery. "Nothing as noble as that."

"What then?"

"I'm going to place you in a cage of my own and make you sing."

CHAPTER 18
PETER

She shudders in my arms, and I feel the fear rippling through her. A part of me regrets my brutal honesty, but I can't bring myself to lie to her. My desire for her is nothing like the gentle affection I'd felt for Tamila or the straight-forward lust I'd experienced with other women.

My need for Sara is darker, tainted by what passed between us and the knowledge that she used to belong to my enemy. I don't want to hurt her, yet I can't deny that her suffering appeals to me in some perverse way. Tormenting her cools my burning rage, satisfies my need to punish and avenge, even as I tell myself I want to heal her, to atone for the pain I inflicted.

When it comes to Sara, I'm a mess of contradictions, and the only thing I'm sure of is that a simple fucking won't be enough.

I want more.

I want to make her mine.

It's tempting to break my promise and take her now, to claim her and ease the hunger consuming me alive. She's completely naked in my embrace, her bare skin rubbing against mine each time she takes a breath. I can smell the flowery shampoo in her damp hair, feel the softness of her breasts resting on my arm, and my cock throbs painfully against the curve of her ass, my body aching with the need to thrust inside her. She'd fight at first, but I could make her like it.

She's not immune to me. I know it. I sense it.

Before the dark impulse can take over, I draw in a breath and let it out slowly. As good as it would feel to fuck Sara, I want her trust as much as her body.

I want her to sing for me of her own accord.

"Go to sleep, ptichka," I murmur when she remains silent, all her questions choked off for now. "You'll be safe tonight."

And ignoring the hunger raging through my body, I close my eyes and sink into a light but restful sleep.

I wake up three times during the night, twice when Sara tries to free herself from my embrace—undoubtedly to escape and do something painful to me—and once when she wakes up from a bad dream. I hold her tighter in each case, and she eventually falls asleep again. After a while, so do I, though the lust gnawing at me only grows more intense throughout the night. By morning, I'm ready to explode, and it takes all of twenty seconds to jerk off when I go use the restroom.

She's still asleep when I come out of the bathroom, and I contemplate getting back under the covers with her. However, it's almost seven, and I want to catch up with Anton before he crashes for the day. I'm also not entirely certain of my self-control; the quick release barely took the edge off my violent craving for her.

If I climb into bed with Sara again, I run the risk of breaking my promise.

Deciding against tempting fate, I quietly dress and slip out of the room.

I'll see Sara again soon. In the meanwhile, there's work to be done.

CHAPTER 19
SARA

I have a scheduled C-section in the morning and an un-scheduled one in the afternoon. In between, I see a woman who has painful menstrual cramps but can't tolerate the usual remedy of hormonal birth control—something I empathize with very much—and another one who's been trying to get pregnant for two years without much success. I schedule an ultrasound for the first one to check for endometriomas and refer the second one to a fertility specialist. As soon as I'm done with that, I get called to the ER to examine a six-months-pregnant woman who's been in a bad car accident. Luckily, I'm able to tell her that the baby is healthy and kicking—the best possible outcome in a head-on collision of that magnitude.

It surprises me that I'm able to focus on my work after last night, but for the first time in months, dark memories don't invade my mind at every turn, and the paranoia of the past month is absent. Perversely, now that I *know* I'm being watched, the idea doesn't fill me with as much anxiety as when I just had that unnerving sensation. I also feel well rested and alert with minimal caffeine consumption, and I suspect it's because I got a solid nine hours of sleep despite the hard body wrapped around me all night.

Or maybe *because* of it. No matter how hard I tried to stay awake last night, the animal warmth coming off Peter's skin and his even breathing lured me to sleep. I woke up a couple of times throughout the night to try to extricate myself from him, but it was impossible. He held me with the intensity of a child clutching his favorite teddy bear, and eventually, I gave in and simply slept, my subconscious mind blissfully unaware that the source of my nightmares was right next to me.

In any case, whatever the reason, I remain calm and focused throughout my shift. It helps that I've managed to suppress all thoughts of Peter and his intentions, shoving them to the back of my mind while I concentrate on my patients. If I let myself dwell on his declaration, I would run out of the hospital screaming, and who knows what my stalker would do then? When I woke up alive and unharmed this morning, I decided that the best course of action is to take it one day at a time and avoid provoking him as much as I can.

Maybe he'll play nice for a while longer, and I'll have time to figure out what to do.

When my shift is over, I head to the locker room and run into Andy in the hallway. She must be just starting her shift, because her scrubs look perfectly pressed and her curly hair is drawn into a neat bun, without a single strand out of place.

By the end of a long shift, most nurses and doctors—myself included—look far more disheveled.

"Hey," she says, stopping in front of me. "Everything okay?"

I blink. "Um, yeah." She can't know about Peter, can she? "Why?"

"You said you weren't feeling well the other night," Andy says, a small frown tugging at her forehead. "When you hightailed it from the club."

"Oh, yeah, sorry about that." I attempt an embarrassed smile. "I had too much to drink, and it hit me hard. I think I puked when I got home, but it's all kind of fuzzy now."

"Ah, I see." A relieved grin replaces the worry on her face. "I thought maybe you were upset about something. You looked like someone shot your favorite pony in front of you."

I laugh and shake my head, though she's not far from the truth. "I'm afraid the only victim was my liver."

Andy laughs, then asks, "What are you doing next Saturday? Tonya and Marsha are planning another girls' night out, but I was thinking of just grabbing dinner and a movie with Larry—both at a reasonable hour, since I have an early shift next Sunday. Want to join us?"

"You and your boyfriend?" I give her a surprised look. "Wouldn't I be the third wheel?"

"Well…" An impish grin lights up her freckled face. "As it so happens, Larry has a very handsome—and very successful—friend who's dying to meet a nice girl. He's a real estate mogul, and he has an impossible list of requirements, but"—she lifts a finger when I'm about to interrupt—"you happen to fit all of them. If you're cool with it, Larry will invite him along, and we could have a nice double date."

I wrinkle my nose. "Oh, I don't know about that—"

"He's a good-looking dude. Here." She pulls a phone out of her pocket, swipes across the screen a few times, and shows me a picture of a guy who looks like a blond Tom Cruise. "See? You could definitely do much worse."

I chuckle. "For sure, but—"

"No buts." She holds up her hand when I'm about to argue. "Just come, and we'll have fun. No pressure to do anything. If you like Larry's friend, great. If not, you and I will bail to join the girls, and Larry can have a boys' night out—he's been hankering for one for ages."

I hesitate, then regretfully shake my head. "Thank you, but I can't." I don't know if Peter poses a threat to Andy or her boyfriend, but I don't want to risk it. With the Russian killer watching my every move, every person around me could become his target.

Until my stalker situation is resolved, it's best if I keep to myself.

Andy's face falls. "Oh, okay. Well, if you change your mind, ping me. Marsha has my number."

"I will, thanks," I say, but Andy is already hurrying away, walking as fast as her white sneakers allow.

On my way home, I listen to Kelly Clarkson's "Stronger" and fight the urge to keep driving until I'm in another state.

Or maybe even in another country. Canada and Mexico both sound appealing, as do Antarctica and Timbuktu. Instead of going to my camera-infested house, I could drive straight to the airport and hop on a plane to somewhere—anywhere.

I'd go to the North Pole if I had a guarantee Peter wouldn't come after me.

Unfortunately, I don't have that guarantee. Just the opposite, in fact. If I run, he'll come after me. I'm sure of that. He's a hunter, a tracker, and he won't rest until he finds me, just like he found all the people on his list. I could go to another hotel or another continent, and it wouldn't make any difference.

He won't leave me alone until he gets what he wants—whatever that is.

My palms feel slippery on the steering wheel, and I realize I'm breathing fast, my calm dissipating as thoughts of last night creep in. I'm still not certain what he's after, but it seems to be something other than just sex.

Something darker and far more twisted.

Realizing I'm on the verge of another panic attack, I switch from Kelly Clarkson to classical music and start doing my breathing exercises. Maybe I'm making a mistake by not going to the FBI. There's at least a chance they might be able to protect me, whereas on my own I stand no chance at all. The best I can hope for is that he'll get bored with me and move on to his next victim, leaving me alive and with most of my sanity intact.

I'm already reaching for my phone when I remember why I didn't call Ryson right away: my parents. I can't disappear and leave them, and it would be selfish to uproot them on the slim chance the FBI would be able to protect us. To explain the necessity for the move, I'd have to tell my parents everything, and I don't know if my dad's heart would survive that kind of stress. He had a triple bypass several years ago, and the doctors advised him to keep stressful activities to a minimum. Learning about a homicidal stalker who tortured me and killed George could literally kill my dad, and might even be dangerous for my mom.

No. I won't do that to them. Getting my breathing under control, I put Kelly Clarkson back on. My parents have a happy, normal life, and I'll do whatever it takes to keep it that way. If that means I have to deal with Peter on my own, so be it.

Hopefully, I'm strong enough to survive whatever he'll dish out.

CHAPTER 20
SARA

What he dishes out is food. Lots of deliciously smelling food.

Stunned, I gape at the spread on my dining room table. There is a whole roasted chicken, a bowl of mashed potatoes, and a big leafy salad—all of it prettily arranged between lit candles and a bottle of white wine.

I figured I might get ambushed in my house tonight, but I didn't expect this.

"Hungry?" a deep, lightly accented voice asks from behind me, and I whirl around, my pulse leaping as Peter Sokolov steps out from the hallway. The front of his hair is wet, as if he just washed his face, and though he's dressed in a blue button-up shirt and a pair of dark jeans, he's not wearing shoes, only socks.

He looks gorgeous—and more dangerous than ever.

"What—" My voice is too high, so I take a breath and try again. "What is this?"

"Dinner," he says, looking amused. "What does it look like?"

"I..." The air in the room thins as he stops a couple of feet from me, the intimate look in his eyes reminding me that I slept naked in his arms. "I'm not hungry."

"No?" He arches his dark eyebrows. "All right, then. Let's go to bed." He moves as if to reach for me, and I jump back.

"No, wait! I could eat."

A smile curves his lips. "I thought so. After you."

He gestures in a courtly semi-circle, and I walk over to the table, trying to swallow my heart back into my chest as he turns off the overhead light, leaving only candlelight as illumination, and follows me to the table.

He pulls out a chair, and I sit in it. Then he walks over to the chair across from me and takes a seat himself. I notice that the table is set with two plates and my formal silverware—the one George liked me to use only for holidays and parties.

Silently, I watch George's killer expertly cut up the chicken and put one of the drumsticks—my favorite part of the chicken—on my plate, along with several spoonfuls of mashed potatoes and a generous portion of the salad.

"Where did you get all this food?" I ask as he loads his own plate.

"I made it." He looks up from his plate. "You like chicken, right?"

I do, but I'm not about to tell him that. "You cook?"

"I dabble." He picks up his knife and fork. "Go ahead, try it."

I push my chair back and get up. "I have to wash my hands." I just came in from the garage, and the OCD doctor in me won't let me touch food without first washing off the hospital germs.

"All right," he says, putting down his utensils, and I realize he intends to wait for me.

My stalker has excellent table manners.

I go into the nearby bathroom and wash my hands, scrubbing between each finger and around my wrists like I always do. By the time I return to the table, he's already poured us each a glass of wine, and the crisp smell of Pinot Grigio mixes with the delicious aromas of the meal, adding to the bizarreness of the situation.

If I didn't know better, I'd think we're on a date.

"How did you know I'd come here instead of going to a hotel?" I ask when I'm seated.

He shrugs. "It was an educated guess. You're bright, so you're unlikely to make the same mistake twice."

"Uh-huh." I pick up my fork and try a bite of mashed potatoes. The rich, buttery flavor is bliss on my tongue, jumpstarting my appetite despite the anxiety roiling my stomach. "That's a lot of cooking to do on an educated guess."

"Yes, well, no risk, no reward, right? Besides, I've seen how you think and reason, Sara. You don't do stupid, pointless things, and going to another hotel would've been precisely that."

My hand tightens around my fork. "Is that right? You think you know me because you've stalked me for a few weeks?"

"No." His eyes gleam in the candlelight. "I don't know you, ptichka—at least not nearly as well as I'd like to."

Ignoring that provocative statement, I focus on my plate. Now that I've had a bite, my mouth is watering for more. Despite what I told Peter earlier, I'm starving, and I gladly dig into the delicious spread on my plate. The chicken is perfectly seasoned, the mashed potatoes are generously buttered, and the green salad is refreshingly tangy with an unusual lemony dressing. I'm so absorbed in eating that I'm halfway done with my plate when a frightening thought occurs to me.

Putting down my fork, I look up at my tormentor. "You didn't drug this or something, right?"

"If I did, it would be too late for you," he points out with amusement. "But no. You can relax. If I were going to drug or poison you, I'd use a syringe. No need to spoil perfectly good food."

I try to not react, but my hand shakes as I reach for my glass of wine. "Great. Glad to hear it."

He smiles at me, and I feel a warm, melting sensation between my legs. To hide my discomfort, I take several gulps of wine and put the glass down before refocusing on my plate.

I am *not* attracted to him. I refuse to be.

We eat in silence until our plates are empty; then Peter puts down his fork and picks up his wine glass. "Tell me something, Sara," he says. "You're twenty-eight now, and you've been a full-fledged doctor for two and a half years. How did you manage that? Were you one of those child geniuses with a super-high IQ?"

I push my empty plate aside. "Your stalking didn't tell you that?"

"I didn't do a deep dive into your background." He takes a sip of wine and puts down his glass. "If you'd rather I do that, I can—or you can just talk to me, and we could get to know each other in a more traditional manner."

I hesitate, then decide it wouldn't hurt to talk to him. The longer we sit at the table, the longer I can postpone bedtime and all that it could entail.

"I'm not a genius," I say, taking a small sip of wine. "I mean, I'm not dumb, but my IQ is within the normal range."

"Then how did you become a doctor at twenty-six when it normally takes at least eight years after college?"

"I was an oops baby," I say. When he continues looking at me, I explain, "I was born three years before my mom went through menopause. She was almost fifty when she got pregnant, and my dad was fifty-eight. They were both professors—they met when he was her Ph.D. advisor, actually, though they didn't start dating until later—and neither of them wanted children. They had their careers, they had a great circle of friends, and they had each other. They were making plans for retirement that year, but instead, I happened."

"How?"

I shrug. "A couple of drinks combined with the conviction that they were too old to worry about a broken condom."

"So they didn't want you?" His gray eyes darken, steel turning to gunmetal, and his mouth tightens.

If I didn't know better, I'd think he's angry on my behalf.

Shaking off the ridiculous thought, I say, "No, they did. At least, once they got over the shock of learning about the pregnancy. It wasn't what they wanted or expected, but once I was there, born healthy despite all odds, they gave me everything. I became the center of their world, their personal little miracle. They had tenure, they had savings, and they embraced their new role as parents with the same dedication they gave their careers. I was showered with attention, taught to read and count to one hundred before I could walk. By the time I started kindergarten, I could read at fifth-grade level and knew basic algebra."

The hard line of his mouth softens. "I see. So you had a huge leg-up on the competition."

"Yes. I skipped two grades in elementary school and would've skipped more, but my parents didn't think it would be good for my social development to be meaningfully younger than my classmates. As it was, I struggled to make friends in school, but that's neither here nor there." I pause to take another sip of wine. "I did end up finishing high school in three years because the curriculum was easy for me and I wanted to start college, and then I finished college in three years because I'd earned a lot of college credits by taking Advanced Placement classes in high school."

"So that's the four years."

I nod. "Yes, that's the four years."

He studies me, and I shift in my chair, uncomfortable with the warmth in his eyes. My wine glass is mostly empty now, and I'm starting to feel the effects, the faint buzz of alcohol chasing away the worst of my anxiety and making me notice irrelevant things, like how his dark hair looks thick and silky to the touch, and how his mouth is soft and hard at the same time. He's looking at me with admiration in his gaze... and something else, something that makes my skin feel hot and tight, as though I'm running a fever.

As if sensing it, Peter leans in, his lids lowering. "Sara..." His voice is low and deep, dangerously seductive. I can feel my breathing picking up as he covers my hand with his big palm and murmurs, "Ptichka, you're—"

"Why do you think George hurt your family?" I yank my hand away, desperate to douse my growing arousal. "What happened to them?"

My question is like a bomb exploding in the sexually charged atmosphere. His gaze turns flat and hard, the warmth disappearing in a flash of icy rage.

"My family?" His hand clenches on the table. "You want to know what happened to them?"

I nod warily, fighting the instinct to jump up and back away. I have the terrifying feeling I just provoked a wounded predator, one who could rip me apart without even trying.

"All right." His chair scrapes across the floor as he stands up. "Come here, and I'll show you."

CHAPTER 21
PETER

She remains seated, frozen in place. A fawn caught in the crosshairs of a hunter's rifle. I know I'm scaring her, but I can't bring myself to care—not with the pain and rage tearing me up inside.

Even after five and a half years, thinking of Pasha and Tamila's deaths has the power to destroy me.

"Come here," I repeat, stepping around the table. Grabbing Sara's arm, I pull her to her feet, ignoring her stiff posture. "You want to know? You want to see what your husband and his cohorts did?"

Her slim arm is tense in my grasp as I reach into my pocket with my free hand and take out my old smartphone. I always carry it with me, though it's not on any network and can't be used to make phone calls. Swiping across the screen with my thumb, I navigate to the last set of pictures.

"Here." I thrust the phone into her free hand. "Take a good look."

Sara's hand shakes as she lifts the phone to her face, and I know the exact moment she lays eyes on the first picture. Her face turns white, and she swallows convulsively before swiping across the screen to view the rest of the photos.

I don't glance at the phone myself—I don't need to. The images are burned into my retinas, etched into my brain like a gruesome tattoo.

I took these pictures the day after I escaped from the soldiers who dragged me away from the scene. They'd already relocated the remaining villagers, but the investigation was just starting, and they hadn't cleaned up the bodies yet. When I returned, the corpses still lay there, covered by flies and crawling insects. I photographed everything: the burned-out buildings, the dark blood stains on the grass, the decomposing bodies and torn limbs, Pasha's tiny hand curled around the toy car... There were things I couldn't capture, like the stench of rotting flesh that hung thickly in the air and the desolate emptiness of an abandoned village, but what I did record is enough.

Sara lowers the phone, and I take it from her bloodless fingers, slipping it back into my pocket.

"That was Daryevo." I release her arm, each word like sandpaper scraping across my throat. "A small village in Dagestan where my wife and son lived."

Sara takes a step back. "What..." She swallows audibly. "What happened there? Why were they killed?"

I take a breath to control the violent anger churning inside me. "Because of some people's arrogance and blind ambition."

Sara gives me an uncomprehending look.

"It was a sting operation designed to capture a small but highly effective terrorist cell based in the Caucasus Mountains," I say harshly. "A group of NATO soldiers acted on information provided by a coalition of Western intelligence agencies. Everything was done under the radar so they wouldn't have to share the glory with the local counterterrorist groups—like the one I headed for Russia."

Sara covers her trembling mouth, and I see she's beginning to understand.

"That's right, ptichka." Stepping toward her, I capture her slender wrist and pull her hand away from her face. "You can guess who was involved in getting the soldiers that false information."

Her eyes are full of horror. "The terrorist cell wasn't there?"

"No." My grip on her wrist is punishingly tight, but I can't make myself relax my fingers. With the memories fresh in my mind, I can't help thinking of her as my dead enemy's wife. "Nothing was there but a peaceful civilian village, and if your husband and the other operatives on his team had checked in with *my* team, they would have known that." My voice grows rougher, my words more biting. "If they hadn't been so fucking arrogant, so greedy for glory, they would've sought help instead of thinking they knew everything—and then they would've learned their source was planted by the terrorists themselves, and my wife and son would still be alive."

I can feel the rapid flutter of Sara's pulse as she stares up at me, and I see she doesn't believe me—not completely, at least. She thinks I'm mad, or at best, misinformed. Her doubt enrages me further, and I force myself to release her wrist before I crush her fragile bones.

She immediately backs away, and I know she senses the violence pulsing under my skin. When I first learned the truth of what happened, I couldn't punish the NATO soldiers or the operatives involved—the cover-up was remarkably fast and thorough—so I took out my fury on the terrorist cell that fed them the false information, followed by anyone dumb enough to stand in my way.

My son's death unleashed the monster within me, and it still roams free.

When there's a meter of distance between us, Sara stops backing away and regards me warily. "Is that why…" She bites her lip. "Is that why you became a fugitive? Because of what happened back then?"

My hands clench into fists, and I turn away, returning to the table. I can't discuss this for even a second longer. Each sentence is like a spray of acid over my heart. I've gotten to the point where I can go several hours without thinking about my family's violent deaths, but talking about what happened brings back the devastation of that day—and the rage that consumed me.

If we stay on this topic, I might lose control and hurt Sara.

One movement at a time. One task at a time. I blank out my mind like I do when I'm on a job, and focus on what needs to be done. In this case, it's clearing the table, putting the leftovers in the fridge, and stacking the dishes in the dishwasher. I focus on those mundane activities, and gradually, my boiling fury eases, as does the urge to do violence.

When I start the dishwasher and turn back toward Sara, I see her watching me warily. She looks like she's about to bolt at any moment, and the fact that she hasn't already means she understands her predicament.

If she runs right now, I won't be gentle when I catch her.

"Let's go upstairs," I say and walk toward her. "It's time to go to bed."

Her hand is icy in my grasp as I lead her up the stairs, her beautiful face pale. If I didn't feel so raw inside, I'd reassure her, tell her I won't hurt her tonight either, but I don't want to make promises I may not be able to keep.

The monster is too close to the surface, too out of control.

"Take off your clothes," I order, releasing her hand when we get to her bedroom. She's wearing skinny jeans and a loose ivory sweater, and though she looks phenomenal in the simple outfit, I want it gone.

I want there to be no barriers between us.

Instead of obeying, Sara backs away. "Please..." She stops halfway between me and the bed. "Please don't do this. I'm sorry about what happened to your family, and if George was in any way responsible—"

"He was." My tone is cutting. "It took years, but I got the names of every soldier and intelligence officer involved in the massacre. There's no mistake, Sara; my list came directly from your very own CIA."

She looks stunned. "You got it from the CIA? But… how? I thought you said they were involved, that George was one of them."

"There are many divisions and factions within the organization. One hand doesn't always know or care what the other one is doing. I know an arms dealer who has a contact there, and he—or rather, his wife—provided the list. But that's neither here nor there." I cross my arms in front of my chest. "Take off your clothes."

Her eyes dart to the bed, then to the door behind me.

"Don't. You don't want to test me tonight, trust me."

Her gaze returns to my face, and I can feel her desperation. "Please, Peter. Please don't do this. What happened to your family was awful, but this won't bring them back. I'm sorry about them, I truly am, but I had nothing to do with—"

"This is not about that." I uncross my arms. "What I want from you has nothing to do with what happened." Except even as I say it, I know it's a lie. My actions are not those of a man courting a woman; they're of a predator stalking its prey. If she weren't who she is—if she were just a random woman—I wouldn't be forcing myself into her life like this.

My desire for her would've been gentle and restrained instead of dangerously obsessive.

Sara gives me a disbelieving look, and I realize she understands that too. I'm not fooling anyone. What's happening between us has everything to do with the dark past we share.

So be it.

I step toward her. "Remove your clothes, Sara. I won't ask again."

She backs away again, then stops, likely realizing she's getting closer to the bed. Even with the thick sweater concealing her curves, I can see her narrow chest heaving as her hands clench and unclench convulsively at her sides.

"All right. If that's how you want it…" I start toward her, but she raises her arms, palms facing me.

"Wait!" Her hands shake as she reaches for her sweater. "I'll do it."

I stop and watch as she pulls the sweater off over her head. Underneath, she's wearing a tight blue tank top that bares her slender shoulders and highlights the soft curves of her breasts. They're not the biggest I've seen, but they suit her ballerina-like frame, and my cock hardens as I recall how those pretty breasts felt resting on my arm last night.

Soon, I'll know how they feel in my hands—and how they taste.

"Go ahead," I say when Sara hesitates again, her gaze darting past me to the door. "Tank top, then jeans."

Her hands shake as she obeys, pulling the top off over her head before reaching for the zipper of her jeans. Under the tank top, she's wearing a utilitarian white bra, and I have to force myself to remain still as she pushes her jeans down her legs, revealing light blue panties. Though I felt her bare skin against mine last night, and saw her undressed several times on the cameras, this is my first time seeing her naked up close, and my heart rate jacks up as I hungrily take in every graceful line and curve of her body.

She's only about average height, but her legs are long, with the lean, shapely muscles of a dancer. Her belly is flat and toned, her slim waist flares into gently feminine hips, and her skin is smooth and pale all over, with not a tan mark in sight.

She's beautiful, this new obsession of mine. Beautiful and scared.

"Now the rest," I say roughly when she kicks off the jeans and stands there trembling, clad in only her bra and panties. I know I'm being cruel, but the raw, aching wound she exposed sucks out whatever little decency and compassion I possess, leaving only lust edged with the irrational need to punish.

I may not want to hurt her, but at this moment, I need to see her suffer.

She reaches for her bra hook in the back, unsnapping it with jerky motions, and I suck in a sharp breath, the pain in my chest drowned by a wave of even more intense desire. I saw her breasts last night, so I know they're gorgeous, but the sight of her taut pink nipples and soft white flesh still punches me like a fist. My heart pounds in a fast, rough rhythm, and it's all I can do to stay in place and not reach for her as she takes off her panties. Her pussy is smooth and hairless—she either waxes regularly or had her pubic hair lasered at some point—and my mouth waters as I imagine dragging my tongue through those delicate folds.

I can't wait to taste her and make her come.

As I'm picturing that, Sara straightens and defiantly raises her chin. "Happy now?" Though her cheeks are bright red, she's making no attempt to cover her body, her hands clenched into small fists at her sides.

Perversely, her little show of bravery softens the dark lust beating at me, and my mouth curves in amusement.

"Not yet, but I will be soon," I say, taking off my own clothes. My movements are swift and economical, designed to accomplish the task as quickly as possible, but her face still flames brighter, her chest rising and falling as she stares at me.

"Come," I say, walking over to her when I'm fully naked. "I know you like to shower before bed."

She blinks, her eyes flying up to my face, and I realize she was staring at my cock—which is so hard it's curving up to my navel.

"You can touch it in the shower if you'd like," I say, my smile widening at her obvious embarrassment. "Come, ptichka. You'll enjoy this."

Clasping her wrist, I lead her to the bathroom.

CHAPTER 22
SARA

I try to maintain my composure—or at least the appearance of it—as Peter drags me to the bathroom, his long fingers wrapped firmly around my wrist. This is definitely not how I imagined this night going when I was walking up the stairs. Despite the lingering darkness in his eyes, my tormentor now seems to be in a light, almost playful mood—a stark contrast to the terrifying rage I glimpsed on his face earlier.

It's as if my forced little striptease calmed whatever demons those horrifying pictures had unleashed.

Nausea crawls through me again as I recall the images, the death and devastation depicted in such gruesome detail. I only looked at them for a few seconds, but I know I'll never be able to forget them. I can't imagine being there in person to take those pictures, much less knowing that it's my family lying there—that the decomposing corpses used to be people I love. The mere thought fills me with such agony that for one heartbreaking moment, I understand what drives my attacker.

I don't excuse it, but I understand it, and pity battles with terror in my chest.

If Peter believes my husband was responsible for those deaths, he had no choice but to come after him. That much is obvious to me. Even before he went rogue, the Russian's profession would've exposed him to the darkest parts of humanity, taught him to embrace violence as a solution—and that's not even taking into account whatever it was that turned him into a killer before age twelve. A man like that wouldn't turn the other cheek; an eye for an eye would be more his speed. He wouldn't care how many innocents he hurt in his quest for vengeance, and he certainly wouldn't blink at torturing an enemy's wife to get to him.

If George had *any* involvement in what happened, I'm lucky to be alive.

Stopping in front of the glass shower stall, my captor releases my wrist, steps inside, and turns on the water. As he plays with the faucet, trying to find the right temperature setting, I glance at the bathroom door. He's wet and distracted, so I'm almost certain I can make it down the stairs and to my car before he catches me. But then what? Do I drive naked to a random hotel and hope he doesn't find me tonight? Run straight to the FBI and beg them to hide me?

Before I can start that internal debate again, Peter steps out of the shower, water droplets glistening on his powerful chest. "Come in," he says, reaching for my arm, and I almost stumble as he pulls me into the stall.

"Careful," he murmurs, steadying me, and I look up to find him watching me with a mix of hunger and dark amusement. "It's slippery in here."

At his innuendo, the flush that hasn't quite left my face blazes back to life. I hate it that he knows about my body's reaction to him—that just moments earlier, he caught me eyeing his erection like a teenage girl seeing her first porn. Granted, he could star in porn with a cock like that, but that's not the point. It shouldn't matter to me that he's a gorgeous male animal; his powerful body is something for me to fear, not desire.

He's a dangerous, possibly mad murderer, and I should regard him as such.

And I do—rationally, at least. However, as he angles the shower toward me, letting the warm water spray hit my back, I realize I'm not nearly as terrified as I was last night—though I should be, after seeing those pictures. If Peter believes what he's told me, then he has every reason to hate me, and whatever attraction he feels toward me is likely of the toxic variety. I don't know why he didn't rape me last night, but I'm almost certain he'll do it tonight. The thought should fill me with dread—and it does—yet the visceral panic I felt in that hotel room is absent. It's as if sleeping in his arms desensitized me to the sheer wrongness of what he's doing to me, to the violation that is his presence in my house and my shower.

For the second time in as many days, we're naked together, and I don't find it nearly as disturbing as I should.

"Close your eyes," Peter says, picking up my shampoo bottle, and I obey, letting him pour the soapy liquid into my hair. Despite his earlier volatile mood, his strong fingers are gentle on my skull as he massages in the shampoo, and I realize he's pampering me again, further disarming me with his bizarrely caring ministrations. I have an incongruous desire to arch my head back, butting against his hands like a cat demanding a petting, but I remain still, not wanting him to know that I enjoy any part of what he's doing to me.

Whatever my tormentor's game is, I refuse to play along.

My determination lasts until he begins massaging my neck, skillfully working out the knots at the base of my skull. I didn't even realize how much tension I carried there until it melted away, the heat of the water combining with his touch to make me feel warm and relaxed in a way I haven't experienced in a very long time.

I try to recall if George has ever washed my hair like this and draw a blank. I can't even remember him showering with me outside of a couple of times early in our relationship, when we were still relatively adventurous in bed. By the time we'd been dating for a year, our sex life had become routine, and George rarely touched me in ways that couldn't directly get me off—and toward the end, he rarely touched me, period.

Over the past couple of days, I've had more physical intimacy with my husband's killer than with my husband during most of our marriage.

When my hair is clean, Peter guides my head under the spray, rinsing out the shampoo, and then applies conditioner to my strands. As he does this, he steps closer, his chest brushing against mine for a second, and my nipples tighten under the hot spray, my sex growing soft and slick as I feel the smooth head of his hard cock against my stomach.

He steps back a moment later, but it's too late. The warm, relaxed feeling transitions into arousal so quickly I have no chance to guard against it. Though he's barely touched me, I'm left breathless and trembling, aching for him. It's a purely physical reaction, I know, yet it fills me with shame. I shouldn't want him or this forced intimacy; nothing about this should appeal to me on any level.

Biting the inside of my cheek to distract myself with pain, I open my eyes and see him pouring body wash into his palm.

"Let me do it," I say tightly, reaching to take the body wash from him, but he shakes his head, a sensual smile curving his lips as he moves the bottle out of my reach.

"Not yet, ptichka. You have to wait your turn."

Stepping behind me, he starts washing my back, and even through the heat of the water, his touch burns me, each stroke of his rough hands intensifying the flames of arousal in my core. I try to focus on something else, anything else, but my heart is racing too fast, my body burning with equal parts shame and desire.

And fear. Though muted for the moment, it's an insidious presence in the back of my mind. I haven't forgotten what the man touching me has done or what he's capable of. Perhaps some other woman in my situation would fight instead of letting him do this, but I don't want him to truly hurt me. Yesterday, he subdued me with pathetic ease, and I know the outcome would be the same today. Except he might not stop once he has me stretched out underneath him.

He might give in to the darkness I glimpsed in his eyes tonight, and the game, whatever it is, would end in some horrible way.

So I stand still and stare straight ahead, watching the water droplets roll down the steam-fogged glass wall as his soapy hands slide over my back, my shoulders, my arms... my sides. It's torture of a different kind, and as his hands move to the front, spreading soap over my quivering stomach before sliding up my ribcage, I can't take it anymore.

"Stop," I whisper breathlessly, my nails digging into my thighs as his fingers brush the underside of my breasts. "Please, Peter, stop."

To my shock, he listens, lowering his hands to my hipbones. "Why?" he murmurs, drawing me against him. His chest molds against my back as his erection presses into my ass. "Because you hate it?" He dips his head, his stubble rasping against my temple as he traces the outer rim of my ear with his tongue. "Or because you love it?"

Either. Both. I can't think clearly enough to make up my mind. My eyes drift shut, and goosebumps pebble my skin as his tongue dips into the hollow behind my ear, turning my insides to liquid mush. I want to push him away, but I don't dare move in case I do something stupid, like tipping my head back toward the tantalizing heat of that wicked mouth.

"What is it you're afraid of, ptichka?" he continues in a soft, dark voice. "Pain?" He bites my earlobe gently. "Or pleasure?" His right hand inches diagonally along my stomach, moving toward the aching nook between my legs with insidious slowness. He's giving me every chance to stop him, but I can't—not even when I realize his destination. All I can do is take quick, shallow breaths as his callus-roughened fingers breach the top of my slit and leisurely part my folds, exposing the sensitive flesh within.

"No answer?" His breath is warm on my temple. "I guess I'll have to find out for myself."

The tip of his finger circles my clit, and my breath stutters in my chest, my mind going strangely blank. It's as if every nerve ending in my body has come to life all at once. I'm hyperaware of his big, hard body pressing against my back and his stubble rasping across my ear, of his large hand resting low on my belly and the hot water spraying down on us. And that finger, that rough yet gentle finger. It's barely touching me, yet my whole body feels like a coiled spring, each muscle rigid with anticipation.

Dimly, I register a strange sound, and realize it's coming from me. It's a moan, mixed with a kind of gasping whimper. It fills me with shame, but the embarrassment only intensifies my arousal, all my senses centering on the pulsing ache in the bundle of nerves he's so cruelly teasing. I can feel the slickness between my thighs, and as his finger presses harder on the exquisitely sensitive flesh, the ache transforms into an unbearable tension, one that grows and intensifies with every second. It's both pleasure and agony, and it's so acute I'm vibrating with it, waves of heat rolling over my skin. I try to hold it off, to stop the tension from cresting, but it's as impossible as holding back the tide.

With a choked gasp, I come, my whole body clenching in a release so intense my vision goes white behind my tightly closed eyelids. It goes on and on, the pleasure radiating out from my core in pulsing waves that leave me dazed and shaking, barely able to stand upright. I try to push my tormentor away, to end the terrifying pleasure, but he tightens his hold on me, and I have no choice but to ride it out, feeling every shameful ripple he forces from my body.

"That's it, ptichka," he breathes when I finally sag against him, panting and drained. "That was so beautiful."

His hand leaves my sex, and I open my eyes, the post-orgasmic lethargy dissipating as the horror of what happened seeps in.

I came. I came at the hands of the man who ended my husband's life.

He starts turning me around to face him, and I finally find the strength to act. With a pained moan, I twist out of his hold and stumble back, nearly crashing into the glass wall behind me. "Don't!" My voice is high and thin, verging on hysterical. "Don't touch me!"

To my surprise, Peter remains still, though I can see he's still hard, still wanting me. Cocking his head to the side, he regards me silently for a few moments, then reaches over and turns off the shower.

"Come out," he says gently, pushing open the door of the stall. "I think we're clean enough."

CHAPTER 23
PETER

I dry myself off with a fluffy white towel; then I grab another one and wrap it around Sara as she steps out of the shower. She looks like she's on the verge of shattering, her hazel eyes glittering with painful brightness, and despite the lust consuming me, I feel something close to pity.

She must hate herself right now. Almost as much as she hates me.

I rub the towel up and down her body, drying her, then wrap it around her wet hair. I know I'm treating her like a child instead of the grown woman that she is, but taking care of her calms me, helps me keep the darker impulses under control.

Helps me remember I don't truly want to hurt her.

Bending down, I swing her up into my arms, and she lets out a startled gasp. "What are you doing?" She pushes at my chest. "Put me down!"

"In a second." Ignoring her attempts to wriggle away, I carry her out of the bathroom. She's light, easy to carry. It's as if her bones are hollow, like those of an actual bird. She's fragile, my Sara, but resilient at the same time.

If I'm careful, she'll bend for me instead of breaking.

Reaching the bed, I put her down, and she grabs the blanket, pulling it over herself to cover her nakedness. Her gaze is filled with desperation as she scrambles backward on the bed, away from me.

"Why are you doing this to me? Why can't you find some other woman to torture?"

"You know why, ptichka." Climbing onto the bed, I yank the blanket out of her grasp. "I have no interest in anyone else."

She jumps off the bed, clearly forgetting the futility of running from me, and I leap after her, catching her before she makes it to the door. My blood is pumping thickly in my veins, the monster rearing up as she struggles in my arms, and it takes all of my self-control not to crush her against a wall and fuck her raw.

If it weren't for the fact that I don't want our first time to be like that, I would already be inside her.

"Stop fighting," I grit out when she continues to writhe in my arms, trying to get away. I can feel my control unraveling, my cock reacting to her twisting movements as if to a lap dance. "I'm warning you, Sara…"

She freezes, comprehending the danger she's in.

I inhale slowly, then release her and step back to minimize the temptation. "Get into bed," I say harshly as she stands there, panting. "We're going to sleep, understand?"

Her eyes widen. "You're not going to—?"

"No," I say grimly. Stepping forward, I take her arm to usher her to the bed. "Not tonight."

No matter how torturous it will be, I'll give Sara more time to get used to me. It's the least I can do to make up for our violent beginning.

She'll be mine soon, but not yet.

Not until I can be sure I won't destroy her.

———

"Are you awake, Papa? Come play with me." A small hand tugs at my wrist. "Please, Papa, come play."

"Let your papa sleep," Tamila chides, rising up on her elbow on the other side of the bed. "He got in late last night."

I roll over onto my back and sit up, yawning. "It's okay, Tamilochka. I'm up." Leaning down, I pick up my son and stand up, lifting him at the same time. Pasha squeals in excitement, his small legs kicking in the air as I hold him above my head.

"You're way too indulgent with him," Tamila mutters, then gets up also, throwing on a robe over her pajamas. "I'll go make us breakfast."

She disappears into the bathroom, and I grin at Pasha. "You want to play, pupsik?" I throw him in the air and catch him, causing him to erupt in shrieks of excited laughter. "Like this?" I throw him again.

"Yeah!" He's laughing so hard now he's practically chortling. "More! Higher!"

I laugh, then throw him in the air a few more times, ignoring the pain in my bruised ribs. I spent the last week hunting down a group of insurgents, and we finally found them yesterday. In the resulting gunfight, I caught a couple of bullets in my vest. Nothing serious, but I could use a few slow days. Still, I wouldn't miss this playtime for the world.

My son is growing up too fast as is.

I wake up with a bittersweet ache swelling my chest. I don't need to open my eyes to know where I am, or to realize I was dreaming. The pain of losing Pasha is too sharp, too deeply embedded for me to mistake the dream-memory for anything else, though it *is* the first time I've experienced a pleasant dream so vividly.

Usually, my dreams about my family are soft and blurry—at least until they turn into graphic nightmares.

I lie still for a few moments, listening to Sara's even breathing and absorbing the feel of her slender body curled up in my arms. She's finally asleep, her overactive mind at rest. She didn't talk to me this evening, just lay there rigidly for almost an hour, and I knew she was beating herself up over what happened in the shower. I thought about talking to her, distracting her from her thoughts, but with the memories fresh in my mind and my body hard and aching, I didn't want to risk the conversation venturing into painful territory.

If she started to defend her husband, I might've lost control and taken her, hurting her in the process.

Inhaling, I draw in the sweet scent of her hair and let the familiar surge of lust chase away the lingering tightness in my chest. It doesn't make a lot of sense, but I'm certain Sara is the reason why, for the first time in five and a half years, I dreamed of my son without also dreaming of his death. Though holding her naked body without fucking her is a form of self-torture, Sara's presence in my bed has the same effect on my dreams as her nearness on my waking moments.

When I'm with her, the agony of my losses is less acute, almost bearable.

Closing my eyes, I blank out my mind and let myself sink back into sleep.

If I'm lucky, I'll meet Pasha in my dreams again.

CHAPTER 24
SARA

*L*ike yesterday, Peter is gone by the time I wake up. I'm glad, because I don't know how I would've faced him this morning. Every time I think about what happened in the shower, I die a little bit inside.

I betrayed George, betrayed his memory in the worst possible way. I met my husband when I was barely eighteen. He was my first serious boyfriend, my first everything. And even when things had begun going south, I remained loyal to him and to our marriage.

Until last night, George had been the only man I'd had sex with, the only one who'd ever made me come.

The pain slams into me, the grief so sharp and sudden it feels like a physical blow. Gasping, I bend over the sink, my toothbrush clutched in my fist. For the past six months, I've been so busy coping with my anxiety and panic attacks, with the guilt of knowing I caused George's death, that I haven't had a chance to truly grieve for my husband. I haven't processed the empty gap that is his absence in my life, haven't dealt with the fact that the man I'd been with for the better part of a decade is gone.

George is dead, and I've been sleeping with his killer.

My stomach roils with nausea as I stare at myself in the bathroom mirror, hating the image looking back at me. The ease with which I orgasmed last night fills me with red-hot shame. Peter barely touched me, barely did anything. He didn't even restrain me that much. If I tried, I might've been able to push him away, but I didn't try.

I just stood there and gave in to the pleasure, and then I slept in my torturer's arms for the second night in a row.

The pain congeals into a thick knot of self-disgust, and I look away from my reflection, unable to bear the censure in the hazel eyes staring back at me. I can't do this, can't play this sick, twisted game Peter is forcing on me. It doesn't matter if he has his reasons, or thinks he does. No amount of suffering excuses what he's done to George, or what he's still doing to me.

My tormentor might be hurt and damaged, but that only makes him more dangerous—to my sanity as well as my safety.

I have to find a way out.

No matter what it takes, I have to get rid of him.

———

I spend most of my on-call shift on autopilot. Thankfully, I don't have any surgeries or anything else critical; otherwise, I might've had to ask another doctor to step in. For once, my mind is not on the needs of my patients, but on what I'm going to have to do to deal with my stalker.

It won't be easy, and it will certainly be dangerous, but I don't see any other choice.

I can't spend another night in the arms of a man I hate.

I'm almost finished for the day when I run into Joe Levinson in the hallway. I walk past him at first, but he calls out my name, and I recognize the tall, lean man with sandy hair.

"Joe, hi," I say, smiling. We had a good time chatting at my parents' dinner on Saturday, and pretty much every other time we've run into each other over the years thanks to the Levinsons' friendship with my parents. Under different circumstances—say, if I hadn't been married, then violently widowed—I might've considered going out on a date with Joe, both to please my parents and because I genuinely like him. He doesn't make my pulse race, but he's a nice guy, and that counts for a lot in my book. "What are you doing here?"

"This," he says ruefully, raising his right hand to display a thickly bandaged finger.

"Oh, no! What happened?"

He makes a face. "I got into a fight with a food processor, and the food processor won."

"Ouch." I wince as I picture that in my mind. "How bad is it?"

"Bad enough that they can't put in stitches. I'm going to have to wait for the bleeding to stop on its own."

"Ooh, sorry. So you came into the ER with this?"

"Yeah, but I obviously overreacted. I mean, there was blood everywhere, and the tip of the finger is pretty much pulp, but they said it'll heal and I might not even have that bad of a scar."

"Oh, that's good. I hope it heals up soon."

He grins at me, his blue eyes twinkling. "Thanks, me too."

I smile back and am about to continue down the hallway when he says, "Hey, Sara…"

I cringe internally at the hesitant expression on his face. "Yes?" I hope he's not about to—

"I was going to call you, but since I ran into you… What are you doing this Friday?" he asks, confirming my suspicion. "Because there's this really great art exhibit downtown, and—"

"I'm sorry. I can't." The refusal is automatic, and it's only when I see the crestfallen look on Joe's face that I realize how rude I'm being. Feeling terrible, I backtrack. "It's not that I don't want to, but I might be on call on Friday, and I don't know if—"

"It's okay. No worries." He puts on a smile that I instantly recognize as fake. I often wear one just like it when covering up emotional turmoil.

Shit. He must like me more than I realized.

"Do you want to do something else instead?" I offer before I can think better of it. "Not Friday, but maybe in a couple of weeks?"

Joe's smile turns genuine, his eyes crinkling attractively at the corners. "Sure. How about dinner the weekend after

173

this one? I know this little Italian place that makes the best lasagna."

"That sounds good," I say, already regretting the impulse. What if I don't manage to resolve my stalker situation by then? It's too late to back out now, though, so I say, "How about we nail down the day and time closer to then? My schedule changes all the time, and—"

"Say no more. I completely understand." He gives me a big grin. "I have your number, so I'll just give you a call next week, and you let me know what time works best for you, okay?"

"Okay. I'll talk to you then," I say and hurry down the hallway before I can stick my foot in my mouth again.

I have one last patient to see, and then I can carry out my mission.

If all goes well, by tomorrow, I'll be free.

CHAPTER 25
PETER

"Are you going to see her again tonight?" Anton asks in Russian, looking up from the laptop as I enter the living room. As usual, the former pilot is dressed in black from head to toe and armed to the teeth, even though our suburban hideout is as safe as it gets. Like the rest of my crew, he's a lethal motherfucker, and though we often rib him about his hipster-ish long hair and thick black beard, he looks exactly like what he is: a former Spetsnaz assassin.

"Of course," I reply, also speaking Russian.

Stopping by the coffee table next to the couch where Anton is sitting, I take off my leather jacket and remove the arsenal of weapons attached to my vest. When I go see Sara, I only bring one gun and a couple of knives with me, all strategically hidden in the inner pockets of my jacket so she doesn't spot them when I'm dressing or undressing. I don't want to scare her or remind her of what I am; she's too intimately acquainted with my skills as is. Besides, I'd be an idiot to trust her around real weapons.

Even a novice can fire a gun and score a lucky shot.

"Yan will be taking the first shift tonight," Anton says, turning his attention back to the computer on his lap. "I have to work out some of the logistics for this Mexico job."

I frown as I remove my bulletproof vest. "I thought we had everything ready."

"Yeah, I thought so too, but it seems Velazquez got into a little altercation with your old buddy Esguerra, and he's beefing up security like crazy. I think he's expecting an attack from Esguerra. Has nothing to do with us, obviously, but still. Complicates matters."

"Fuck." Julian Esguerra's involvement, however indirect, definitely complicates matters, and not just because he inadvertently spooked our target. The Colombian arms dealer holds a serious grudge against me. Though I saved the bastard's life, I endangered his wife in the process, and that's not something he'll ever forgive. He's not actively hunting me down, but if he catches word that I'm in Mexico, so close to his turf, he might make good on his promise to kill me.

Come to think of it, I'm close to his turf here in Illinois, too. His wife's parents live in Oak Lawn, not too far from Sara's place in Homer Glen. I doubt he'll visit here anytime soon, but if he does, and our paths cross somehow, I may have no choice but to deal with him.

Oh, well. I'll worry about that if it happens. There's no way I'm leaving here until I'm done with Sara.

"Yeah," Anton mutters, glowering at the computer. "Fuck, indeed."

I leave him to it and head into the kitchen to grab a beer from the fridge. Today, I handled a local job personally, leaving Yan's twin brother Ilya to watch over Sara, and I'm still hopped up on adrenaline, my senses extra sharp and my mind starkly clear. It's strange that killing can make one feel so alive, but it does.

As anyone in my field of work knows, life and death are but a slice of a blade apart, and wielding that blade is one of the greatest thrills there is.

I gulp down half a bottle of beer, eat a handful of nuts from a bowl on the counter, and go back to the living room. In a little bit, I'll head over to Sara's house to make dinner for us, and the snack should tide me over until then. Before that, however, Anton and I have to catch up.

The Mexico job is a big one, and we can't afford to fuck it up.

"So what's the latest?" I ask, sitting down next to Anton on the couch. Placing my beer on the coffee table, I peer at the computer screen. "How much of our plan are we going to have to scrap?"

"Pretty much all of it," Anton growls. "The guards' schedules are a mess, there are new security cameras everywhere, and Velazquez is instituting patrols around the compound perimeter."

"All right. Let's get to it."

Over the next hour, we come up with a new plan of attack on Velazquez, one that takes into account the heavier security on his compound. Instead of coming in to assassinate him at night, as originally planned, we're going to go in at lunchtime because that's when only a few newbie guards will be on watch. It's stupid, but most people, including Mexican cartel leaders who should know better, feel safer in the daytime. It's one of the most common problems I've encountered during my security consultant days, and I've always advised my clients to have equally strong protections in place regardless of whether the sun is up or down.

"Did the transfer go through?" I ask when we're done, and Anton nods.

"Seven million euros as agreed, with the other half to come upon job completion. Should keep us in beer and peanuts for a while."

I chuckle dryly. Anton and two other members of my old team—the Ivanov twins—joined me two years ago, after I got my list and approached them for help, promising to make them wealthy in return for throwing in their lot with me. They agreed, both out of friendship and because they'd been growing increasingly disillusioned with the Russian government. With the team in place, I switched from security consulting to more lucrative—and flexible— wet work, using my connections to get high-paying gigs for us. I needed the money to finance my revenge and stay ahead of the authorities, and the guys needed a new challenge. While elimination of the people on my list took priority, we carried out a number of paid hits along the way and built up our reputation in the underworld. Now we specialize in eliminating difficult targets all over the world and get paid enormous sums of money for jobs everyone else is too scared to touch. Most often, our clients are dangerous, insanely rich criminals, and our targets tend to be that too—like Carlos Velazquez, head of the Juarez Cartel.

As far as my crew is concerned, there isn't much difference between tracking down terrorists and taking out crime lords. Or bumping off whoever gets in our way. We've all lost whatever passes for conscience and morality ages ago.

"Heading out?" Anton asks, closing the laptop when I get up and put on my jacket. "Going to be with her all night again?"

"Probably." I pat my jacket, making sure my weapons are well concealed. "Most likely."

Anton sighs and stands up, leaving the laptop on the couch. "You know this is nuts, right? If you want her so much, just fucking take her and be done with it. I'm tired of these local ten-grand gigs; the stupid thugs don't even put up a fight. If we don't have another real job before Mexico, I'll go out of my fucking mind."

"You're always welcome to strike out on your own," I point out, and suppress a chuckle when Anton gives me the middle finger in reply. Even if we weren't friends, he wouldn't leave the team. My connections are the reason we get all this lucrative business. In the process of obtaining the list, I've ventured deep into the criminal underworld and gotten to know many of the key players. As skilled as my guys are, they wouldn't be half as successful without me, and they know it.

"Have fun," Anton calls out as I head for the exit, and I pretend not to hear as he mutters something about obsessed stalkers and poor tortured women.

He doesn't understand why I'm doing this to Sara, and I'm not inclined to explain.

Especially since I don't understand it myself.

CHAPTER 26
SARA

The mouthwatering smell of buttery seafood and roasted garlic greets me when I walk into the house, my handbag hanging casually over my shoulder. As I hoped, once again the dining room table is set with candles, and a bottle of white wine is chilling in a bucket of ice. Only the food is different today; it looks like we're having seafood linguini for the main course, with calamari and a tomato-mozzarella salad for the appetizers.

The setup couldn't be more perfect if I tried.

Act normal. Stay calm. He can't know what you're planning.

"Italian night, huh?" I say as Peter turns from the kitchen counter, where he was chopping up something that looks like basil. My heart is thumping erratically in my chest, but I succeed in keeping my tone coolly sarcastic. "What's tomorrow? Japanese? Chinese?"

"If you wish," he says, walking over to the table to sprinkle the chopped basil on the mozzarella. "Though I'm less familiar with those cuisines, so we might have to order in."

"Uh-huh." My gaze falls to his hands as he brushes the remnants of the basil off his fingers. A warm, shivery sensation curls through me as I remember how those fingers touched me with devastating pleasure, making me unravel in his arms.

No. Don't go there.

Desperate to distract myself, I focus on his outfit. Today, he's wearing a black button-up shirt with the sleeves rolled up, and my throat goes dry at the sight of his tan, muscular forearms, the left one covered by tattoos all the way down to the wrist. Inked guys aren't normally my thing, but the intricate tattoos suit him, emphasizing the power flexing under that smooth, hair-dusted skin. I've always been drawn to strong, masculine forearms, and Peter has the best I've ever seen. George worked out, so he had nice arms too, but they were nowhere near as powerfully cut as these.

Ugh, stop. Self-disgust burns in my throat as I realize what I'm doing. At no point should I be comparing my husband, a normal, peaceful man, to a killer whose life revolves around violence and vengeance. Obviously, Peter Sokolov is in better shape; he has to be, to kill all those people and evade the authorities. His body is a weapon, honed by years of battle, while George was a journalist, a writer who spent most of his time with his computer.

Except... if I were to believe Peter, my husband *wasn't* a journalist. He was a spy operating in the same shadow world as the monster puttering around my kitchen.

Bands of tension loop around my forehead, and I push all thoughts of my husband's alleged deception away, focusing on the rest of my stalker's outfit: another pair of dark jeans and black socks with no shoes. For a second, it makes me wonder if Peter has something against wearing shoes, but then I recall that in some cultures, it's considered disrespectful and unclean to wear outside shoes inside the house.

Is the Russian culture like that, and if so, is the man who tortured me in this very kitchen showing, in some very roundabout way, that he respects me?

"Go ahead, wash your hands or whatever you need to do," he says, dimming the lights before sitting down at the table and uncorking the wine. "The food is getting cold."

"You didn't have to wait for me," I say and go to the nearby bathroom to wash my hands. I hate how he acts like he knows all my habits, but I'm not about to compromise my health to spite him.

"Really, I mean it," I say when I return. "You didn't have to be here at all. You know feeding me isn't part of your stalker duties, right?"

He grins as I take a seat across from him and hang my handbag on the back of my chair. "Is that right?"

"That's what all the stalker job postings say." I spear a piece of tomato and mozzarella with my fork and bring it to my plate. My hand is steady, showing nothing of the anxiety shredding me inside. I want to clutch my bag against me, keep it on my lap and within easy reach, but if I do, he'll get suspicious. I'm already taking a chance by hanging it on my chair when I normally plop it carelessly on the couch in the family room. I'm hoping he ascribes that to the fact that I came straight to the kitchen/dining area instead of making my usual detour to the couch.

"Well, if that's what they say, who am I to argue?" Peter pours us each a glass of wine before placing some of the mozzarella salad on his plate. "I'm no expert."

"You haven't stalked other women before?"

He cuts a piece of mozzarella, brings it to his mouth, and chews it slowly. "Not like this, no," he says when he's done.

"Oh?" I find myself morbidly curious. "How did you stalk them?"

He gives me a level look. "Trust me, you don't want to know."

He's probably right, but since there's a chance I might not see him after tonight, I feel a bizarre urge to find out more about him. "No, I actually do," I say, drawing comfort from the handbag strap brushing against my back. "I want to know. Tell me."

He hesitates, then says, "The majority of my assignments have always been men, but I've followed women as part of my job, too. Different jobs, different women, different reasons. Back in Russia, it was often the wives and girlfriends of the men who threatened my country; we followed and questioned them to locate our real targets. Later, when I became a fugitive, I tracked a couple of women as part of my work for various cartel leaders, arms dealers, and such; usually it was because they posed a threat of some kind, or betrayed the men I worked for."

The bite of tomato I just consumed feels stuck in my throat. "You just... tracked them?"

"Not always." He reaches for the linguini, winds a fork in it, and brings a sizable portion of the pasta to his plate without spilling any of the buttery sauce. "Sometimes I had to do more."

The tips of my fingers are starting to feel cold. I know I should shut up, but instead, I hear myself asking, "What did you have to do?"

"It depended on the situation. One time, my quarry was a nurse who sold out my employer—the arms dealer I mentioned to you before—to some terrorist clients of his. As a result, his then-girlfriend was kidnapped, and he was nearly killed rescuing her. It was an ugly situation, and when I found the nurse, I had to resort to an ugly solution." He pauses, his gray eyes gleaming. "Do you want me to elaborate?"

"No, that's..." I reach for my glass of wine and take a big gulp. "That's okay."

He nods and begins eating. I have no appetite anymore, but I force myself to follow his example, transferring some pasta onto my plate. It's delicious, the seafood and the pasta perfectly cooked and coated in the rich, savory sauce, but I can barely taste it. I'm dying to reach into my bag and take out the little vial sitting there, but for that, I need Peter to be distracted, to look away from his wine glass for at least twenty seconds. I timed it back in the hospital, practicing with a vial of water: five seconds to open the vial, five more to reach across the table and tip the contents of the vial into the wine glass, and three more to yank my hand back and compose myself. That's about thirteen seconds, not twenty, but I can't have him suspect anything, so I need the extra cushion.

"So, tell me about your day, Sara," he says after most of the linguini on his plate is gone. Looking up, he pins me with a cool silver gaze. "Anything interesting happen?"

My stomach contracts, knotting around the linguini I forced down my throat. Peter couldn't know about me running into Joe, could he? My tormentor hasn't said anything, but if in his mind, this weird thing between us is some kind of courtship, he might object to me talking to—and making plans with—other men.

"Um, no." To my relief, my voice sounds relatively normal. I'm getting better at functioning under extreme stress. "I mean, one woman came in with extra-heavy spotting and turned out to have miscarried twins, and we had a fifteen-year-old girl come in with a *planned* pregnancy—she's always wanted to be a mom, she said—but that wouldn't be all that interesting for you, I'm sure."

"That's not true." He puts his fork down and leans back in his chair. "I find your work fascinating."

"You do?"

He nods. "You're a doctor, but not just someone who preserves life and cures disease. You *bring* life into this world, Sara, helping women when they're at their most vulnerable—and most beautiful."

I inhale, staring at him. This man—this *killer*—couldn't possibly understand, could he? "You think... pregnant women are beautiful?"

"Not just pregnant women. The whole process is beautiful," he says, and I realize that he does understand. "Don't you think so?" he asks when I continue looking at him in mute shock. "How life comes about, how a tiny bundle of cells grows and changes before emerging into the world? Don't you find that beautiful, Sara? Miraculous, even?"

I pick up my wine glass and take a sip before responding. "I do." My voice sounds thick when I finally manage to speak. "Of course I do. I just didn't expect you to feel that way."

"Why?"

"Isn't it obvious?" I put down my glass. "You take life. You hurt people."

"Yes, I do," he agrees, unblinking. "But that only makes my appreciation for it stronger. When you understand the fragility of *being*, the sheer transience of it—when you see how easy it is to snuff something out of existence—you value life more, not less."

"So why do it, then? Why destroy something you value? How can you reconcile being a killer with—"

"With finding human life beautiful? It's easy." He leans in, his gray eyes dark in the flickering light of the candles. "You see, death is part of life, Sara. An ugly part, sure, but there's no beauty without ugliness, just as there's no happiness without sorrow. We live in a world of contrasts, not absolutes. Our minds are designed to compare, to perceive changes. Everything we are, everything we do as human

187

beings, relies on the basic fact that X is different from Y—better, worse, hotter, colder, darker, lighter, whatever it may be—but only in comparison. In a vacuum, X has no beauty, just as Y has no ugliness. It's the contrast between them that enables us to value one over the other, to make a choice and derive happiness from it."

My throat feels inexplicably tight. "So you what? Bring joy to the world with your work? Make everyone happy?"

"No, of course not." Peter picks up his wine glass and swirls the liquid inside. "I have no delusions about what I am and what I do. But that doesn't mean I don't comprehend the beauty in your work, Sara. One can live in the darkness and see the light of the sun; it's even brighter that way."

"I…" My palms are slippery with sweat as I pick up my wine glass and surreptitiously reach into my bag with my free hand. As fascinating as this is, I have to act before it's too late. There's no guarantee he'll pour himself a second glass. "I've never thought of it that way."

"No reason why you should." He puts his glass down and smiles at me. It's his dark, magnetic smile, the one that always sends heat surging to my core. "You've led a very different life, ptichka. A gentler life."

"Right." My breaths are shallow as I pick up my glass and bring it to my lips. "I guess I have—until you came into it."

His expression turns somber. "That's true. For what it's worth—"

My glass slips out of my fingers, the contents spilling out onto the table in front of me. "Oops." I jump up, as if embarrassed. "So sorry about that. Let me—"

"No, no, sit." He stands up, just as I hoped he would. Though he's in my house, he likes to play at being a good host. "I'll take care of this."

It takes him only a few strides to reach the paper towel rack on the counter, but that's all the time I need to open the vial. *Six, seven, eight, nine...* I do the mental count as I pour the contents into his glass. *Ten, eleven, twelve.* He turns back, paper towels in hand, and I give him a sheepish smile as I sink back into my chair, the empty glass vial dropped back into my bag. My back is soaked with icy sweat, and my hands are shaking from adrenaline, but my task is done.

Now I just need him to drink the wine.

"Here, let me help," I say, reaching for a napkin as he mops up the spilled wine on the table, but he waves me away.

"It's all good, don't worry." He carries my wine-soaked plate to the garbage and dumps the remnants of my pasta— that could've been another opportunity, I note with a corner of my brain—and then returns with a clean plate.

"Thank you," I say, trying to sound grateful instead of gleeful as he swaps my wine glass for a new one and pours me more wine before adding some to his own glass. "Sorry I'm such a klutz."

"No worries." He looks coolly amused as he sits down again. "Normally, you're very graceful. It's one of the things I like most about you: how precise and controlled your movements are. Is it because of your medical training? Steady hand for surgery and all that?"

Don't act nervous. Whatever you do, don't act nervous.

"Yes, that's part of it," I reply, doing my best to keep my tone even. "I also took ballet when I was a child, and my instructor was a stickler for precision and good technique. Our hands had to be positioned just so, our feet turned just so. She'd make us practice each position, each step until we got it completely right, and if we ever slipped from good form, we'd have to go back and practice whatever we got wrong again, sometimes for the duration of an entire class."

He picks up his glass and swirls the liquid inside again. "That's interesting. I've always thought you looked like a dancer. You have the posture and the body type."

"I do?" *Drink. Please drink.*

He puts the glass down and fixes me with an enigmatic stare. "Definitely. But you don't dance anymore, do you?"

"No." *Come on, pick up the glass again.* "I quit ballet when I started high school, though I did a little salsa later in college."

"Why did you quit ballet?" His hand shifts closer to the glass, as if he's going to pick it up again. "I imagine you must've been good at it."

"Not good enough to do it professionally, at least not without a lot of additional training. And my parents didn't want that for me." My pulse speeds up in anticipation as his fingers curl around the stem of the glass. "The earnings potential of a dancer is fairly limited, and so is the length of her career. Most stop dancing in their twenties and have to find something else to do with their lives."

"How practical," he muses, lifting the glass. "Did that matter to you or to your parents?"

"Did what matter?" I try not to stare at the wine glass as it hovers a few inches from his lips. *Come on, just drink it.*

"The earnings potential." He swirls the wine again, seeming to derive pleasure from the sight of the light-colored liquid circling the glass walls. "Did you want to be a rich, successful doctor?"

I force myself to look away from the hypnotic movement of the wine. "Sure. Who doesn't?" The anticipation is eating me alive, so I distract myself by picking up my own wine glass and taking a big sip. *Please mimic me subconsciously and drink. Come on, just take a few sips.*

"I don't know," he murmurs. "Maybe a little girl who'd much rather be a ballerina or a singer?"

I blink, briefly distracted from his non-drinking. "A singer?" Why would he say that? Nobody outside of my seventh-grade counselor knew of that particular ambition.

Even at ten, I knew better than to bring up something so impractical with my parents—especially after they told me their views on ballet.

"You have a beautiful singing voice," Peter says, still toying with his wine glass. "It's only logical that at some point, you might've considered performing. And unlike a dancer's, a successful singing career doesn't have to end early. Many older singers are highly respected."

"I suppose that's true." I eye his glass again, my frustration growing. It's like he's torturing me, seeing how long I can take before cracking. To tame my impatience, I take a big sip of my own wine and say, "How do you even know what kind of singing voice I have? Oh, wait, never mind. Your listening devices, right?"

He nods, not the least bit remorseful. "Yes, you often sing when you're alone."

I gulp down some more wine. At any other time, his casual disregard for my privacy would've maddened me, but right now, all my attention is on the stupid wine. *Why isn't he drinking it?*

"So you really think I have a good singing voice?" I ask, then realize I should probably sound more outraged. In a more acerbic tone, I add, "Since I unwittingly performed for you, you might as well give me your honest opinion."

His eyes crinkle at the corners as he lowers the glass again. "Your voice is beautiful, ptichka. I already told you so, and I have no reason to lie."

Oh my God, just drink the fucking wine! To prevent myself from yelling that out loud, I take a breath and paste a pretty smile on my lips. "Yes, well, you *are* trying to get into my pants. Like any woman will tell you, flattery helps with that."

He laughs and picks up his glass again. "True. Except I have a feeling I could compliment you from now 'till eternity, and it wouldn't change a thing."

"You never know." I keep my tone light and flirty despite the cold sweat sliding down my spine. If he's not drinking on his own, I have to force his hand.

We can't end this dinner until he takes at least a few good sips.

Lifting my glass, I smile wider and say, "Why don't we drink to that? To women's vanity and you flattering me?"

"Why don't we, indeed?" He lifts his glass and clinks it against mine. "To you, ptichka, and your gorgeous voice."

We each bring our glasses to our lips, but before I can take a sip, his fingers loosen around the stem of his glass.

"Oops," he murmurs as the glass tips forward, spilling the wine in front of him in the exact replica of my earlier goof. His eyes gleam darkly. "My bad."

I cease breathing, my blood crystallizing in my veins. "You... you—"

"Knew that you added a little something to my drink? Yes, of course." His voice remains soft, but I can now discern the lethal note within. "You think no one's ever tried to poison me before?"

My pulse is in hyperdrive, yet I can't make myself move as he stands up and circles around the table, approaching me with the sleek grace of a predator. All I can do is stare at him, seeing the rage simmering in those metallic eyes.

He's going to kill me now. He's going to kill me for this. "I wasn't..." Terror is a toxic burn in my veins. "It wasn't—"

"No?" Stopping next to me, he reaches into my bag and pulls out the empty vial. I should run, or at least make an attempt at it, but I'm not brave enough to provoke him further. So I remain still, scarcely breathing as he brings the vial to his nose and sniffs it.

"Ah, yes," he murmurs, lowering his hand. "A little diazepam. I couldn't smell it in the wine, but it's clear like this." He puts the vial on the table in front of me. "You got it at the hospital, I assume?"

"I… Yes." There's no point in denying it. The evidence is literally in front of me.

"Hmm." He props his hip against the table and gazes down at me. "And what were you going to do when you had me knocked out, ptichka? Deliver me to the FBI?"

I nod, the words frozen in my throat as I stare up at him. With his big body looming over me, I feel like the little bird he compared me to: small and terrified in the shadow of a hawk.

His sensuous mouth twists in a parody of a smile. "I see. And you think it would've been that easy? Just knock me out and done?"

I blink up at him, uncomprehending.

"You think I don't have a contingency plan for that?" he clarifies, and I flinch as he lifts his hand. But all he does is pick up a lock of my hair and brush the ends of it against my jaw, the gesture tender yet cruelly mocking at the same time. "For you trying to kill or disable me in some way?"

"You… you do?"

His lids lower, his gaze dropping to my mouth. "Of course." The lock of hair brushes over my lips, the ends tickling the sensitive flesh, and my stomach contracts into a hard ball as he says softly, "At this very moment, my men are monitoring your house and everything in the ten-block radius, as well as the little screen that displays my vital signs." His eyes meet mine. "Do you want to guess what they would've done had my blood pressure dropped unexpectedly?"

I mutely shake my head. If Peter's men are anything like him—and they must be, to do his bidding—I'd rather not know the specifics of what I just narrowly avoided.

His smile takes on a dark edge. "Yes, that's probably wise, ptichka. Ignorance is bliss and all that."

I gather the scraps of my courage. "What are you going to do to me?"

"What do you think I'm going to do?" He tilts his head, the smile darkening another fraction. "Punish you? Hurt you?"

My heart drums in my throat. "Are you?"

He looks at me for a few long moments, his smile dimming, then shakes his head. "No, Sara." There is a strangely weary note in his voice. "Not today."

Pushing away from the table, he begins gathering the dishes, and I sag in my chair, relieved yet drained of all hope.

If he's not lying about his men—and I have no reason to think he is—I'm even more trapped than I thought.

CHAPTER 27
PETER

It shouldn't hurt, knowing that she wants to get rid of me. It shouldn't feel like blades of fire slicing across my chest. Any person in Sara's situation would fight back; it's only logical and expected.

It shouldn't hurt, but it does, and no matter what I tell myself as I lead Sara upstairs, the monster inside me snarls and howls, demanding that I do exactly as she feared and punish her for this transgression.

When we get to the bedroom, I don't make her take her clothes off in front of me again; I'm too close to the edge to guarantee my self-control. I already tested it too much during dinner, playing along with her innocent, *I didn't just drug your wine* routine. I knew what she did right away—the wine spill was too out of character for her—but I wanted to see how good of an actress she is, and so I continued to converse with her, to pretend I was clueless and gullible, an idiot about to fall for one of the oldest tricks in the book.

"You can take a shower," I say, nodding toward the bathroom when she stops next to the bed, her gaze darting nervously from me to the bed and back. "I'll be here when you return."

Relief flashes across her face, and she disappears into the bathroom. I use the opportunity to go downstairs and take a quick rinse in one of the other bathrooms.

Though I showered after today's job, I want to be extra clean for her.

She's still showering when I return to the bedroom, so I carefully fold my clothes and leave them on the dresser before getting into bed. I gave myself a quick release with my hand earlier today, but my desire for Sara hasn't abated, and I know I won't be able to play this game much longer.

I'm going to take her and make her mine.

If not tonight, then very soon.

Sara's shower is long, so long that I know she's using it as a way to avoid me, but I don't mind. I use the time to empty my mind and cool the residual anger burning inside me. By the time she finally emerges from the bathroom, wrapped in a towel, I have the monster under control and can smile at her coolly.

"Come," I say, patting the bed next to me. I'm trying like hell not to think about how slick and soft her pussy felt yesterday, but it's impossible. I want to feel that silky wetness wrapped around my cock, want to hear her moan as I drive into her. I want to taste that plush mouth and see her hazel eyes go soft and unfocused as I bring her to her peak again and again.

I want her, and I can't have her.

Not yet, at least.

She approaches uncertainly, as wary as a wild gazelle, and just as graceful. I want to grab her and drag her into bed, but I remain still, letting her come to me of her own accord. This way, I can pretend that she doesn't hate me, that seeing me imprisoned or dead wouldn't give her the greatest joy.

This way, I can imagine that someday, she may *choose* to be with me.

"Take off that towel and come here," I order when she pauses half a meter away from the bed, but she doesn't move, her hands clutching the towel in front of her chest.

"Are we going to sleep? Just sleep?" she asks in an unsteady voice, and I nod, though I'm painfully hard just from seeing her. If I could be sure that I would maintain control throughout, I'd take her tonight, or at least give her another orgasm, but the best I can do is hold her and force myself to go to sleep. Even that will be torture, but I'll bear it. I won't force her when she's expecting me to hurt her; no matter how difficult it is, I won't live up to her fears.

"Just sleep," I promise, and hope she can't hear the raging hunger in my voice. "We're just going to sleep."

She hesitates for another second, then steps up to the bed, dropping the wet towel on the floor as she slips under the blanket. All I see is a flash of naked skin, but it's enough for lust to punch me in the gut. Bracing myself, I pull her against me and bite back a groan as her soft ass nestles against my groin, her skin damp and extra warm from the long shower. She has a beautiful ass, my little doctor, tight and shapely, and my dick throbs with the need to be inside her, to feel those smooth cheeks pressing against my balls as I pound into her, taking her again and again.

Closing my eyes, I inhale the sweet scent of her shampoo and concentrate on controlling my breathing. After a while, I feel the tension in her muscles easing, and I know she's starting to relax, to believe I won't assault her despite the hard cock she must feel pressing against her.

Slow and easy, I tell myself as I breathe in and out. *Control and focus. Pain means nothing. Discomfort means nothing.* It's a mantra I taught myself during my time in Camp Larko, and it's true. Pain, hunger, thirst, lust—it's all chemistry and electrical impulses, a way for the brain to communicate with the body. Wanting Sara won't kill me, any more than the six months I spent in solitary did when I was fourteen. The torture of unfulfilled desire is nothing compared to the hell of being locked in a room barely big enough to be called a cage, with no one to talk to and nothing to do. It's nothing compared to the agony of a shiv slashing through your kidney, or a giant fist nearly knocking out your eye.

If I survived juvenile prison in Siberia, I'll survive not having Sara.

For a little bit longer, at least.

CHAPTER 28
SARA

"How about you, Sara?"

"Huh?" I look up from my plate to stare blankly at Marsha, who must've just asked me something.

Andy rolls her eyes. "She's in la-la land again. Leave her alone, Marsha."

"Sorry, I'm just distracted," I say, pushing back a lock of hair that escaped from my ponytail. I'm pretty sure my hair is a crooked mess today, but I keep forgetting to get to a mirror to fix it. In general, all I can think about this morning is that when I go home tonight, *he* will be waiting for me there.

Peter Sokolov, the man I can't escape.

"I asked if you want to join me and Tonya this Saturday," Marsha says, looking more amused than annoyed. "Andy just said she's in; she'll hang out with her boyfriend some other time. How about you, Sara?"

"Oh, sorry, I can't," I say, pushing my plate away. I ran into the nurses in the cafeteria while grabbing a quick breakfast, and they talked me into joining them for a sit-down meal. "I promised my parents I'll go see them."

That last part is a lie, but I figure it's better than explaining that I don't want to put my friends on the radar of a certain Russian killer—or whoever he'll have watching me.

"That's too bad," Marsha says. "Tonya's going to get us back into that club. You seemed to like it there, I recall. Tonya says that cute bartender has been asking about you."

I frown. "He has?"

"Yep," Tonya confirms. "He said something weird, though. He thought he saw some guy with you, acting all proprietary, like he was your boyfriend or something. I told him he must've been mistaken, because you definitely left alone that night. Right? You don't have a secret boyfriend stashed somewhere, do you?"

Ice trickles down my spine even as my face turns uncomfortably hot. "No, definitely not."

"Really?" Marsha says, sounding fascinated. "Then why are you blushing? And clutching that fork like you want to stab someone?"

I glance down at my hand and see that she's right. I'm gripping the utensil so hard my knuckles have turned white. Forcing my fingers to relax, I give an awkward laugh and say, "Sorry. I was drunk that night, and I'm a little embarrassed about that. I think I must've danced with some random guy, and that's what your bartender friend saw, Tonya."

Andy frowns. "Is that random guy the reason you ran out of there like that? You looked almost… frightened."

"What? No, I was just drunk." I force another embarrassed laugh. "You know how it is when you think you're going to puke at any moment? Well, that was me that night."

"Okay," Tonya says. "I'll tell Rick—that's the bartender—that you're available. In case you ever join us at the club again, that is."

"Oh, I…" My face heats up again. "No, that's okay. I'm not really ready to date and—"

"No worries." Tonya pats my hand, her slim fingers cool on my skin. "I won't give him your number or anything. You can maintain your 'princess in a tower' mystique. Only makes them hotter, if you ask me."

"What?" I gape at her. "What do you mean by that?"

"She means that you have the whole untouchable thing going on," Andy says through a mouthful of eggs. "It's hard to describe, but it's like you give off this ice princess vibe, only not cold, you know? Kind of like if Jackie-O and Princess Diana decided to slum it by working among us regular folks, if that makes sense."

"No, not really." I frown at the red-headed girl. "You're saying I come across as stuck-up?"

"No, not stuck-up, just different," Marsha says. "Andy didn't explain it well. You're just… classy. Maybe it's all that ballet you did when you were younger, but you look like someone taught you to curtsy and walk with a book balanced on your head. Like you know which fork to use at a formal dinner and how to make small talk with the ambassador of whatever."

"What?" I burst out laughing. "That's ridiculous. I mean, George and I had been to a few formal fundraisers, but that was his thing, not mine. If I had a choice, I'd live in yoga pants and sneakers; you know that, Marsha. For God's sake, I listen to Britney Spears and dance to hip-hop and R&B."

"I know, hon, but that's just the way you look, not the way you are," Marsha says, taking out a small mirror to re-apply her red lipstick. Swiping on a coat with a practiced hand, she puts away the mirror and the lipstick and says, "It's a good thing, trust me. Take me, for instance. I could try to class it up all I want, but guys take one look at me and decide I'm easy. Doesn't matter what I wear or how I act; they just see my hair, tits, and ass, and figure I put out."

"That's because you do put out," Tonya points out with a grin.

Marsha huffs and flicks back her blond waves. "Yeah, but that's neither here nor there. My point is, *she*"—she jerks her thumb at me—"couldn't look easy if she tried. Any guy looking at her knows—he just *knows*—he's going to have to work for it. Like dinners with parents and ring on the finger kind of work."

"That's not true," I object. "I slept with George long before we got married."

Andy rolls her eyes. "Yeah, but how long were you dating before you slept with him?"

"A few months," I say, frowning. "But I was just eighteen, and—"

"See? A few months," Tonya says, elbowing Marsha. "And how long do *you* make them wait?"

Marsha chuckles. "At least a few hours."

"Well, there you go," Andy says. "And you wonder why those jerks never call you again. My mom always said, 'The fastest way to lose a guy is to sleep with him.' Sara's got it right: act cool and distant, so when you so much as smile at a guy, he falls all over himself."

"Oh, please." I busy myself with the remnants of my breakfast. "It's the twenty-first century. I think men know better than to—"

"Nope," Marsha says cheerfully. "They don't. If something comes easy, they don't value it as much. I know that, and I'm okay with being a good-time girl. Most of the time, I don't *want* those jerks to call me, and the couple of times that I do..." She sighs. "Well, it's just not meant to be, I guess. In any case, life's too short to waste it being something other than what you are. By the time you get to be my age, you figure that out."

"Uh-huh, sure." Tonya stuffs the last of her bagel into her mouth. "Tell us more, Oh Wise Old One."

"Shut up," Marsha grumbles, throwing a balled-up napkin at her. It hits Andy, who immediately retaliates with a napkin projectile of her own, and I duck, laughing, as the breakfast devolves into a full-on napkin fight.

It's not until I'm walking out of the cafeteria, still chuckling over what happened, that I realize the nurses didn't just lighten my mood and distract me from thoughts of Peter.

They also gave me an idea.

My on-call shift doesn't end until late evening, but I still go to the clinic afterward. It's open twenty-four hours, and they always need me. On my end, I want to delay going home for as long as I can. The idea brewing in my mind makes my stomach cramp, and the last thing I want is to face my stalker.

As usual, they're glad to see me at the clinic. Despite the late hour, the waiting room is packed with women of all ages, many accompanied by crying children. In addition to providing OB-GYN services to low-income women, the clinic staff often treat their children for minor illnesses— something the patients, and nearby ER departments, greatly appreciate.

"Busy night?" I ask Lydia, the middle-aged reception- ist, and she nods, looking harried. She's one of the only two salaried staff members at the clinic; everyone else, includ- ing all the doctors and nurses, are volunteers like me. It makes for an unpredictable schedule but enables the clinic to provide pro bono care to the community while operat- ing solely on donations.

"Here," Lydia says, thrusting the sign-in sheet into my hand. "Start with the five names on the bottom."

I take the sheet and go to the little room that functions as my office/exam room. Putting my things down, I wash my hands, splash some cold water on my face, and step out into the waiting room to call in the first patient.

My first three patients end up being easy—one needs birth control, another wants to get tested for STDs, a third needs a pregnancy confirmation—but the fourth one, a pretty seventeen-year-old named Monica Jackson, complains of prolonged period bleeding. When I examine her, I find vaginal tearing and other signs of sexual trauma, and when I ask her about it, she breaks down crying and admits that her stepfather assaulted her.

I calm her down, collect a rape kit, treat her injuries, and give her the phone number of a women's shelter where she can stay if she feels unsafe at home. I also suggest she contact the police, but she's adamant about not filing charges.

"My mother would kill me," she says, her brown eyes red-rimmed and hopeless. "She says he's a good provider, and we're lucky to have him. He's got priors, so if I say anything, he'll get put away, and we'll end up on the street again. I don't give a fuck—I'd sooner turn tricks in an alley than live with that asshole—but my brother's only five, and he'll end up in a foster home. Right now, I take care of him when my mother can't, and I don't want him taken away from me."

She starts crying again, and I squeeze her small hand, my heart aching at her plight. Though the paperwork Monica filled out says she's seventeen, with her petite build and baby-round cheeks, she looks barely old enough to be in high school. I often see girls like her come through here, and it shatters me each time, knowing there's only so much I can do to help. If she were on her own, it would be easy to extract her from this situation, but with the little brother in the mix, the best I can do is call Child Services, and that might lead to the very thing my patient dreads: having her brother in foster care without her.

"I'm so sorry, Monica," I say when she calms down. "I still think going to the police is the best option for you and your brother. Isn't there anyone else you could turn to? A family friend? A relative, perhaps?"

The girl's expression turns hollow. "No." Jumping off the table, she pulls on her clothes. "Thanks for seeing me, Dr. Cobakis. Take care."

She walks out of the room, and I stare after her, wanting to cry. The girl is in an impossible situation, and I can't help her. I can never help girls like her. Except—

"Wait!" I grab my bag and run after her. "Monica, wait!"

"She already left," Lydia says when I burst into the reception area. "What happened? Did she forget something?"

"Sort of." I don't bother explaining further. Rushing to the door, I step out and survey the dark, deserted street. Monica's small, dark-haired figure is already at the end of the block, walking fast, so I run after her, desperate to do something at least this once.

"Monica, wait!"

She must hear me, because she stops and turns.

"Dr. Cobakis?" she says in surprise when I catch up to her.

I stop, panting from the exertion, and rummage inside my bag. "How much do you need to tide you over?" I ask breathlessly, pulling out my checkbook and a pen.

"What?" She gapes at me as though I've turned into an alien.

"If you go to the police and they take your stepfather away, how much will you and your mother need to *not* end up on the street?"

She blinks. "Our rent is twelve hundred a month, and my mother's disability check covers about half of it. If we could last until this summer, I'd get a full-time job and pitch in, but—"

"Okay, hold on." I prop the checkbook against the side of a building and write out a check for five thousand dollars. I planned to use that money to send my parents on an anniversary cruise this summer, but I'll come up with a less costly gift.

My parents won't mind, I'm sure.

Tearing off the check, I hand it to the girl and say, "Take this and go to the police. He deserves to be in jail."

Her rounded chin quivers, and for a moment, I'm afraid she'll start crying again. But she just accepts the check with trembling fingers. "I... I don't even know how to thank you. This is—" Her young voice breaks. "This is just—"

"It's okay." I put my checkbook away and smile at the girl. "Go cash it in, and put the bastard away, okay? Promise me you'll do that?"

"I promise," the girl says, stuffing the check into her jeans pocket. "I promise, Dr. Cobakis. Thank you. Thank you so much."

"It's okay. Go now. It's late, and you shouldn't be out alone."

The girl hesitates, then throws her arms around me in a quick hug. "Thank you," she whispers again, and then she's off, her small figure bobbing between the streetlights before disappearing from sight.

I stand there until she's gone, and then I turn to go back to the clinic. My bank account just took a serious hit, but I feel as jubilant as if I've won the lottery. For the first time since I've started working at the clinic, I've truly helped someone, and it feels amazing.

The cold wind slaps me in the face as I start walking back, and I realize I forgot my coat at the clinic. It doesn't matter, though. I'm glowing with an inner joy that's no match for the chilly March evening.

I can't fix my own life, but maybe I just helped fix Monica's.

I'm less than half a block from the clinic when a flicker of shadow on the right catches my attention. My heart jumps, and adrenaline floods my veins as two home-less-looking men step out from the narrow alley-like space between two houses, the light from the street reflecting off the gleaming blades of their knives.

"Your bag," the taller one snarls, gesturing toward me with the knife, and even from this distance, I catch the nauseating stench of body odor, alcohol, and vomit. "Give it here, bitch. Now."

I reach for the bag before he even finishes speaking, but my icy fingers are clumsy, and the bag falls off my shoulder.

"You fucking bitch! Give it here, I said!" he hisses, in-creasingly agitated, and I realize he's on something. Meth? Coke? Either way, he's unstable, and his partner—who started giggling like a hyena—must be too.

I have to pacify them. Quickly.

"Hold on, I'm giving it to you, I promise." Shaking, I kneel to pick up the bag so I can hand it to them, but before I can get up, a blur of motion cuts in front of me.

Gasping, I fall back, catching myself on my palms as a tall, dark figure rams into my attackers, moving with a speed and agility that seems almost superhuman. The three of them disappear back into the shadowed alley, and I hear two panicked cries, followed by a strange wet gurgle. Then something metallic clatters on the pavement. Twice.

Oh God. Oh God, oh God, oh God.

I scramble backward, barely noticing the asphalt scraping the skin off my palms as my rescuer steps out of the alley, and I see the two men behind him crumple like puppets with their strings cut off. A dark liquid spreads out from under their prone bodies, and the coppery tang of blood fills the air, mixing with something even more foul.

He killed them, I realize in dazed stupor. He just fucking *killed* them.

The blast of terror injects me with fresh adrenaline, and I jump to my feet, a scream rising in my throat. But before it can escape, the dark figure steps toward me, and the streetlight illuminates his face.

His familiar, exotically handsome face.

"Did they hurt you?" Peter Sokolov's voice is as hard as his metallic gaze, and once again, I find myself paralyzed, terrified yet unable to move an inch as he comes toward me, his thick eyebrows drawn into a forbidding scowl. It's the countenance of a killer, the visage of the monster beneath the human mask, yet there's something more there too.

Something almost like concern.

"I…" I don't know what I was going to say because in the next moment, I find myself enfolded in his arms, held so tightly against his powerful chest that I can hardly breathe. The heat of his large body surrounds me, shielding me from the icy wind and making me realize how cold I am, how frozen inside. The full horror of what I just witnessed hasn't settled in yet, but already I'm starting to feel numb, my thoughts scattered and sluggish as the cold burrows deeper into me, anesthetizing me against the trauma.

Shock, I diagnose on autopilot. I'm going into shock.

"Shhh, ptichka. It's all right. It's going to be all right." Peter's voice is low and soothing, his grip loosening until he's cradling me with startling tenderness, and I realize the odd gasping sounds I'm hearing are coming from me. I'm struggling to breathe, my throat closing up as though during a panic attack.

No, not as though—I *am* having a panic attack.

He must recognize it too, because he pulls away and gazes down at me, his gray eyes narrowed in worry. "Breathe," he commands, his hands tightening on my shoulders. "Breathe, Sara. Slowly and deeply. That's it, ptichka. And again. Breathe…"

I follow his voice, letting him act as my therapist, and gradually, the choking sensation fades, my breathing evening out. I focus on that, on just breathing normally and not thinking, because if I think about what just happened—if I glance at the alley to the right and see the puppet-like bodies—I might pass out.

"There, that's good." He pulls me against him again, his big hand stroking my hair as I stand with my face pressed against his chest. "You're okay, ptichka. Everything is okay."

Okay? I want to laugh and scream at the same time. In what world are two dead bodies in an alley "okay?" I'm shaking now, both from the cold wind and the shock, and I know I'm on the verge of losing it again. I'm no stranger to blood and injury, and I've seen death in the hospital as well, but the way those two men crumpled, like they're nothing, like they're just sacks of meat and bones—

I stop before my thoughts can veer too far down that path, but my throat already feels tight again, my shaking intensifying.

"Shhh," Peter soothes again, rocking me gently back and forth. He must feel me trembling. "They can't hurt you. It's over. It's all over. Come, let's get you home."

I open my mouth to object, to insist on calling the police or an ambulance or someone, but before I can squeeze out a single word, he bends down and lifts me into his arms. He does it effortlessly, as though I weigh nothing. As though it's normal to carry a woman battling a panic attack away from the scene of a double homicide.

As though he does this every day—which, for all I know, he might.

I finally find my voice. "Put me down." It's a thin, hollow whisper, barely a sound, but it's better than nothing. My hands manage to move as well, pushing at his shoulders as he strides down the street. "Please. I—I can walk."

"It's okay." He glances down, his gaze reassuring. "We're almost there."

"Almost where?" I ask, but then I see his destination.

It's a black SUV parked on the corner a block away from my clinic. A tall man with a thick black beard is leaning against the side of it, and as we approach, Peter says something to him in a foreign language, his voice low and urgent.

The man responds in the same language—most likely Russian, I realize dazedly—and then pulls out a sleek smartphone, swiping across the screen with quick, furious gestures. Lifting it to his ear, he spews out more rapid-fire Russian as Peter opens the car door and carefully deposits me on the back seat.

My tormentor wasn't lying about having a team. This man must be one of his helpers.

"I'll be right with you, ptichka," Peter murmurs in English, brushing my hair off my face with that same bizarre tenderness, and then he backs out and closes the door behind him, leaving me alone in the warm interior of the car.

I sit still for a couple of seconds, watching him speak to the bearded man, and then I spring into action.

Scrambling across the backseat, I grab the door handle on the opposite side from where the two men are standing and push the door open, nearly tumbling out of the car in my haste to get away. My thoughts and reactions are still slow from shock, but I've recovered enough to comprehend one very important fact.

Two men were killed in front of me, and if I don't do something about it, I'm an accessory to their murders.

The cold wind bites at me, and my lungs burn as I sprint toward the clinic. Behind me, I hear a shout, followed by rapid footsteps, and I know they're chasing after me. My only hope is to get inside the clinic before they catch me. As a wanted man, Peter shouldn't be willing to risk exposure. Once I'm safe inside, I can catch my breath and figure out what to do, how to best inform the police about what happened.

I'm less than a hundred feet away from my destination when a hard arm loops around my ribcage, and a strong hand slaps over my mouth, muffling my scream. "You really like me to chase after you, don't you?" a familiar voice growls in my ear, and then I hear a car approaching.

I double my efforts to get free, kicking at Peter's shins and clawing at his hand over my face, but it's futile. I hear a car door open, and then Peter is stuffing me inside, much less carefully this time.

"*Yezhay*," he barks at the bearded driver, and then we're speeding away, leaving the clinic and the scene of the crime behind.

CHAPTER 29
PETER

"**Y**an and Ilya are on it," Anton informs me in Russian as he takes a right onto the street leading to Sara's house. "They got there before anyone stumbled onto the scene."

"Good." I glance at Sara, who's sitting next to me in the backseat, silent and deathly pale. "Tell them to thoroughly dispose of the remains. We don't want body parts turning up anywhere. Also, they need to bring her car back to her house."

"Yeah, they know." Anton meets my gaze in the mirror. "What are you going to do with her? You really freaked her out."

"I'll figure something out."

I'm glad Sara can't understand what we're saying; otherwise, she'd be even more horrified. I shouldn't have killed those methheads in front of her, but they were threatening her with knives, and I lost it. All I could see was Tamila's body lying there, broken and bloodied, and the thought that it could've been Sara—that if I hadn't been there, one of those strung-out vagrants could've killed *her—made my blood turn to volcanic ice. I don't even remember making a conscious decision; I acted purely on instinct. It took only seconds to disarm them and slice their throats, and by the time their bodies hit the ground, it was too late.*

Sara saw them die.

She saw me kill them.

"Can you take Ilya's shift for the rest of the night?" I ask Anton when we stop in front of Sara's house. With the big oaks shading the driveway and the nearest neighbors a good distance away, the place is nice and private—great in a situation like this. It's too bad she's selling the house; I've grown to really like it.

"No problem," Anton replies. "I'll be around. You going to be here until morning?"

"Yes." I glance at Sara, who's still staring straight ahead, seemingly oblivious to our arrival. "I'll be with her."

Taking Sara's hand, I tell her in English, "We're here, ptichka. Come on, let's get you home."

Her slender fingers are icy in my grip; she's still in shock. However, as I help her out of the car, she looks up at me and asks hoarsely, "What about the clinic?"

"What about it?"

"They'll wonder what happened to me."

"No, they won't." I dip my hand into my pocket and pull out her phone, which I got from her bag during our trip. "I sent them this." I show her the text message about having to see to an emergency at the hospital.

"Oh." She gives me a perplexed look. "You sent this?"

I nod, slipping the phone back into my pocket as I lead her away from the car. "You were a little out of it during the ride." That's actually an understatement; after I dragged her into the car, she stopped fighting and became almost catatonic.

She blinks. "But… what about the bodies?"

"That's taken care of, too," I assure her. "Nothing will tie you to that scene. You're safe."

Sara visibly shudders, so I quickly usher her into the house, opening the door with keys I fished out from her bag earlier. I have my own pair of keys—I had them made a month ago, when I returned for her—but I'd rather Sara not know that. If she changes the locks again, it'll be annoying to go through the process a second time.

"Here, sit," I say, leading her to the couch. "I'll make you some chamomile tea."

"No, I…" She twists out of my hold. "I have to wash my hands."

"All right." I remember she has a thing about that. "Go for it."

She disappears around the corner into the bathroom, and I walk over to the kitchen sink to soap up as well. I was careful to keep out of the spray of blood as I sliced those men's throats, but I still find a few small red stains on my forearms.

Hopefully, Sara hasn't seen them.

I wash my hands and forearms, then turn on the electric tea kettle. When the water boils, I make two cups of tea and carry them over to the table. Sara is not back yet, so I decide to check on her.

Walking over to the bathroom, I knock on the door. "Everything okay?"

There's no answer, only the sound of running water. Worried, I try the door handle but find it locked.

"Sara?"

No response.

"Sara, open the door."

Nothing.

I take a calming breath and say in a softer voice, "Ptichka, I know you're upset, but if you don't open the door now, I'll have no choice but to break it." Or to pick the lock, but I don't say that. Breaking the door sounds way more threatening.

The water turns off, but the door remains locked.

"Sara. I'm giving you to the count of five. One. Two. Three—"

The lock clicks.

Relieved, I push the door open—and realize I was right to be concerned. Sara is sitting on the floor, her back against the tub and her knees drawn up to her chest. She's not making a sound, but her face is streaked with tears, and she's shaking.

Fuck. I really shouldn't have killed them in front of her.

"Sara..." I kneel next to her, and she scoots to the side, away from me. Ignoring her reaction, I gently grasp her arm and pull her into my embrace. "I won't hurt you, ptichka," I whisper into her hair when I feel her shaking intensify. "You're safe with me."

A stifled sob escapes her throat, then another and another, and suddenly, she's clinging to me, her slender arms folding around my neck as she begins to cry in earnest. I rub her back in soothing circles as she shakes with uncontrollable sobs, and she grips me tighter, burying her face against my neck. I feel the wetness of her tears, and I'm reminded of that time in the kitchen, when I was trying to calm her after the waterboarding. The memory sickens me; I can't imagine doing that to her now, can't picture hurting her for any reason.

She's not just a person to me now; she's my world, and I will protect her from everyone and everything.

It takes a long time for her sobs to ease, so long that my legs feel stiff when I finally get up and gently pull her to her feet.

"Come," I murmur, wrapping a supportive arm around her back as I lead out of the bathroom. "Let's have a little tea and get you off to bed. You must be exhausted."

She sniffles and whispers hoarsely, "No tea."

"Okay, no tea. In that case, let's get you to sleep." I bend to lift her into my arms.

She doesn't object to me carrying her, just lays her head on my shoulder and loops her arms around my neck. Her breathing is still ragged from all the crying, but she's calming down. That pleases me, as does the needy way she's clinging to me. I don't know if it's the aftermath of the trauma, or if I'm finally wearing down her resistance, but her holding on to me like this, with no trace of fear or mistrust, fills my chest with a special kind of warmth, one that lessens the icy hollowness around my heart.

With Sara, I'm coming alive again, and I want more of that feeling.

CHAPTER 30
SARA

He's gentle with me in the shower, his touch tender and incongruously platonic as he washes me from head to toe. I stand still; that's all I'm capable of at the moment—just standing. Nothing bothers me right now, not my nakedness and not even his. Now that my emotional storm has passed, I feel empty, a fog of exhaustion dulling all my thoughts and feelings. I'm beyond desire, beyond anxiety and fear; all that exists is guilt.

Terrible, soul-crushing guilt from the knowledge that two more men died because of me.

They died because I let a killer into my life and fed his obsession.

It's clear to me now, so perfectly obvious I don't know why I didn't see this before. I'm toxic—a danger to everyone around me. Today, the victims were two druggies; tomorrow, it might be my friends or family. Nobody is safe around me for as long as Peter wants me, and everything I've done has only fueled his obsession.

From the beginning, I've played the game wrong, and two men paid for that with their lives.

"Here, step out," Peter commands, and I exit the shower, letting him wrap a thick towel around me. He dries me with it, once again treating me like a child, and I let him, because I'm too exhausted to do anything else. Besides, all this—crying in his arms, clinging to him, having him take care of me—works well for the new strategy I'm going to implement.

Since he wants me, I'm going to let him have me.

It's not a particularly brilliant strategy, nor is it in any way guaranteed to work. It might even backfire. But at this point, I have little to lose. I've tried pushing him away, and he's still here, still a threat. So now I have to try something different.

I have to make him lose interest in me.

It was the conversation at breakfast that gave me the idea. What if the nurses are right, and I give off some kind of "ice princess" vibe, one that intrigues my stalker? What if, by refusing him, I'm making him want me more?

The fastest way to lose a guy is to sleep with him. It's a stupid saying, but Andy's mother isn't the only one who believes that. I've heard that sentiment dozens of times, usually from the parents of teenagers who got pregnant because their families insisted on teaching them the values of abstinence instead of birth control. It's an old-fashioned, sexist stereotype about the male/female dynamic, one that's predicated on the insulting premise that women are like toilet paper, something to be used once and discarded.

I've always scoffed when I heard stuff like this, but at the same time, I know there are men who act that way, who pursue women until they get them into bed, and then quickly lose interest. But it's not because they think women should be pure—at least, not usually. They just derive the greatest pleasure from the chase. They enjoy the anticipation more than the consummation, and once they score, they move on, seeking out fresher pastures.

I don't know if my stalker falls into that category, but it's possible—probable, even. He's a stunningly handsome man, and he's undoubtedly used to women falling head over heels for his dangerous alpha appeal. I've never known anyone quite like him, but I've seen shades of that arrogance in popular college athletes, Wall Street executives, and overpaid male surgeons. Men like that—the ones at the top of the food chain—perceive any hint of reluctance as a challenge; it intrigues them, makes them more inclined to pursue a woman, not less.

If that's the case—and I'm desperately hoping it is—then the easiest way to get rid of Peter Sokolov may be to give him exactly what he wants: me, willing, in his bed. For whatever reason, the Russian killer seems to have drawn the line at rape, preferring to just force himself into my life, so it's up to me to give him the green light.

If I want this nightmare to end, I'll have to willingly have sex with my tormentor.

"Come on, lie down," Peter urges when we get to the bed. Removing the towel around me, he gently guides me under the blanket. "You'll feel better in the morning, I promise." Once again, his touch is platonic, almost clinical, but I know he wants me. I see how hard he is as he climbs under the blanket next to me, feel the tension rolling off him as he turns off the lights and pulls me into his embrace, tucking me against his big warm body in the familiar spooning position.

He wants me, but he won't take me—not until I give my consent.

I lie still for a few moments, trying to convince myself to do it. My stomach feels like a raccoon is battling a hamster inside, and exhaustion is a thick, smothering layer over my brain. With my eyes raw and my head aching from crying, the last thing I want is sex, but maybe that's why I should do it tonight.

Maybe I'll feel less awful about it if I don't enjoy it.

Bracing myself, I shift slightly, moving my ass an inch closer to Peter's groin. He stiffens, his breathing growing more labored, and I repeat the maneuver, rubbing against him as I shift back and forth on the pretext of getting more comfortable. With his thickly muscled arm folded across my ribcage, I have a very limited range of motion, but it doesn't matter. We're both naked, and the slightest brush of his skin against mine is electrifying, so filled with sensations that each of my nerve endings stands at attention. I can't see anything in the pitch-black darkness of the room, but I can feel the crispness of his leg hair on the back of my thighs, smell his clean male scent, and my own breathing speeds up, my heart pounding furiously in my chest as his cock grows even harder, pressing against my ass like the barrel of a gun.

That's it, come on. Ignoring the anxiety constricting my throat, I shimmy my hips a little more. I can't bring myself to actually turn around and embrace him, but maybe with a little encouragement, his control will break, and he'll reach for me. I won't object; I won't do anything to stop him. I'll let him fuck me, maybe even pretend to enjoy it a little, so I don't pose a challenge in that respect. I'll just lie there and take it, and then it will all be over.

I'll be a willing but boring lay, and he'll get tired of me.

That's the plan, at least, but as I continue moving, I realize some of my exhaustion is fading, only to be replaced by a warm, liquid feeling that originates deep in my core. With the darkness veiling everything, it's easy to pretend that none of this is real, that I'm having another one of those twisted dreams.

"Sara, ptichka…" His hoarse whisper sounds strained. "If you want to go to sleep, you might want to stop moving."

I still for a second, then slowly and deliberately shift against him again. "What if…" I lick my dry lips. "What if I don't want to go to sleep?"

Peter's body turns to stone behind me, his arm tightening across my ribcage. For a brief, irrational moment, I fear that he might refuse, that despite all indications, he doesn't really want me, but then I find myself flipped onto my back, his heavy weight pressing me down as the bedside lamp comes on.

I blink, momentarily blinded by the light, and as his face comes into focus, I see that his gray eyes are narrowed, his jaw clenched tight as he holds himself up with one elbow. He looks furious, and for one horrible second, I wonder if I misinterpreted it all—if I made a huge error.

"Are you playing games with me, Sara?" His voice is low and hard, his accent stronger than usual as he captures my wrists and pins them to the pillow above my head with one big hand. "Trying to see how far you can push me?"

I stare up at him, a dark tingle crawling over my skin. This is so much like my dreams it's uncanny. And at the same time, it's different. My drug-fogged memory had painted him in harsh, cruel strokes, more monster than man, but that was wrong. There's nothing monstrous about the lethally beautiful face gazing down at me. The dreams had underestimated the potency of his magnetic appeal, omitting the sensuous softness of his lips, the strong, noble line of his nose, the way his thick dark eyebrows pull together over those intense metallic eyes... He's gorgeous, this terrifying stalker of mine, and as I lie there, pinned under his hard, warm body, I feel the dark tingle intensify, turning into something dangerous and forbidden. My nipples tighten, and a wave of heat rolls through me, my inner muscles clenching on a surge of aching need.

I don't want this man. I *can't* want him. Yet even as I tell myself this, I know it's a lie, a falsehood born of wishful thinking. Whatever it is that draws him to me works both ways, the pull of connection between us as strong as it is irrational. I do want him. More than that, I *need* him. My body doesn't care that he just killed two people in front of me, that I despise him with all my being. His touch doesn't repulse me; it arouses me, my desire stoked by the intimacy he's forced on me over the last few days and the twisted pleasure I've known in his embrace.

By the unnatural, perverse tenderness that has no place in our violent relationship.

He's still waiting for my response, his eyes narrowed, and I know I can back out of this, pretend it was a big misunderstanding. But if I do, he'll continue stalking me, undermining my resistance day by day until I cave, and in the meantime, everyone around me will be in danger.

"No games," I whisper into the tense silence. "The condoms are in the nightstand drawer."

He inhales, his fingers tightening around my wrists, and I see the exact moment he processes what I'm saying. His nostrils flare and his pupils dilate, the look of fury on his face transforming into one of dark, unbridled hunger. Reaching into the drawer with his free hand, he pulls out a foil packet, rips it open with his teeth, and rolls the condom onto his large, jutting cock.

My heartbeat jumps, anxiety tightening my ribcage, but it's too late.

Lowering his head, Peter captures my lips with his.

CHAPTER 31
SARA

I don't know why, but I never expected him to kiss me, to place his mouth on mine and feast on me as though he's starving. Because that's what it feels like: as if he's consuming me, taking in my essence, my very being. His lips and tongue ravage my mouth, devouring me, taking the air right out of my lungs. His free hand burrows into my hair, holding me still for the voracious kiss, and it's all I can do not to melt into the sheets. Because he doesn't just take; he gives. He gives so much pleasure I'm overwhelmed by it, overtaken by his taste and scent and feel.

He kisses me until I'm flushed and burning, until I can barely recall what it felt like not to kiss him, not to inhale his warm, minty breath. Until all thoughts of who and what we are are gone, and I'm arching against him, mindless with need, desperate for more of his touch, of this dizzying, scorching pleasure. My fingertips tingle from his tight grip on my wrists, and his body is heavy on top of mine, but I want more.

I want to lose myself in his merciless embrace, to dissolve in him and disappear.

He releases my lips to trail burning kisses over my face and neck, and I gulp in air, my heart racing and my skin pebbling from the electrifying pleasure. With each breath I take, my nipples rub against his muscled chest, and wetness slicks my inner thighs, my body preparing itself for him, for this act I shouldn't want, shouldn't crave with such violent intensity.

Breathing raggedly, he lifts his head, and I see an answering hunger in his silver gaze, a dark need mixed with something disturbingly possessive. His hand releases my hair and moves down my body, cupping my breast. "Sara…" My name is a rough exhale on his lips as his thumb grazes across my aching nipple. "You are so beautiful, ptichka… everything I've dreamed of and more."

His fervent words sear through me, filling me with warmth that goes down to my core—and sets off alarm bells in my mind. This feels too much like the consummation of a loving romance, and as his knee wedges between my thighs, the sensual fog engulfing me lifts for a moment. With a jolt of clarity, I process what's happening, and horror douses my desire.

What am I doing? How can I be enjoying this on any level? It's one thing to stoically bear a monster's touch for the greater good, but to actually want him—to let him act as though we're lovers—is sick, utterly insane. Even with my wrists restrained, there's no use pretending I'm unwilling, that my body doesn't crave him in the most perverse ways.

The broad head of his cock nudges at my folds, and my breathing turns shallow, my muscles stiffening in sudden panic. I can't do it—not like this. It's too much like lovemaking. He's still looking at me, his gray eyes filled with burning heat, and I know I have to tell him to stop, to end this—

He pushes into me in one hard stroke, and I forget what I was going to say. I forget everything but the stark, brutal sensation of his cock entering my body. His uncompromising hardness forces apart tight inner tissues, and despite my arousal, I feel a stinging burn as he presses deeper, ignoring the resistance of clenched muscles. It's been a long time for me, and he's big, both thicker and longer than George. My heart drums violently in my chest as my body yields reluctantly to the rough penetration, and with a mix of disappointment and bitter relief, I realize my fears were for naught.

This is nothing like lovemaking.

When he's all the way in, he stops, his eyes glittering with dark hunger, and a different kind of tension invades my body, banishing the last of unwelcome arousal and stiffening my resolve. The sensual allure of his looks is still there, but I now see the monster behind the handsome face, the killer who tortured me and ripped apart my life. There's no longer any ambiguity in what I'm feeling, no ambivalence of any kind. My stalker, the man I hate, is violating my body, and I'm glad. I'm glad because his cruelty hurts less than his tenderness, his ruthlessness less frightening than his mercy.

Sucking in a bracing breath, I prepare to endure a hard, rough fucking, but he doesn't move. His face is taut with lust, his body so tense he's vibrating with it, but he doesn't thrust, and I realize he caught on to my discomfort and is giving me time to adjust.

In his own way, he's trying to be gentle—which is the last thing I want.

Gathering my courage, I run my tongue over my lips and watch the hunger in his eyes intensify.

"Do it," I whisper, flexing my inner muscles. I can feel him throbbing inside me, hard and thick and dangerous. "Just fucking do it."

He stares down at me, and I sense his struggle, feel the monster doing battle with the man. I'm not the only one with mixed emotions here. There is a part of Peter that hates me too, that sees in me a reminder of his tragedy. He wants me, but he also wants to hurt me, to make me pay for what happened to his wife and son. He might not realize this himself, but I know it. I feel it. Our connection was forged in loss and pain, our intimacy born in torture. There's nothing normal about his attraction to me; it's as twisted as my response to him.

His vengeance is what binds us, and no amount of gentleness can change that fact.

I see the exact moment the monster starts to win the battle. Peter's jaw tightens as he withdraws partway, then plunges back in with a hard thrust. "Is this what you want from me?" His voice is low and rough, his gray eyes filled with growing darkness. He flexes his hips, and I gasp as he spears deeper into me, his hand tightening around my wrists. "Tell me, Sara. Is this what you want?"

I can still say no, let the man restrain the beast, but I've chosen my path and I'm not backing down. Maybe this final act of vengeance is what we both need, the punishment required for my absolution.

Maybe if he unleashes his darkness on me, we might both finally be free.

"Yes," I whisper and brace myself. "That's precisely what I want."

CHAPTER 32
PETER

I don't know what I expected, but as I gaze into Sara's hazel eyes and see the hatred there, I feel my fantasies dissolving, the lies I fed myself evaporating in the harsh light of truth. Her body might respond to me, but I'm still her enemy—and she is mine. Even with her silky pussy clasping my throbbing cock, the desire thrumming in my blood is tinged with violence, my need for her darker than anything I've known.

I don't just want to fuck her; I want to break her open, to wreak my vengeance on her delicate flesh.

"Sara..." I claw for remnants of my sanity, for something to hold on to as a mindless red tide descends on me, the vicious lash of hunger undermining my control. "You don't know what you're—"

"Just fucking do it," she whispers again, holding my gaze defiantly, and the last thread of my restraint snaps.

With a low, harsh groan, I pull back and surge into her, scarcely registering the way her pussy clenches in panicked resistance, the tender inner tissues giving way under my assault. She's wet, but she's tight, almost as small as a virgin, and even in a haze of lust, I realize what it means.

She hasn't had sex in a while—likely not since her husband.

The man whose arrogance killed my son.

My desire turns even darker, fueled by a surge of agony-born rage, and I lower my head, capturing Sara's mouth again. Only this time, I can't hold back, and the kiss is hard and savage, as violent as the emotions tearing me apart. The delicious feel of her, the sweet scent, the wet, silky texture of her mouth—it all drives me insane, and I taste the copper of her blood as my teeth sink into her lower lip, breaking the tender skin. It should stop me, or at least make me pause, but instead, it just whets my appetite. I need this from her: her pain, her suffering. It's as if a stranger has taken over my body, twisting my craving for her into a need to punish, to make her pay for her husband's sins. Possessing Sara this way is both heaven and hell, the violent pleasure of fucking her mixing with the bitter knowledge that I failed to keep my promise.

I'm hurting the woman I wanted to heal, the one who makes me feel so alive.

I don't know if it's that realization, or the tears I see on her face when I lift my head, but the surge of rage starts to fade, the red haze dissipating even as my desire reaches a new peak. My balls draw up, the pre-orgasmic tension curling at the base of my spine, yet I find myself painfully aware of the bird-like slenderness of her wrists in my grasp—and the terrified stiffness of her body as I violate her silky flesh.

Her eyes lock on mine, and I see pain in the hazel depths, mixed with perverse satisfaction. I'm making it easy for her, adding fuel to the fire of her hatred. This is what she expected from me all along, what she feared and wanted at the same time.

After tonight, I'll never be anything more than the man who hurt her, who abused her in the cruelest way.

No. Fuck, no. I clench my teeth and force myself to stop, fighting the rising swell of orgasm. Releasing her wrists, I withdraw from her and move down her body, ignoring the agonizing hardness of my cock. Settling between her parted thighs, I grip her knees and lower my head.

"What are you—" she begins dazedly, but I'm already licking her soft pussy, running my tongue between her pink, swollen folds. She's wet, but not as wet as I'd like, so I set out to remedy that, using every skill I've learned over my thirty-five years.

"Wait, Peter, don't..." She reaches down, trying to push me away as I tongue her clit, and when that fails, she attempts to close her legs. "This is not—"

"Hush." I use my grip on her knees to keep her thighs open. "Just lie back and relax."

"No, I—" She gasps, clutching fistfuls of my hair as I pull her clit into my mouth. I begin sucking on it with strong, rhythmic motions, and the tension in her leg muscles slackens, her breath catching audibly in her throat. I can feel her growing slick under my tongue, and I take advantage of her distraction by moving my right hand up to her pussy.

"That's it, ptichka, just relax…" I blow cool air across her clit and am rewarded with a soft moan before her thighs tense again. She's trying to resist, to reject the pleasure, but I already have my elbow in place, preventing her from crushing my head between her legs. She's breathing hard now, her hands tightening in my hair as I resume sucking on her clit, and I push two fingers into her tight, wet opening, curving them inside her until I feel the soft, spongy wall of her G-spot. Her pussy clamps tight, quivering around my fingers, and her hips arch off the bed as I intensify my sucking. She's close, I can sense it. My heart is thumping heavily in my chest, my breathing coming fast as the ache in my balls grows unbearable, but I restrain myself until I'm certain she's on the verge. Then, and only then, I give in to my own need.

Pulling my fingers out, I move up, covering her with my body, and line my cock against her swollen entrance.

"Come with me," I say hoarsely, meeting her gaze as I penetrate her in one hard stroke, and her body obeys me, her tight, wet flesh clenching around me, milking my cock just as the orgasm hits me. Her beautiful eyes go soft and unfocused, her face twisting with ecstasy as her fingers dig into my sides, and I hear her choked cry as my seed spurts out. It feels like every muscle in my body is vibrating at the same time, my lungs working like bellows as the pleasure blasts through me in scorching waves, and as I collapse on top of her, I know that this is it.

I'll never want another woman again.

I don't know how long it takes until the aftershocks die down, but by the time I find the strength to push myself up on my elbows, Sara has recovered enough to realize what happened, and horror creeps across her face. Like me, she's breathing hard, her cheeks flushed with post-coital glow, but there's no joy in her gaze, only the sharp glitter of tears.

She's regretting this, beating herself up again, and I won't stand for it.

"Don't." I dip my head to kiss her cheeks as the tears spill out, streaking down her temples. "Don't, ptichka. Don't feel bad. You did nothing wrong. It was all me. I hurt you, remember? I gave you no choice."

Her breath trembles on her lips as I rain kisses across her face, and I feel her shaking underneath me, her hands twisting in the sheets as the tears keep coming. I'm still inside her, my softening cock buried in her body, yet she's trying not to touch me, to curl in on herself and reject the connection between us.

I wanted her pain and I got it—and it's tearing me up inside.

I don't know what to do, how to calm her, so I just keep kissing her, stroking her as gently as I can. The thirst for vengeance is gone, and all that's left is regret. Once again, I'm the cause of Sara's suffering, and this time, it's infinitely worse. This time, I know her.

I know her, and I care.

She's still crying when I withdraw from her and get up to dispose of the condom in the bathroom. When I return with a wet towel, I find her curled on her side, with the blanket drawn up to her neck.

"Here, let me clean you up," I murmur, pulling the blanket off her naked body, and when she doesn't object, I run the towel over her soft folds, soothing the sore, swollen flesh and wiping away the evidence of her desire. She's no longer crying, but her eyes are still wet, and the moment I'm done, she huddles back under the blanket, pulling it over her head.

I'm about to climb into bed with her when I hear the vibration of my phone on the nightstand, where I left it in case of emergencies.

Frowning, I pick it up and glance at the screen.

Change of plans, the message from Anton reads. *Velazquez is moving to the Guadalajara compound in 2 days. It's tomorrow or never.*

I bite back a curse, fighting an urge to throw the phone across the room. Of all the shitty timing… We just finished working out all the logistics of the plan and were going to strike in six days. But if our target is changing locations, we're back to square one in terms of planning. It might take several weeks to scope out Velazquez's Guadalajara compound, and our client, a rival drug lord, is already getting antsy. He wants Velazquez gone as of yesterday, and he won't look kindly upon a delay.

Anton is right. We have to act now.

Get the plane and the supplies ready, I text back. *We're flying out early morning.*

Got it, Anton responds. *I assume you want the Americans on her?*

Yes, I text. *Tell them to stay close near the clinic.*

The last time my team and I had to go out of the country on a job, I hired a few locals to watch over Sara in our absence and report to me on her movements. They're highly vetted, and though I don't trust them nearly as much as my guys, so far I've been pleased with their services.

They should be able to protect her while I'm gone.

Setting my phone alarm to go off in four hours, I climb under the blanket with Sara and pull her into my embrace, curving my body around hers from the back. She stiffens but doesn't pull away, and as I close my eyes, breathing in her scent, a feeling of peace settles over me.

Nothing is resolved between us, but for some reason, I'm certain that it will be, confident that we'll make this work, whatever "this" turns out to be. It's the only way, because I can't picture my life without her.

Sara is mine, and I'd die before I set her free.

CHAPTER 33
SARA

A persistent buzzing drags me out of sound sleep. For a second, I'm so disoriented I think it's the middle of the night.

Rolling over onto my side, I blindly grope for the vibrating phone. "Hello," I croak, grabbing it from the nightstand without opening my eyes. My lashes feel glued together, my head so heavy I can barely lift it off the pillow.

"Dr. Cobakis, we have a patient going into premature labor, and Dr. Tomlinson was called away on a family matter. You're next in line to be on call. Can you be here soon?"

I sit up, a spike of adrenaline chasing away the worst of my drowsiness. "Um…" I blink the sleep out of my eyes and realize sunlight is seeping in through the cracks in the drapes. The alarm clock by the bed reads 6:45—less than an hour before I need to get up for work anyway. "Yes. I can be there in about an hour."

"Thank you. We'll see you soon."

The second the scheduling coordinator hangs up, I jump off the bed to rush to the shower—and stop dead, feeling the soreness deep inside. Memories of last night rush in, scorching hot and toxic, and all remnants of grogginess fade.

I had sex with Peter Sokolov last night.

He hurt me, and I came in his arms.

For a moment, those two facts seem irreconcilable, like an ice storm in July. I've never been into pain—just the opposite. The couple of times George and I explored kink, the light spanking he gave me distracted me from my orgasm instead of turning me on. I don't understand how I could've come after such rough sex, how I could've found pleasure when my body felt torn and battered.

And that orgasm wasn't the only one. My tormentor woke me up in the middle of the night by sliding into me, his fingers skillfully teasing my clit, and despite being sore, I came within minutes, my body responding to him even as my mind screamed in protest. Afterward, I cried myself back to sleep while he held me, stroking my back as though he cared.

No wonder I felt so groggy; with all the sex and crying, I only got a few hours of sleep.

Swallowing the ball of shame in my throat, I force myself to keep moving. I have to get dressed and go to the hospital. No matter how it feels right now, my life didn't end last night. I have no idea if I did the right thing by encouraging Peter to bed me, but what's done is done, and I have to move on.

The good news is that I don't have to see him again until tonight.

Maybe by then, the idea of facing him won't make me want to die.

The day flies by in a blur of work, and by the time I come home, I'm both exhausted and starved. I was so busy I skipped lunch, and though I'm dreading another night with my stalker, I have to admit that I'm looking forward to his cooking.

Peter Sokolov might be a psychopath, but he's an excellent chef.

To my surprise—and a small measure of disappointment—no delicious smells greet me as I walk in from the garage. The house is dark and empty, and I know without going from room to room that he's not there. I can feel it. My home seems colder, less vibrant, as if whatever dark energy Peter Sokolov emits was giving it a vitality of sorts.

Still, I call out, "Hello? Peter?"

Nothing.

"Are you there?"

No response.

Could my plan have worked so quickly? Is it possible that one taste satisfied whatever sick craving my stalker had for me?

Puzzled, I walk over to the refrigerator and take out a frozen dinner to pop into the microwave. It's the healthy, organic kind, Thai noodles and vegetables in some kind of not overly sugary sauce, but it's still dinner in a box. Too bad it's the only thing I have energy for tonight. I should've grabbed something from the hospital cafeteria, but I think I was subconsciously counting on being fed at home.

Shaking my head at the ridiculousness of it all, I turn on the microwave and go wash my hands.

My tormentor is gone, and that's a good thing.

I just need to convince my stomach of that.

He's still not there when I wake up, and though I have the vague sensation of being watched as I drive to work, I can't detect anyone following me. Same thing when I get to the hospital and go about my day. I'm paranoid enough to feel eyes on me all the time, but the sensation is not nearly as intense as it used to be.

If I didn't know I have a real stalker, I'd chalk it up to my imagination.

My parents call when I'm on my lunch hour and invite me over for dinner on Friday. I give them a noncommittal response—I don't want to expose them to any danger either—and then I call the clinic.

"Hey, Lydia, how's it going?" I ask, trying not to sound nervous. "How's everything been?"

"Hi, Dr. Cobakis." The receptionist's voice turns extra warm. "Glad to hear from you. Everything's going well. Not too busy for now, but it's probably going to pick up in the afternoon. Will you be able to come in again this week?"

"Yes, I think so. Um, Lydia…" I hesitate, unsure how to ask her what I want to know. I haven't seen anything on the news about the murders, but that doesn't mean the bodies haven't been found. "You haven't seen or heard anything... unusual, have you?"

"Unusual?" Lydia sounds confused. "Like what?"

"Oh, nothing in particular." To allay any suspicion, I add, "I was just thinking about that one patient, Monica Jackson... You haven't heard from her, right? The young dark-haired girl I saw yesterday?"

To my surprise, Lydia says, "Oh, that. Yes, actually. She dropped by a couple of hours ago and left a message for you. Something along the lines of 'thank you and he's now behind bars.' She didn't explain, just said that you'd understand. Any of that make sense to you?"

"Yes." Despite my tension, a big grin cuts across my face. "Yes, it makes perfect sense. Thanks for letting me know. I'll see you later this week."

I hang up, still grinning, and go scrub up for my afternoon C-section.

I have no idea how Peter made the evidence of his crime disappear, but he did, and now it seems like some good came out of that awful evening.

There might be no escape for me, but Monica is free.

————

My house is again dark and empty when I get home that evening, and as I get ready for bed, I'm aware of a peculiar melancholy. Having Peter in my house was terrifying, but he was still a human presence. Now I'm alone again, as I've been for the past two years, and the feeling of loneliness is sharper than ever, my bed colder and emptier than I recall it being.

Maybe I should get a dog. A big one that I would spoil by letting it sleep with me. That way, I'd have someone to greet me when I came home, and I wouldn't miss something as perverse as my husband's killer holding me at night.

Yes, I'll get a dog, I decide, climbing into bed and pulling the blanket over myself. Once I sell the house, I'll rent a place closer to the hospital and make sure it's dog-friendly—maybe near a park of some kind.

A dog will give me what I need, and I'll be able to forget about Peter Sokolov.

That is, assuming he forgot about me.

CHAPTER 34
SARA

By Monday, I'm almost convinced that Peter left for good. Over the weekend, I scoured my house from top to bottom in an effort to uncover his hidden cameras, but either they're all gone or they're concealed in such a way that a layman like myself has no hopes of finding them. Alternatively, they might not have been there in the first place, and my stalker knew the things he knew in some other way. Either way, there's been no sign of him, no contact of any kind. I spent most of the weekend at the clinic, and though I felt eyes on me as I walked to my car, it could've been remnants of my paranoia.

Maybe my nightmare is finally over.

It's silly, but the knowledge that I drove Peter away with sex stings a little. I hoped that once I stopped being the unattainable "ice princess," he'd leave me alone, but I didn't expect the results to be quite so immediate. Maybe I'm bad in bed? I must be, if one time was all it took for Peter to realize I'd never live up to whatever fantasy he had in his mind.

After stalking me for weeks, my tormentor abandoned me after just one night.

It's a good thing, of course. There are no more dinners, no more showers where I'm cared for like a child. No more dangerous killers wrapped around me at night, fucking with my mind and seducing my body. I go about my days as I've done for the past several months, only I feel stronger, less shattered inside. Confronting the source of my nightmares has done more for my mental wellbeing than months of therapy, and I can't help but be grateful for that.

Even with shame gnawing at me whenever I think of the orgasms he gave me, I feel better, more like my old self.

"So, tell me how you've been, Sara," Dr. Evans says when I finally go see him after his vacation. He's bronzed from the sun, his thin face for once glowing with health. "How did the Open House go?"

"My realtor is fielding a couple of offers," I reply, crossing my legs. For some reason, today I feel uncomfortable in this office, like I no longer belong here. Shaking the feeling away, I elaborate, "They're both lower than I'd like, so we're trying to play them off against one another."

"Ah, good. So some progress on that front." He tilts his head. "And maybe on other fronts as well?"

I nod, unsurprised by the therapist's perceptiveness. "Yes, my paranoia is better, and so are my nightmares. I was even able to turn on the water in the kitchen sink on Saturday."

"Really?" His eyebrows rise. "That's wonderful to hear. Anything in particular bring it on?"

Oh, you know, just having the man who tortured me and killed my husband reappear in my life.

"I don't know," I say with a shrug. "Maybe it's time. It's been almost seven months."

"Yes," Dr. Evans says gently, "but you should know that's nothing in the timeline of human grief and PTSD."

"Right." I look down at my hands and notice a rather ragged-looking hangnail on the left thumb. It might be time to get a manicure. "I guess I'm lucky then."

"Indeed."

When I look up, Dr. Evans is regarding me with that same thoughtful expression. "How is your social life?" he asks, and I feel a fiery blush creep across my face.

"I see," Dr. Evans says when I don't answer right away. "Anything you'd like to talk about?"

"No, it's… it's nothing." My face burns even hotter when he gives me a disbelieving look. I can't tell him about Peter, so I scramble for something plausible. "I mean, I did go out with some coworkers a couple of weeks back and had a good time…"

"Ah." He seems to accept my answer at face value. "And how did it make you feel, having 'a good time?'"

"It made me feel… great." I think back to dancing at the club, letting the beat of the music thump through me. "It made me feel alive."

"Excellent." Dr. Evans scribbles down some notes. "And have you gone out again since?"

"No, I haven't had the opportunity." It's a lie—I could've gone out with Marsha and the girls this past Saturday—but I can't explain to the therapist that I'm trying to protect my friends by minimizing contact with them. Doctor-patient privilege has its limits, and disclosing that I've been in contact with a wanted criminal—and that I witnessed two murders last week—could prompt Dr. Evans to go to the police and endanger us both.

In general, coming here today was a bad idea. I can't talk about the things I really need to discuss, and he won't be able to help me work through my complicated feelings without understanding the full story. That's why I'm feeling uncomfortable, I realize: I can't let Dr. Evans in anymore.

My phone vibrates in my bag, and I eagerly pounce on the distraction. Fishing the phone out, I see it's a text from the hospital.

"Please excuse me," I say, getting up and dropping the phone back into my bag. "A patient has just gone into premature labor and needs my assistance."

"Of course." Unfolding his lanky frame, Dr. Evans rises to his feet and shakes my hand. "We'll continue next week. As always, it's been a pleasure."

"Thank you. Same here," I say and make a mental note to cancel my next week's appointment. "Have a wonderful rest of the day."

And leaving the therapist's office, I rush to the hospital, for once grateful for the unpredictability of my work.

I don't know if it's the session with Dr. Evans or the bet-ter sleep in the last few days, but that night, I find myself tossing and turning, drifting off only to jerk awake, heart hammering from some undefined anxiety. The emptiness of my bed grates at me, my loneliness a painful hole in my chest. I want to believe that I'm missing George, that it's his arms I'm longing for, but when the uneasy sleep claims me, it's steel-gray eyes that invade my dreams, not soft brown ones.

In those dreams, I'm dancing, performing in front of my tormentor like a professional ballerina. I'm dressed as one too, in a light yellow dress with stiff, feathery wings in the back. As I twirl and fly across the stage, I feel lighter than fog, more graceful than a wisp of smoke. But inside, I burn with passion. My movements come from deep within my soul, my body speaking through dance with the raw honesty of beauty.

I miss you, this plié says. *I want you*, that pirouette con-firms. I say with my body what I can't say through words, and he watches me, his face dark and enigmatic. Red drop-lets decorate his hands, and I know without asking that it's blood, that he took another life today. It should disgust me, but all I care about is whether he wants me, whether he feels the heat that devours me from within.

Please, I beg with my movements, hinging in a grace-ful arc in front of him. *Please give me this. I need the truth. Please tell me.*

But he doesn't say anything. He just watches me, and I know there's nothing I can do, no way I can convince him. So I dance closer, pulled by a dark attraction, and when

I'm within his reach, he lifts his arms, his blood-splattered hands closing around my shoulders.

"Peter…" I sway toward him, that terrible longing twisting my insides, but his eyes are cold, so cold they burn.

He doesn't want me anymore. I know it. I see it.

Still, I reach for him, my hand lifting to his hard-edged face. I want him—I need him—so much. But before I can touch him, he murmurs, "Goodbye, ptichka," and shoves me away.

I tumble backward, falling off the stage. My dress flutters in the air for a brief second, and then my wings crumple as I hit the floor. Even before the shock of the impact reverberates through me, I know that this is it.

My body is broken, and so is my soul.

"Peter," I moan with my last breath, but it's too late.

He's gone for good.

I wake up with my face wet with tears and my heart heavy with grief. It's pitch black in the room, and in the darkness, it doesn't matter that I can't rationally miss a man I hate. The dream is so vivid in my mind it feels as if I truly lost him… as if I died from the rejection at his hands. I know what I'm grieving must be my real losses—George and the life we were supposed to have—but with my bed empty and my body aching for a hard, warm embrace, it feels like I miss *him*.

Peter.

The man I have every reason to despise.

Squeezing my eyes shut, I roll up into a small ball under the blanket and hug a pillow to myself. I don't need Dr. Evans to tell me that what I'm feeling can't possibly be real, that at best, it's a bizarre version of Stockholm Syndrome. One does *not* fall for one's stalker; it simply doesn't happen. I haven't even known Peter Sokolov that long. He's been in my life for what? A week? Two? The days since the club outing have felt like years, but in reality, hardly any time has passed.

Of course, he's been in my nightmares for much longer.

For the first time, I allow myself to really think about my tormentor—to wonder about him as a man. What had he been like with his family? It should've been difficult to imagine such a ruthless killer in a domestic setting, but for some reason, I have no problem picturing him playing with a child or making dinner with his wife. Maybe it's the gentle way he took care of me, but I feel like there's something within him that transcends the monstrous things he's done, something vulnerable and deeply human.

He must've loved his family, to dedicate himself to vengeance so completely.

The pictures on his phone surface in my mind, making my chest squeeze with pain. False information, that's what Peter blamed for those atrocities. Is it possible that George had been the one to provide that information? That my handsome, peaceful husband, who loved barbecues and reading the newspaper in bed, had really been a spy who'd made such a terrible error? It seems unbelievable, yet there must've been a reason Peter came after George, why he went to such lengths to murder him.

Unless Peter made a huge error himself, George hadn't been what he seemed.

Tightening my grip on the pillow, I process that realization, letting the knowledge fully settle in. Over the past week and a half, I've avoided thinking of my stalker's revelations, but I can no longer push the truth away.

Between the FBI protection that came out of nowhere and the growing distance between me and George after our marriage, it's entirely possible that my husband had fooled me—that he'd lied to me and everyone else for the better part of a decade.

My life had been even more of an illusion than I'd known.

When I fall asleep an hour later, it's with the bitter taste of betrayal on my tongue and a fresh determination in my mind.

Come tomorrow morning, I'm going to accept one of the offers on my house. I need a fresh start, and I'm going to get it. Maybe in a new place, I'll forget both George's duplicity and *him*.

If Peter Sokolov is gone for good, I might be able to finally start living.

CHAPTER 35
SARA

*O*n Thursday, I sign the papers, selling my house to a lawyer couple moving to the area from Chicago. They have two children in elementary school and a baby on the way, and they need the five bedrooms. Though their offer is three percent below market value and a couple of thousand dollars less than the other offer I received, I went with the lawyers because they're paying cash and can close on the house quickly.

If there are no issues with the inspection, I'll be moving out in less than three weeks.

Feeling energized, I ask another doctor to cover for me on Friday and spend the day looking for apartments to rent. I settle on a small one-bedroom within walking distance of the hospital, in a pet-friendly condo building. It's a little dated, and the closet space is almost nonexistent, but since I'm planning to get rid of everything that reminds me of my old life, I don't mind.

Fresh start, here I come.

My excitement lasts until the evening, when I get home and feel the emptiness of the house again. My dinner is another box from the freezer, and despite my best efforts, I can't help thinking about Peter, wondering where he is and what he's doing. It occurred to me yesterday that there could be another reason why he's gone, and the thought has been gnawing at me ever since.

The authorities could've captured or killed him.

I don't know why I didn't think of this possibility before yesterday, but now I can't get it out of my mind. It would obviously be a good thing—I'd be truly safe if he were dead or in custody—but every time I think about it, my chest feels tight and heavy, and something bizarrely like tears prickles at my eyes.

I don't want Peter Sokolov in my life, but I can't bear the thought of him dead, either.

It's stupid, so very stupid. Yes, we had sex that night—and he gave me orgasms more than once—but I'm not some virginal teenager who believes sleeping together means eternal love. The only feeling between us other than hatred is animal lust, an attraction of the most basic kind. That much I can accept; as a doctor, I know how potent biology can be, having seen the evidence of smart people making stupid decisions in the throes of passion. It's disturbing that I wanted my husband's killer on any level, but to fear for his wellbeing is something else.

Something far more insane.

I do not miss Peter, I tell myself as I toss and turn in my empty bed. Whatever loneliness I'm feeling is a function of too much stress and not enough time with my friends and family. Once a little more time passes, and the threat of my stalker is completely gone, I'll go out with Marsha and the nurses and maybe even consider a date with Joe.

Okay, maybe not the latter—I turned him down when he called a few days ago, and I still can't work up any regret—but I'll definitely go out dancing again.

One way or another, my new life will start soon.

CHAPTER 36
PETER

She's sleeping when I enter the room, her slender body swaddled in a blanket from head to toe. Quietly, I turn on the lights and stop, my breath catching in my chest. During the past two weeks, as I lay recuperating from the stab wound I sustained in Mexico, I've entertained myself by watching her on the house cameras and devouring the Americans' reports on her activities. I know everything she's done, everyone she's spoken to, all the places she's gone. That should've lessened the feeling of separation, but seeing her like this, with her shiny chestnut hair spread over her pillow, steals the air from my lungs and sends a stab of longing through me.

My Sara. I missed her so fucking much.

I approach the bed, curling my hands into fists to contain the need to reach for her, to grab her and never let her go.

Two weeks. For two impossibly long weeks, I couldn't return for her because I'd missed the knife hidden in one guard's boot. Granted, I was dealing with another guard pointing an AR15 at me, but that's no excuse for sloppiness.

I was distracted on the job, and that nearly cost me my life. An inch to the right, and I'd have been laid up way longer than two weeks. Maybe permanently.

"What the fuck, man?" Ilya grumbled as he and his brother patched me up after the mission was over. "He almost nicked your kidney. You have to watch your fucking back."

"That's what I have you two for," I managed to say, and then the blood loss got the better of me, preventing me from explaining the reason for my distraction. It was just as well. The truth is, I missed the knife coming at me because, as I was staring down the barrel of the AR15, I thought not of my team or my mission, but of Sara and never seeing her again.

My obsession with her almost became my downfall.

Sitting down on the edge of the bed, I carefully pull the blanket off her. She's sleeping naked, as always, and lust roars in my veins at the sight of her slim, graceful curves. She doesn't wake up, just huffs like a disgruntled kitten at the loss of the blanket, and I feel something soft slither into my chest. My heart fills with a warm glow even as my cock stiffens further and my pulse picks up pace.

I have to have her. Now.

Getting up, I swiftly strip off my clothes and place them on the dresser, making sure my weapons are well hidden. The jerky movements pull at the fresh scar on my stomach, but I want her so much the pain scarcely registers. Putting on a condom, I climb into bed with her and roll her over onto her back, settling between her legs.

My touch wakes her up. Her eyelids fly open, her hazel eyes panicked and dazed at the same time, and I smile as I grasp her wrists and pin them by her shoulders. It's a predatory smile, I know, but I can't help myself.

Even with the warm feeling in my chest, my hunger for her is dark, as violent as it is all-consuming.

"Hello, ptichka," I murmur, watching the shock creep into her eyes as her gaze clears. "I'm sorry I was gone for so long. It couldn't be helped."

"You're... you're back." Her chest rises up and down in an uneven rhythm, her nipples like hard pink berries on her deliciously round breasts. "What are you—why are you back?"

"Because I'd never leave you." I lean down and inhale her scent, delicate and warm, as captivating as Sara herself. Lightly nibbling on her ear, I whisper against her neck, "Did you think I would just walk away?"

She shivers underneath me, her breathing speeding up, and I know if I reach between her legs, I'll find her hot and wet, ready for me. She wants me—or at least her body does—and my cock throbs at the knowledge, eager to fill her, to feel the tight, slick embrace of her pussy. First, though, I want an answer to my question.

Raising my head, I pin her with my gaze. "Did you think I'd leave, Sara?"

Her face is a mask of confusion as she blinks up at me. "Well, yes. I mean, you were gone, and I thought—I hoped…" She stops, frowning. "Why did you leave if you didn't get bored with me?"

"Bored with you?" Does she not realize that I literally think about her all the time, even in the heat of battle? That I can't go an hour without checking on her whereabouts or spend a night without seeing her in my dreams? Holding her gaze, I slowly shake my head. "No, ptichka. I didn't get bored with you—nor will I ever."

Out of the corner of my eye, I see her slender fingers flex, and I realize I'm still holding her wrists pinned next to her shoulders, my grip as tight as if I'm afraid she would escape. She wouldn't, of course—even with my recent injury, she's no match for my reflexes or strength—but I like having her like this, restrained underneath me, naked and helpless. It's part of my fucked-up feelings for her, this need to dominate, to have her always at my mercy.

"Don't," she whispers, but her tongue flicks out to wet her soft pink lips, and the hunger within me intensifies, my balls tightening as blood rushes to my groin. There's something so pure about her, something so gentle and innocent in the graceful lines of her heart-shaped face. It's as if she's been untouched by life, uncorrupted by all the vileness I deal with daily. It makes the things I want to do to her that much more dirty, that much more wrong, yet I know I will do them all.

Right and wrong has never been my strong suit.

Lowering my head, I taste her lips, keeping my kiss gentle despite the aching stiffness of my cock. Even with the dark urges gnawing at me, I don't want to hurt her today—not after the last time. I still can't define what she means to me, but I know she's mine to care for, mine to coddle and protect. I don't want her to fear pain from my touch—even if I sometimes want to inflict it.

I don't know what I want from her, but I know it's more than this.

She's unresponsive at first, her lips sealed against the probing of my tongue, but I keep kissing her, and eventually, her lips soften, letting me into the warm recesses of her mouth. She tastes delicious, like a hint of minty toothpaste and herself, and I can't suppress a groan as the head of my cock brushes against her inner thigh. I want to be inside her, to feel her hot, slick walls squeezing me tight, but I resist the temptation, focusing on seducing her, on giving her so much pleasure she'll forget the pain I caused.

I don't know how long I tease and caress her lips, but after a while, I feel the tentative touch of her tongue. She's responding to me, kissing me back, and as her body softens underneath me, my heartbeat spikes, the need to have her drumming in my chest. Breathing raggedly, I move from her lips to the tender skin of her neck, then her collarbone and the plush softness of her breasts. She moans as my lips close over her nipple, and I feel her arch underneath me, her hips rising off the bed to press her pussy against me.

Growling low in my throat, I turn my attention to the other breast, sucking on it until Sara's moans grow in volume, and she's writhing underneath me, her hands flexing convulsively as I hold her wrists. When I lift my head, I see that her face is flushed, her eyes squeezed shut and her head tipped back in sensual abandon.

It's time. Fuck, it's way past time.

Releasing her nipple, I move up, lining my hard cock against the entrance to her body.

"Do you want this?" I ask hoarsely as her eyelids flutter open, revealing eyes hazy with desire. "Tell me you want this, ptichka. Tell me you missed me when I was gone."

Sara's lips part, but no words emerge, and I know she's not ready to admit it, to accept the connection that exists between us. I might have her body, but I'll have to fight harder for her mind and heart. And I will, because that's what I need from her, I realize: for her to be completely mine, to want me and need me as much as I need her.

Lowering my head, I kiss her lips again, then release one of her wrists to guide my cock into her hot, slick opening. She's still incredibly tight, but this time, I manage to go slow, to work myself in inch by inch until I'm buried in her to the hilt. She clutches at my side with her free hand, her delicate nails digging into my skin as she pants against my ear, and I feel her inner walls flex as I begin to move inside her, sliding in and out in a slow, deliberate rhythm. My own desire is at a fever pitch, and it's all I can do to keep my strokes steady, grinding against her clit each time I bottom out inside her.

"Yes, that's it," I groan, feeling her muscles tighten as her breathing speeds up. "Come for me, ptichka. Let me feel you come."

She cries out as I pick up my pace, and I grip her hip, squeezing the tight flesh of her ass as I hammer into her, fucking her so hard the bed creaks underneath us. I can't get enough of her, of her silky softness and sweet scent, and I drive deeper into her body, wanting to meld with her, to sink so far into her I'd be permanently etched inside her flesh.

Her cries grow louder, more frantic, and I feel her pussy clenching, her hips rising off the bed as she reaches her peak. Her contractions are the last straw; with a hoarse shout, I explode, grinding my pelvis against hers as my cock jerks and pulses in release, flooding the condom with my seed.

Panting, I roll off her and gather her against me, holding her tight as our breathing slows. With my hunger sated, I become aware of the dull pulsing of the healing wound on my abdomen. The doctors warned me to take it easy for a few weeks, but I forgot about that, too consumed by Sara and the incandescent pleasure of possessing her.

After a minute, I get up to get rid of the condom, and when I return, Sara is sitting up in bed, her slim form wrapped in a blanket like the last time. Only today, there are no tears; her eyes are dry, her gaze locked defiantly on my face as I cross the room.

Maybe she's beginning to accept the reality of us, to understand there's no shame in wanting me.

"Why are you back?" she asks as I sit down next to her, and I hear the despair behind the bravado.

I was wrong. She's still far from accepting me.

Lifting my hand, I tuck a shiny strand of hair behind her ear. With the blanket wrapped around her and her chestnut waves in disarray, my pretty doctor looks young and vulnerable, more girl than woman. Seeing her like this makes me want to protect her, shelter her from the cruelty of my world.

Too bad I'm part of that world—and maybe the cruelest of them all.

"I never left," I answer, lowering my hand. "At least I didn't mean to leave—not for this long. I had a job to do, but it should've only taken a day or two."

"A job?" She blinks at me. "What kind of job?"

I consider not telling her, or at least glossing over some of the harsher realities of my work, but I decide against it. Sara's opinion of me can't get much worse, so she might as well know the full truth.

"My team carries out certain missions," I say carefully, observing her reaction. "Jobs that few others can handle with the same level of skill and discretion. Our clients generally operate in the shadows, and so do the targets we're paid to eliminate."

The post-sex flush on her cheeks fades, leaving her face starkly pale. "You're an assassin? Your team… kills people for hire?"

I nod. "Not just anyone, but yes. Our targets tend to be quite dangerous themselves, often with multiple layers of security that we have to penetrate. That's how I ended up with this." I point to the fresh scar on my stomach and see her eyes widen as she takes it in—likely for the first time. I doubt she got a good look at me as I was fucking her.

"How did this happen?" she asks, looking up from my stomach. Her face is even paler now, her porcelain skin taking on a greenish tint. "Is that a knife wound?"

"Yes. As to how, a moment of inattention on my part." It still pisses me off that I didn't see the guard behind me reach for his knife while I was dealing with his gun-wielding partner. "I should've been more careful."

She swallows and studies my scar again. "If it's so dangerous, why do you do it?" she asks after a moment, her eyes returning to my face.

"Because hiding from the authorities isn't cheap," I say. So far, Sara's taking my revelation better than I expected, though I guess seeing me kill those two druggies might've prepared her for something like this. "The work pays extremely well, and it's a good fit with my skill set. I used to consult for some of our clients before this, but running my own business is better. I have more freedom and flexibility—something that became important to me when I got my list."

Her lips tighten. "The list that my husband was on?"

"Yes."

Her gaze drops to her lap, but not before I glimpse a flash of anger in the soft hazel depths. It bothers her that I feel no remorse about that, but I'm not about to fake it. That *ublyudok*—that bastard husband of hers—deserved a much worse death than he received, and the only thing I regret is that he was a vegetable when I came for him. That and the fact that, for a brief instant, I hesitated before pulling the trigger.

I hesitated because I thought of Sara instead of my dead wife and son.

The recollection fills me with familiar rage and pain, and I force myself to take a slow, deep breath. If I didn't feel so relaxed after fucking her, it would've been next to impossible to contain the agony flooding my chest, but as it is, I'm able to control myself—even when Sara gets up and excuses herself to go to the bathroom, still wrapped in the blanket.

She's giving me the silent treatment, but it doesn't bother me. It's already after midnight, and there will be plenty of time to talk tomorrow.

Stretching out on the bed, I wait for Sara to return. It's just as well she chose to cut short our little powwow. Though I barely exerted myself today, I feel as tired as after a mission. My body is still in recovery mode, a fact that frustrates me. I hate it when I'm not in battle-ready shape; weakness of any kind makes me feel antsy and unsettled.

Sara takes her time in the bathroom, but eventually, she reappears and lies down next to me, pointedly not sharing the blanket with me. Equal parts annoyed and amused, I pull the blanket off her and arrange it over both of us when I have her where she belongs: in my arms, with her tight little butt pressing against my groin.

"Good night," I murmur, kissing the back of her neck, and when she doesn't respond, I close my eyes, ignoring the twitching of my hardening cock.

As much as I'd like to fuck her again, I need rest, and so does she.

I can be patient. After all, I'll have her again tomorrow—and every day after that.

CHAPTER 37
SARA

I wake up to the smell of coffee and bacon and the feeling of sunlight on my face. Confused, I open my eyes and see that it's a half hour before my alarm is due to go off. As I attempt to process that, memories of last night invade my mind, and I groan, pulling the blanket over my head.

My Russian stalker is back—and cooking breakfast in my house.

After a minute, I convince myself to get up and go through my usual morning routine. Yes, my husband's killer fucked me again last night—and made me come— but the world didn't end, and I have to act accordingly.

I have to ignore the self-loathing knotting my insides and go to work.

Ten minutes later, I go downstairs, dressed and freshly showered. It's strange, but I don't feel any differently about Peter now that I know what he does for work. I've been thinking about him as a killer for so long that knowing he and his team do it for money hardly fazes me. However, it does reinforce my conviction that he's dangerous—and that I need to tread carefully if I'm to avoid putting those I care about in his crosshairs.

"I hope you like bacon and scrambled eggs," he says as I enter the kitchen. Like me, he's fully dressed, minus shoes and the leather jacket hanging on one of the kitchen chairs. Once again, his clothes are dark, and the sight of him by the stove, so powerfully male and lethally handsome, jacks up my pulse and makes my stomach clench with something unsettling.

Something that feels suspiciously like excitement.

Pushing the thought away, I fold my arms in front of my chest and prop my hip against the counter. "Sure," I answer evenly, ignoring my racing heartbeat. "Who doesn't?"

As good as it would feel to throw the food in his face, I don't want to provoke him until I figure out a new strategy.

"That's what I figured." He skillfully plates the eggs and bacon, then pours us each a cup of coffee.

Deciding that I might as well help out, I pick up the cups and carry them to the table. He brings the plates, and we sit down to eat breakfast.

The eggs are excellent, flavorful and fluffy, and the bacon is perfectly crisped. Even the coffee is unusually good, as though he used some secret recipe with my Keurig. Not that I expected anything else; each meal he's fed me has been outstanding.

If the assassin/stalker thing doesn't work out, my tormentor could consider a career as a chef.

The thought is so ridiculous I snicker into my coffee, prompting Peter to look up from his plate, eyebrows raised in a silent question.

"I was just thinking that you could do this professionally," I explain, shoving a forkful of eggs into my mouth. Maybe this is another betrayal of George's memory, but I can't help remembering that my husband had never once made breakfast for me. A couple of times while we were dating, he attempted a romantic dinner—takeout Chinese with some candles—but otherwise, I either cooked or we went out.

"Thank you." A smile touches Peter's lips at my compliment. "I'm glad you like it."

"Uh-huh." I focus on consuming what's on my plate and trying not to flush as I recall how those sculpted lips felt on my neck, my breasts, my nipples... I want to believe that he caught me off-guard last night, that my response to him was the result of a sleep-clouded mind, but the excitement humming in my veins this morning belies that assumption.

Some sick part of me is glad to see him—and relieved that he's alive.

Idiot, I chastise myself. Peter Sokolov is a wanted fugitive, a monster who took two lives in front of me after torturing me and killing George. A stalker whose presence in my life introduces innumerable complications and poses a threat to everyone around me.

It's not just wrong to want him here; it's downright pathological.

Still, as I finish my eggs and gulp down my coffee, I'm aware of a peculiar lightness in my chest. The house no longer feels huge and oppressive around me, the kitchen bright and warm instead of cold and threatening. *He* fills the space now, dominating it with his large body and the frightening force of his personality, and though he's the last person I should want for companionship, I don't feel the crushing pressure of loneliness when I'm with him.

A dog, I remind myself. *All you need is a dog.* And in the next breath, I realize there could be a problem with that—and with my new life plan in general.

"You know I'm moving out in a couple of weeks, right?" I say, putting down my empty cup. "I signed papers to sell the house."

Peter's expression doesn't change. "Yes, I know."

"Of course you do." My hands curl on the table, my nails digging into my palms. "You probably had me watched while you were gone. Those eyes on me—that wasn't my imagination, was it?"

"I couldn't leave you unprotected," he says with an un-apologetic shrug.

"Right." I take a breath and consciously relax my hands. "Well, I'm moving to an apartment soon, and I'm pretty sure you won't be able to come and go like this—at least not without the neighbors seeing you every day. So you might as well find some other woman to torture and stalk. There are plenty who live in semi-rural areas."

The corners of his mouth twitch. "I'm sure there are. Too bad I don't want any of them."

I drum my fingers on the table. "Really? What about the rest of the people on your list? Or did you murder them all?"

"There's one left, and he's proving elusive so far," he says, and I stare at him blankly before shaking my head.

I'm not prepared to go there today.

"Fine," I say in an attempt to regroup. "So what's it going to take for you to leave *me* alone?"

"A bullet to the brain or the heart," he answers, unblinking, and my stomach lurches as I realize he's completely serious.

He has no intention of walking away from me. Ever.

All the lightness and excitement fade, leaving me with the stark terror of my reality. No amount of delicious meals, mind-blowing orgasms, or tender cuddling makes up for the fact that I'm a de-facto prisoner of this lethal man, a killer who doesn't blink at violence and torture. His obsession with me is as dangerous as the man himself, his feelings as twisted as the dark past we share.

A monster is fixated on me, and there's no escape.

My legs are unsteady as I get up, pushing my chair back. "I have to go to work," I say tightly, and before he can object, I grab my bag and hurry to the garage.

Peter makes no move to stop me, but as I'm getting into the car, he comes to stand in the doorway, his darkly handsome face set in an unreadable mask.

"I'll see you when you get back," he says as I start the car, and I know he means it.

My tormentor is back, and he's not going away.

CHAPTER 38
SARA

True to his word, Peter is there when I get home from work that day, and I'm so tired and stressed that I'm tempted to just give in and eat the dinner he made—a savory-smelling rice pilaf with mushrooms and peas. But I can't. I can't keep playing along with this madness, acting as though this is somehow normal.

If my stalker is not going to leave me alone, there's no point in my compliance. I might as well make things as difficult for him as I can.

Ignoring the table he set, I go upstairs while he's pouring us wine. Entering the bedroom, I lock the door and go into the bathroom to splash cold water on my face.

I've tried everything except outright resistance, and I'm desperate enough to try that.

Face freshly washed, I come out and sit down on the bed, waiting to see what's going to happen next. I have no intention of unlocking that door and letting him in, or of cooperating in any way.

I'm done playing house with a monster. If he wants me, he's going to have to force me.

My stomach growls with hunger, and I kick myself for not eating before coming here. I was just so frazzled from thinking about Peter all day that I drove home on autopilot, my mind occupied with my impossible situation. Now that I know about his team and their assassination missions, I'm even less convinced that the FBI would be able to protect me if I went to them.

I don't think *anyone* can protect me from him.

A knock on the bedroom door drags me out of my despairing thoughts.

"Come down, ptichka," Peter says from the other side. "Dinner is getting cold."

My whole body tenses, but I don't respond.

Another knock. Then the door handle rattles. "Sara." Peter's voice hardens. "Open the door."

I get up, too unsettled to sit still, but I make no move toward the door.

"Sara. Open this door. Now."

I remain standing, my hands flexing at my sides. Before coming home, I considered getting a weapon, but I remembered what he told me about his men monitoring his vitals and dismissed the idea. I don't know how the monitoring works, but it's entirely possible he's wearing some kind of device that measures his pulse and/or blood pressure. Maybe even an implant. I've heard of things like that, though I've never encountered them. In any case, if what Peter told me is true, I can't hurt him in any meaning-ful way without risking my own life and possibly the lives of those close to me.

Men who kill for money wouldn't hesitate to avenge their boss in the most brutal ways.

"You have five seconds to open this door."

Fighting a sense of déjà vu, I sink my teeth into my lower lip but keep still, even as my heart thuds sickly and cold sweat pours down my spine. As much as I don't want him to hurt me, I don't want to live like this either, too afraid to stand up for myself, meekly going along with a madman's demands. The last time I locked a door on him, I was in shock, so overwhelmed and terrified from seeing him kill those two men that I acted on autopilot. Now, however, my action is deliberate.

I need to know how far he'll go, what he's willing to do to get his way.

He doesn't count out loud this time, so I count in my head. *One, two, three, four, five…* I wait for his kick to rattle the door, but instead, I hear footsteps heading down the hall.

The breath I'm holding escapes in a relieved whoosh. Is it possible? Could he have given up and decided to leave me alone tonight? I wouldn't have expected that, but he's surprised me before. Maybe his reluctance to force me still holds; maybe he's drawing a line at breaking down the bed-room door and—

The footsteps return, and the door handle rattles again before something metallic scratches against it. My heart skips a beat, then resumes its furious thudding.

He's picking the lock on the door.

The cool deliberateness of that action is somehow scarier than if he'd simply kicked down the door. My tormentor is not acting out of anger; he's fully in control and knows exactly what he's doing.

The metallic scratching lasts for less than a minute. I know because I watch the blinking numbers on the alarm clock on my nightstand. Then the door swings open, and Peter steps in, his gait radiating restrained rage and his face set in cold, hard lines.

Fighting the urge to run, I raise my chin and stare up at him as he stops in front of me, his big body towering over my much shorter frame.

"Come to dinner." His voice is quiet, soft even, but I hear the pulsing darkness underneath. He's hanging on to his control by a thread, and if I had any hope left, I'd back down out of self-preservation. But I'm all out of strategies, and at some point, self-preservation has to take a back seat to self-respect.

Recklessly, I shake my head. "I'm not doing this."

His nostrils flare. "Doing what? Eating?"

My stomach chooses that moment to growl again, and I flush at the unfortunate timing. "I'm not eating with *you*," I say as evenly as I can manage. "Nor am I sleeping with you—or doing anything else for that matter."

"No?" Dark amusement creeps into the gray iciness of his gaze. "Are you sure about that, ptichka?"

My hands ball at my sides. "I want you out of my house. Now."

"Or what?" He steps closer, crowding me with his large body until I have no choice but to back up in the direction of the bed. "Or what, Sara?"

I want to threaten him with the police or FBI, but we both know that if I could've gone to them, I would've already done so. There's nothing I can do to force him out of my life, and that's the crux of the matter.

Ignoring the icy sweat trickling down my back, I lift my chin higher. "I'm done with this, Peter."

"This?" He steps closer, cocking his head to the side.

"This sick relationship fantasy you've cooked up," I clarify. He's too close for comfort, invading my personal space like he belongs there. His masculine scent surrounds me, the heat coming off his big body warming my insides, and I step back again, trying to ignore the melting sensation between my thighs and the aching tautness of my nipples.

I can't be this close to him without remembering how it feels to be even closer, to be joined with him in the most intimate of ways.

"A sick relationship fantasy?" His eyebrows arch mockingly. "That's a little harsh, don't you think?"

"I. Am. Done," I repeat, enunciating each word. My heart slams anxiously against my ribcage, but I'm determined not to back down or let him distract me with a discussion of our messed-up relationship. "If you want to cook in my kitchen, go ahead, but short of force-feeding me, you can't make me eat with you—or do anything else with you of my own accord."

"Oh, ptichka." Peter's voice is soft, his gaze almost sympathetic. "You have no idea how wrong you are."

His lips curve in that imperfect, magnetic smile, and my stomach flips as he comes even closer. Desperate for some distance, I take another step back, only to feel the back of my knees press against the bed.

I'm trapped, caught by him once again.

Mercilessly, he steps closer, and my sex clenches as his hands curl around my shoulders. "Come downstairs with me, Sara," he says softly. "You're hungry, and you'll feel better once you eat. And while you're eating, we can talk."

"About what?" I ask, my voice tight. The heat of his palms burns even through the thick layer of my sweater, and it's all I can do to keep my breathing semi-steady as pernicious arousal curls in my core. "We have nothing to talk about."

"I think we do," he says, and I see the monster behind the dark silver of his gaze. "You see, Sara, if you don't want to be with me here, we can be together someplace else. The fantasy can be made real—but solely on my terms."

CHAPTER 39
PETER

She's shaking as I lead her downstairs, and I know it's as much from anger as fear. I suppose her reaction should bother me, but I'm too angry myself. Yesterday, and today at breakfast, I could've sworn she was glad to see me, relieved that I came back. But tonight, she's back to being cold and distant, and I won't stand for it.

It's time the gloves came off.

"Sit," I tell her when we get to the kitchen table, and she plops down in a chair, a defiant expression on her pretty face. She's determined to make things difficult, and I'm just as determined not to let her.

Taking a breath to steady myself, I turn off the bright overhead lights and light the candles. Then I plate the risotto I made and bring it over to her before getting my own food. I'm as hungry as she is, so as soon as I sit down, I dig into the food, figuring the discussion of our relationship can wait a couple of minutes.

Unfortunately, Sara doesn't share that opinion. "What did you mean, 'the fantasy can be made real?'" she asks, her voice tense as she toys with her fork. "What exactly are you saying?"

I make her wait until I'm done chewing; then I put down my fork and give her a level look. "I'm saying that you living in this house, going to work, and interacting with your friends is a privilege I'm allowing," I say calmly and watch her blanch. "Other men in my position wouldn't have been nearly so accommodating—and I don't have to be either. I want you, and I have the power to take you. It's as simple as that. If you don't like our existing relationship dynamic, I will change it—but not in a way you'll enjoy."

Her hand trembles as she reaches for the glass of wine I poured earlier. "So you'll what? Kidnap me? Take me away from everyone and everything?"

"Yes, ptichka. That's precisely what I'll do if I can't make the current situation work." I resume eating, giving her time to process my words. I know I'm being harsh, but I need to squash this little rebellion, make her understand just how precarious her position is.

There's no line I won't cross when it comes to her. She's going to be mine one way or another.

Sara stares at me, the glass shaking in her grasp; then she puts it down without taking a single sip. "So why haven't you done this already? Why all this?" She sweeps her hand out in a broad gesture, nearly knocking over the glass and one of the candle holders.

"Careful there," I say, moving both objects out of her reach. "If I didn't know better, I'd think you're trying to drug me again."

Her teeth audibly grind together. "Tell me," she demands, her hand curling into a fist next to her untouched plate. "Why haven't you kidnapped me already? Surely you have no moral qualms about that."

I sigh and put my fork down. Maybe I should've promised her a discussion after the meal, not during. "Because I like what you do," I say, picking up my wine glass and taking a sip. "With babies, with women. I think your work is admirable, and I don't want to take you away from that—or from your parents."

"But you will if you have to."

"Yes." I put down the glass and pick up my fork again. "I will."

She studies me for a few seconds, then picks up her own fork, and for a couple of minutes, we eat in an uneasy silence. I can practically hear her thinking, her agile mind struggling to find a solution.

It's too bad for her that one doesn't exist.

When Sara's plate is half-empty, she pushes it away and asks in a strained voice, "Did you stalk her too?"

My eyebrows lift as I pick up my wine glass. "Who?"

"Your wife," Sara says, and my hand tightens on the wine stem, nearly snapping the fragile glass in half. Instinctively, I brace for the agonizing pain and fury, but all I feel is a dull echo of loss, accompanied by a bittersweet ache at the memories.

"No," I say, and surprise myself by smiling fondly. "I didn't. If anything, she stalked me."

CHAPTER 40
SARA

Shocked, I stare at my tormentor, caught off-guard by that soft, almost tender smile. I fully expected him to explode at the question, and as I watched his fingers tighten on the glass stem, I was sure he would.

Instead, he smiled.

Chewing on my lower lip, I consider dropping the topic, but even with the threat of kidnapping looming over me, I can't resist the chance to learn more about him.

"What do you mean?" I ask, picking up my wine glass. The risotto is amazing, but my stomach is tied in knots, preventing me from finishing my portion. Wine, though, I could use.

Maybe if I drink enough, I'll forget his terrifying promise.

"We met when I was passing through her village almost nine years ago." Peter leans back in his chair, a wine glass cradled in his big hand. The candlelight casts a soft, warm glow over his handsome features, and if it weren't for the stress-induced adrenaline in my veins, I could've bought into the illusion of a romantic dinner, into the fantasy he's trying so hard to create.

"My team was tracking a group of insurgents in the mountains," he continues, his gaze turning distant as he relives the memory. "It was winter, and it was cold. Unbelievably cold. I knew we had to crash someplace warm for the night, so I asked the villagers to rent us a couple of rooms. Only one woman was brave enough to do so, and that was Tamila."

I take a sip of wine, fascinated despite myself. "She lived by herself?"

Peter nods. "She was only twenty at the time, but she had a small house of her own. Her aunt died and left it to her. It was unheard of in her village, for a young woman to live on her own, but Tamila was never big on rules. Her parents wanted her to marry one of the village elders, a man who could give them a dowry of five goats, but Tamila found him repulsive and was delaying the marriage as much as she could. Needless to say, her parents weren't pleased, and by the time my men and I came to the village, she was desperate to change her situation."

I gulp down the rest of my wine as he continues. "I didn't know any of this, of course. I just saw a beautiful young woman, who, for whatever reason, welcomed three half-frozen Spetsnaz soldiers into her home. She gave her bedroom to my guys and put me into the second, smaller room, saying that she herself would sleep on the couch."

"But she didn't," I guess as he leans in to pour me more wine. My stomach feels tight, something uncomfortably like jealousy roiling my insides. "She came to you."

"Yes, she did." He smiles again, and I hide my discomfort by drinking more wine. I don't know why picturing him with this "beautiful young woman" bothers me, but it does, and it's all I can do to listen calmly as he says, "I didn't turn her down, naturally. No straight man would. She was shy and relatively inexperienced but not a virgin, and when we left in the morning, I promised to swing by the village on the way back. Which I did, two months later, only to learn that she was pregnant with my child."

I blink. "You didn't use protection?"

"I did—the first time. The second time, I was asleep when she started rubbing against me, and by the time I woke up fully, I was inside her and too far gone to remember the condom."

My mouth drops open. "She got pregnant on purpose?"

He shrugs. "She claimed she didn't, but I suspect otherwise. She lived in a conservative Muslim village, and she'd had a lover before me. She never told me who he was, but if she'd gone through with the marriage to the elder—or if she'd turned him down and married someone else from her village—she could've been publicly exposed and cast out by her husband. A non-Muslim foreigner like me was her best bet at avoiding that fate, and she seized the opportunity when she saw it. It's admirable, really. She took a risk, and it paid off."

"Because you married her."

He nods. "I did—after the paternity test confirmed her claim."

"That's... very noble of you." I feel inexplicably relieved that he didn't fall head over heels for this girl. "Not many men would've been willing to marry a woman they didn't love for the sake of the child."

Peter shrugs again. "I didn't want my son exposed to ridicule or growing up without a father, and marrying his mother was the best way to ensure that. Besides, I grew to care for Tamila after my son was born."

"I see." Jealousy bites at me again. To distract myself, I drain my second glass of wine and grab the bottle to pour myself more. "So she trapped you, but it worked out." My palms are sweaty, and the bottle almost slips out of my hand, the wine splashing into my glass with such force that some liquid spills over the rim.

"Thirsty?" Peter's gray eyes gleam with amusement as he reaches over to take the bottle from me. "Maybe I should get you some water or tea instead?"

I vehemently shake my head, then realize the motion made the room spin a little. He might be right; I haven't had much to eat, and I should probably slow down on the wine. Except my anxiety is melting away with each sip, and it feels too good to stop.

"I'm fine," I say, picking up my glass again. I might regret this at work tomorrow, but I need the warm buzz the alcohol brings. "So you grew to care for Tamila. And she continued living in that village?"

"Yes." His face tightens; we must be getting close to the painful memories. Confirming my suspicion, he says roughly, "I figured she and Pasha—that's what we named my son—would be safer there. She wanted to live with me in my apartment in Moscow, but I was always traveling for work, and I didn't want to leave her in an unfamiliar city on her own. I promised I'd take her to Moscow for a visit when Pasha was older, but until then, I thought it would be better if she stayed close to her family, and my son grew up breathing fresh mountain air instead of city smog."

The mouthful of wine I swallowed burns though my tightening throat. "I'm sorry," I murmur, putting down my glass. And I *am* sorry for him. I despise Peter for what he's doing to me, but my heart still aches for his pain, for the loss that led him down this dark path. I can only imagine the guilt and agony he must be feeling, knowing that he inadvertently made the wrong choices, that his desire to protect his family led to their demise.

It's something I can relate to, having killed my own husband not once, but twice.

Peter nods, acknowledging my words, then gets up to clear off the table. I keep drinking my wine as he loads the dishes into the dishwasher, and the warm buzz in my veins intensifies, the candles in front of me attracting my attention with the hypnotic flickering of the flames.

"Let's go to bed," he says, and I look up to see him drying his hands with the kitchen towel. I must've zoned off for a bit, watching the candles. That, or he's insanely fast with his cleanup. Most likely, though, I zoned off—which means I'm more buzzed than I thought.

"Bed?" I force myself to focus as he comes up to me and clasps my wrist, pulling me to my feet. Despite the wine-induced softness around the edges of my vision, I re-member the reason I was upset, and as he tugs me toward the stairs, the tightness in my stomach returns, my pulse picking up pace. "I don't want to sleep with you."

He glances at me, his fingers tightening on my wrist. "I'm not interested in sleep."

My anxiety grows. "I don't want to have sex with you either."

"No?" He stops at the foot of the stairs and turns me to face him. "So if I reached into your jeans right now, I wouldn't find your panties soaked through? Your little pussy swollen and needy, just waiting to be filled by my cock?"

Heat climbs up my neck and blazes all the way up to my hairline. I *am* wet, both from before and from the way he's looking at me now. It's like he wants to devour me, like his dirty words are turning him on as much as they're arousing me. The mental haziness from the wine isn't help-ing, either, and I realize I made a mistake, trying to drown my sorrows.

Resisting him with my head clear is difficult enough; like this, it's nearly impossible.

Still, I have to try. "I don't—"

"Ptichka..." He lifts his hand, curving his big palm around my jaw. His thumb strokes over my cheek as he gazes down at me, his eyes like molten steel. "Do we need to discuss alternative arrangements again?"

I stare at him, ice crystals forming in my veins. For the first time, I comprehend the full extent of his ultimatum. He doesn't just expect me to stop fighting him over meals;

he wants me fully compliant, welcoming him into my bed as though we're in a real relationship.

As though he didn't murder my husband and forcibly invade my life.

"No," I whisper, closing my eyes as he bends his head and brushes his lips over mine… softly, gently. His tenderness tears me into pieces, juxtaposed as it is with the looming horror of his threat. If I fight him on this, he'll kidnap me, take away all remnants of my freedom.

If I resist him, I'll lose everything that matters, and if I don't, I'll lose myself.

I stumble as Peter leads me up the stairs, so he lifts me into his powerful arms, carrying me up the steps with ease. His strength is both terrifying and seductive. I know what it's like to have it turned against me, yet something primitive within me is drawn to it, attracted by the promise of safety it provides.

When we reach the bedroom, he lowers me to my feet and undresses me, pulling off my sweater and jeans in a calm, unhurried manner. Only the dark heat in his silver gaze betrays his hunger, the desire that he'll stop at nothing to satisfy.

Once I'm naked, he undresses too, and I spot a metallic glint inside his jacket as he hangs it on a chair. A gun? A knife? The idea of him bringing weapons into the bedroom should terrify me, but I'm too overwhelmed to react, my emotions already veering from shock to anger to icy fear. And underneath it all is a strange, illogical relief.

With all my choices gone, I can give in.

It's the only way.

A tear trickles down my cheek as he approaches me, fully naked and aroused, his large body a study of hard angles and sculpted muscles, of violent beauty and dangerous masculinity. Monsters shouldn't look like this, shouldn't be as mesmerizing as they are lethal.

It's too hard on one's sanity.

"Don't cry, ptichka," he murmurs, stopping in front of me. His fingers brush across my cheeks, wiping away the moisture. "I won't hurt you. It's really not as bad as you think."

Not as bad as I think? I want to laugh, but instead I just shake my head, my mind hazy both from the wine I consumed and the heat his nearness generates. He's right: I do want him. I ache for him, my body burning with a need so strong I can scarcely contain it. And at the same time, I hate him.

I hate him for what he's doing—and what he's making me feel.

His fingers slide into my hair, cupping my skull, and I close my eyes as he kisses me again, his other hand gripping my hip to draw me closer to him. His erection presses against my stomach, huge and hard, but his kiss is gentle, his lips coaxing out the sensations instead of forcing them.

It feels good, so unbelievably good that for a moment, I forget I have no choice in this. My hands grip his sides, feeling the hard flex of muscle, and my lips part as the heat builds inside me. Taking advantage, he licks inside my mouth, his tongue bringing with it the dizzying taste of wine and sweet seduction. This isn't our first time, but in this kiss, there is a sense of exploration, of sensual discovery and tender wonder.

He kisses me like I'm the most precious, most desirable thing he's ever known.

My head spins from the bone-melting pleasure, and it's tempting to lose myself completely, to give in to the illusion of his caring. The way he holds me speaks of raw need, but also of something deeper, something that resonates with the most vulnerable corners of my heart.

Something that fills the well of loneliness left by the ruins of my marriage.

I don't know how long Peter kisses me like this, but by the time he lifts his head, we're both breathing raggedly, and the heat circling through my body is a full-blown conflagration.

Dazed, I open my eyes and meet his gaze as he bears me down to the bed. There's no coldness in the gray metallic depths, no seething darkness, nothing but that hungry tenderness, and as he settles between my thighs, covering me with his powerful body, I know it could be easy.

I could stop fighting and buy into the fantasy, embrace this darker version of the fairy tale.

"Sara..." His strong palm curves around my face, framing it with aching gentleness, and the pain that spears through my chest is as potent as it is perverse. He's looking at me like I'm his everything, like he wants to make my every dream come true. It's what I've always wanted, always needed—but not with my husband's killer.

Gathering the crumbling pieces of my sanity, I close my eyes, shutting out the silvery lure of that hypnotic gaze. *No choice*, I remind myself as his lips descend on mine with another searing kiss. *No choice*, I chant silently as I hear the ripping of a foil packet and feel his hair-roughened legs press against the tender insides of my thighs, opening them wider to let his cock nestle against my sex. *No choice*, I cry out in my mind as he thrusts inside me, stretching me, filling me... making me burn with scorching need.

It's wrong, it's sick, but it takes less than a minute before I come, his hard, driving rhythm hurling me over the edge with an intensity that wrenches a scream from my throat and brings tears to my eyes. My body shudders in dark ecstasy, clenching around his thick length, and I cry out his name, raking my nails down his back as he continues fucking me, taking me to the peak twice more before he comes himself.

In the aftermath, I lie draped over him, our limbs tangled together as he lazily strokes my back. With my head pillowed on his shoulder, I hear the steady thumping of his heart, and the glow of sexual satisfaction gives way to the familiar tangle of shame and desolation.

I hate him, and I hate myself.

I hate myself because something perverse inside me was glad for his ultimatum.

It felt good not to have a choice.

"You won't be moving in a couple of weeks," he murmurs, not pausing in his gentle stroking. "The lawyer couple no longer owns this house—I do. Or rather one of my shell corporations does."

I should be surprised, but I'm not. I must've expected this on some level. My fingers tighten, crushing the corner of the pillow. "Did you threaten them? Kill them?"

He chuckles, his powerful chest moving underneath me. "I paid them double what the house is worth. Same goes for your would-be landlord. He's well compensated for the lease you broke."

I close my eyes, so relieved I could cry. I don't know what I would've done if someone else had suffered because of me, how I could've lived with myself.

When I'm sure my voice won't shake, I pull back and meet his shadowed gaze. "So that's it? We're just going to go on like this?"

"We are… for now." His eyes gleam darkly. "Afterward, we'll see."

And tugging me back down to his shoulder, he drapes his arm around me, holding me as though that's where I belong.

PART III

CHAPTER 41
SARA

As the days pass, we fall into a bizarre pattern of domesticity. Every evening, Peter makes a delicious dinner for us, and the food is already waiting on the table when I walk in. We eat together, and then he fucks me, often taking me twice or more before we fall asleep. If he's there in the morning when I wake up—and he frequently is—he also feeds me breakfast.

It's as if I acquired a house husband, only one who does black-ops-style assassinations in his spare time.

"What do you do all day?" I ask when I come home after a particularly grueling day in the hospital and discover a gourmet meal of lamb chops and beet-based Russian salad. "You don't just stay here and cook, right?"

"No, of course not." He gives me an amused look. "What we do takes a lot of logistical planning, so I work with my guys on that, and also take care of the business side of things."

"The business side of things?"

"Client interactions, securing payments, investment and distribution of funds, acquisition of weapons and supplies, that sort of thing," he replies, and I listen in fascination as he gives me a glimpse into a world where insane sums of money exchange hands and assassination is a method of business expansion.

"We do a lot of work for the cartels and other powerful organizations and individuals," he tells me as we polish off the lamb. "The Mexico job, for instance, was a case of one cartel leader hiring us to eliminate his rival so he could move into his territory. Other clients of ours include Russian oligarchs, dictators of various flavors, Middle Eastern royals, and a few of the better-run mafia organizations. Sometimes, if we're between jobs, we'll take on some smaller gigs, dealing with local thugs and such, but those pay next to nothing so we consider them pro-bono work, a way for us to stay sharp in downtime."

"Right, pro bono." I don't try to hide my sarcasm. "Like my work at the clinic."

"Exactly like that," Peter says, and grins. He knows he's shocking me, and he's doing it on purpose. It's a game he plays sometimes, horrifying me and then seducing me into welcoming his touch despite the revulsion I feel—or should feel.

It's part of the sickness of our relationship that almost nothing he says or does has any lasting effect on my desire for him. My inability to resist him is a bleeding ulcer in my chest, and I can't heal it no matter what I do. Each time I eat the food he makes, each time I sleep in his arms and find pleasure in his touch, the wound reopens, leaving me sick with shame and crippled with self-loathing.

I'm living in domestic bliss with my husband's murderer, and it's not nearly as terrible as it should be.

Part of the issue is that after our first time, Peter hasn't hurt me. Not physically, at least. I feel the violence within him, but when he touches me, he's careful to control himself, to stop the darkness from spilling out. It helps that I can't fight him outright; with his kidnapping threat hanging over my head, I have no choice but to comply with his demands—or so I tell myself.

It's the only way I can justify what's happening, how I'm beginning to need the man I hate.

If all he wanted from me was sex, it would be easy, but Peter seems determined to take care of me as well. From the romantic home-cooked meals to the nightly cuddling, I'm showered with attention, pampered and even groomed at times. We don't go out on dates—I assume because he doesn't want to show his face in public—but with the way he treats me, I could easily be his highly spoiled girlfriend.

"Why do you like doing this?" I ask when he's brushing my hair after washing me in the shower. "Is this some kind of weird kink of yours?"

He shoots me an amused look in the mirror. "Maybe. With you, it seems to be, for sure."

"No, but seriously, what do you get out of this? You know I'm not a child, right?"

Peter's mouth tightens, and I realize I inadvertently hit a nerve. We don't speak about his family much, but I know that his son was only a toddler when he was killed. Could it be that in some twisted way, I'm a substitute for his dead family? That he fixated on me because he needed to care for someone… anyone?

Could my Russian killer need love so much he'd settle for its perversion?

It's a tantalizing thought, especially since by the end of the second week, I find myself growing addicted to the comfort and pleasure Peter provides. At the end of a long shift, I physically crave the neck and foot rubs he often gives me, and it's a struggle not to salivate each time I pull into the garage and smell the delicious aromas from the kitchen.

I'm not only becoming used to my stalker's presence in my life; I'm starting to enjoy it.

Or at least some parts of it. I'm still far from enthusiastic about the bodyguards who follow me wherever I go. I almost never see them, but I can sense them watching me, and it both unsettles and irritates me.

"I'm not going to run, you know," I tell Peter when we lie in bed one night. "You can call off your watchdogs."

"They're there for your protection," he says, and I know it's something he has no intention of compromising on. For whatever reason, he's convinced that I'm in some kind of danger, something that he, of all people, needs to protect me from.

"What are you afraid of?" I ask, tracing the hard ridges of his abs with my finger. "Do you think some madman might invade my home? Maybe waterboard me and kill my husband?"

I glance up to find him grinning, as though I said something funny.

"What?" I say, goaded. "You think this is a joke?"

His expression turns serious. "No, ptichka. I don't think that at all. For what it's worth, I'm sorry for hurting you that time. I should've found another way."

"Right. Another way to kill George."

Feeling sick, I push away from him and escape into the bathroom—the only place my tormentor lets me be alone. Sometimes, I almost forget how everything began, my mind conveniently skipping over the horrors of our early relationship.

It's as if something inside me wants me to fall in line with Peter's fantasy, to pretend that all of this is real.

"So you never told me what happened between you and George," Peter says as we're having a leisurely Sunday brunch some three weeks after his return. "Why weren't you the perfect couple everyone thought you were? You didn't know what he really did, so what went wrong?"

The piece of poached egg I'm chewing sticks in my throat, and I have to gulp down most of my coffee to wash it down. "What makes you think something went wrong?" My voice is too high, but Peter caught me totally off-guard. Usually, he tends to avoid the topic of my dead husband— probably to foster the illusion of a normal relationship.

"Because that's what you told me," he answers calmly. "While you were on the drug I gave you."

I gape at him, unable to believe he went there again. Ever since our conversation about the bodyguards last week—and my subsequent crying in the bathroom—we've been tiptoeing around the topic of what he did to me, neither one willing to poke at that raw wound.

"That's..." Suppressing my shock, I compose myself. "That's none of your business."

"Did he beat you?" Peter leans in, his metallic eyes darkening. "Hurt you in some way?"

"What? No!"

"Was he a pedophile? A necrophiliac?"

I take a calming breath. "No, of course not."

"Did he cheat on you? Do drugs? Abuse animals?"

"He started drinking, okay?" I snap, goaded. "He started drinking, and he never stopped."

"Ah." Peter leans back in his chair. "An alcoholic then. Interesting."

"Is it?" I ask bitterly. Picking up my plate, I walk over to dump the remnants of my breakfast in the trash and put the plate in the dishwasher. "You like hearing that the man I knew and loved since I was eighteen—the man I *married*—transformed after our wedding without apparent cause? That in a matter of months, he became someone I could hardly recognize?"

"No, ptichka." He comes up behind me, and my breath catches as he pulls me against him, brushing aside my hair to kiss my neck. His breath warms my skin as he murmurs, "I don't like hearing that at all."

"I just... I never understood it." I turn around in his arms, the old hurt welling up as I meet Peter's gaze. "Everything was going so well. I finished med school, we bought this house and got married... He was traveling a lot for work, so he didn't mind my residency hours, and in return, I didn't mind all the travel. And then—" I stop, realizing I'm confiding in George's killer.

"And then what?" he prompts, his fingers curling around my palm. "What happened then, Sara?"

I bite my lip, but the temptation to tell him everything, to expose the full truth for once, is too strong to deny. I'm exhausted from pretending, from wearing the mask of perfection everyone expects to see.

Pulling my hand out of his grip, I walk over to sit down at the table. Peter joins me there, and after a moment, I begin talking.

"Everything changed several months after our marriage," I say quietly. "In a span of a few weeks, my warm, fun-loving husband became a cold, distant stranger, one who kept pushing me away no matter what I did. He started having these strange moods, cut down on work travel, and"—I take a breath—"began drinking."

Peter's eyebrows lift. "He never drank before?"

"Not like that. He'd have a few drinks when we went out with friends, or a glass of wine with dinner. It wasn't anything out of the ordinary—nothing I wasn't in the habit of doing myself. This was different. We're talking black-out drunk three, four nights a week."

"That *is* a lot. Did you ever confront him about it?"

A bitter laugh rips from my throat. "Confront him? All I did was confront him about it. The first few times it happened, he explained it as stress at work, then a boys' night out, then a need to relax, and then…" I bite my lip. "Then he started blaming me."

"You?" A frown knits Peter's forehead. "How could he possibly blame you?"

"Because I wouldn't leave him alone about it. I kept nagging, wanting him to go to rehab, to attend AA, to talk to someone—anyone—who could help. I asked the same questions over and over again, trying to understand why this was happening, what caused him to change like that." My chest constricts with remembered pain. "Things were going so well before, you see. My parents, all our friends— everyone was overjoyed with our marriage, and we had this bright future ahead of us. There was no reason for this, nothing I could latch on to to explain his sudden transformation. I kept prying and pushing, and he kept drinking, more and more. And then I—" I drag in air through a tightening throat. "Then I told him I couldn't live like this, that he had to choose between our marriage and his drinking."

"And he chose the drinking."

"No." I shake my head. "Not at first. We ended up in the classic substance abuse cycle, where he'd beg me to stay, promise to do better, and I'd believe him, but after a week or two, things would go back to how they were before. And when I'd point out his moods and ask him to see a psychiatrist, he'd lash out at me, claiming *I* was the reason he was drinking."

Peter's frown deepens. "His moods?"

"That's what I called them. Maybe it was clinical depression or some other form of mental illness, but since he refused to see a shrink, we never got an actual diagnosis. The moods started right before the drinking. We'd be doing something together, and suddenly, he'd seem completely out of it, like he'd mentally go into a different world. He'd get distracted and weirdly anxious—jumpy even. It was like he was on something, but I don't think he was. At least, it didn't look like drugs to me. He'd just go somewhere else in his mind, and there was no talking to him when he was like that, no way to get him to calm down and just be *present*."

"Sara…" A strange expression steals over Peter's face. "When did you say this all began?"

"Just a few months after we got married," I answer, frowning. "So at this point, about five and half years ago. Why?" And then it dawns on me. "You're not suggesting that—"

"That your husband's transformation might've had something to do with his role in the Daryevo massacre? Why not?" Peter leans in, his eyes narrowing. "Think about it. Five and a half years ago, Cobakis provided information that resulted in the slaughter of dozens of innocent people, including women and children. Whether it was out of ambition or greed or sheer stupidity, he fucked up, and he fucked up big. You say he was a good man? Someone who had a conscience? Well, how would a man like that feel about causing the slaughter of innocents? How would he live with all that blood on his hands?"

I recoil, the horrible truth of his words slamming into me like a bullet. I don't know why I didn't connect the dots before, but now that Peter said it, it makes perfect sense. When I first learned about George's deception, it occurred to me that his real job might've been behind his transformation, but I was so busy coping with Peter's invasion of my life—and trying not to dwell on his revelations—that I didn't pursue the thought to its logical conclusion.

I didn't consider that the tragic events that brought my tormentor into my life could be the same ones that ruined my marriage… that our fates have been intertwined for much longer than I thought.

Feeling like I'm about to be sick, I stand up, my legs shaking. "You're right." My voice is choked and raw. "It had to be guilt that drove him to drink. All this time, I wondered if it was something I said or did, if our marriage disappointed him somehow, and it was this all along. "

Peter nods, his face set in grim lines. "Unless your husband caused multiple massacres throughout his career, this is the only thing that makes sense."

I inhale raggedly and turn away, walking over to the window looking out into the back yard. The enormous oaks stand like guardians outside, their branches bare of leaves despite the hints of spring in the warming air. I feel like those oaks right now, stripped, bared in all my ugliness. And at the same time, I feel lighter.

The drinking, at least, was not my fault.

"The accident happened because of me, you know," I say quietly when Peter comes up to stand next to me. He's not looking at me, his profile hard and uncompromising, and though I know he's battling his own demons, his presence comforts me on some fundamental level.

I'm not alone with him by my side.

"How?" he asks without turning his head. "The report said he was alone in the vehicle."

"He drank the night before. Drank so much he puked several times throughout the night." I shudder, remembering the smell of vomit, of sickness and lies and broken hopes. Holding myself together by a thread, I continue. "By morning, I was done. I was done with his excuses, with the endless accusations sprinkled with promises to do better. I realized that George and I weren't special in any way; we were just another alcoholic and his too-stupid-to-see-it wife. It wasn't a rough patch we were going through. Our marriage was simply broken."

I stop, my voice shaking too much to continue, when a big, warm hand wraps around my palm. Peter's expression is unchanged, his gaze trained on the view outside the window, but the silent gesture of support steadies me, giving me courage to continue.

"He was still passed out when I went to work, so I confronted him when I returned," I say as steadily as I can manage. "I told him to pack his bags and get out, said I was filing for divorce the next day. We got into a huge fight, and both said hurtful things, and I—" I gulp down the lump in my throat. "I forced him out of the house."

Peter glances at me with mild surprise. "How could you have forced him out? He wasn't the biggest guy I've seen, but he must've outweighed you by at least fifty pounds."

I blink, distracted by the odd question. "I threw his car keys and his bag in the garage and yelled at him to get out."

"I see." To my shock, a faint smile touches the edges of Peter's mouth. "And you think you're at fault because he drove and got into an accident?"

"I *am* at fault. The police said he had double the legal amount of alcohol in his blood. He was drinking, and I forced him to drive. I threw him out and—"

"You threw his *keys* out, not him," Peter says, the smile disappearing as his fingers tighten around my hand. "He was a grown man, both bigger and stronger than you. If he wanted to stay in the house, he could've done so. Besides, did you know he was drinking when you told him to get out?"

I frown. "No, of course not. I had just come from work, and he didn't look drunk, but—"

"But nothing." Peter's voice is as hard as his gaze. "You did what you had to. Alcoholics can appear functional with a lot of drinks in their system. I should know; I've seen plenty of this in Russia. It wasn't your responsibility to check on his blood alcohol levels before sending him packing. If he was too drunk to drive, he had no business getting behind the wheel. He could've called a cab, or asked you to give him a ride to a hotel. Hell, he could've slept it off in your garage and *then* driven."

"I…" It's my turn to stare out the window. "I know that."

"Do you?" Releasing my hand, Peter captures my chin, forcing me to meet his gaze. "Somehow I doubt that, ptichka. Have you told anyone what really happened?"

My stomach twists, an unpleasant, heavy ache settling low in my belly. "Not exactly. I mean, the cops knew he was drinking, but…"

"But they didn't know it was habitual, did they?" Peter guesses, lowering his hand. "No one knew except you."

I look away, feeling the familiar burn of shame. I know it's the classic spousal mistake, but I just couldn't bring myself to air out our dirty laundry, to admit that the marriage everyone praised was rotten inside. Initially, it was pride, mixed with equal amounts of denial. I was supposed to be smart, a young doctor with a bright future ahead of her. How could I have made that kind of error? Were there warnings signs that I missed? And if not, how could this have happened to the wonderful man I married, the golden boy everyone said had so much promise? Surely, it was a temporary situation, a fluke in an otherwise perfect life. And by the time I realized the drinking was here to stay, there was another reason to keep quiet.

"My dad had a heart attack about a year into my marriage," I say, staring at the naked branches swaying in the wind. "It was a bad one. He almost died. After the triple bypass, the doctors told him to keep stress to a minimum."

"Ah. And learning that his beloved daughter's husband turned into a raging alcoholic would've been stressful."

"Yes." I could've stopped at that, let Peter think I was simply a good daughter, but some strange compulsion makes me blurt out, "That wasn't all, though. I was afraid of what people would say and the judgments they'd make. George was good at hiding his addiction from everyone—in hindsight, I guess the acting skills should've been a clue about the whole spying bit—and I also became a pro at pretending. The nature of our work helped with that. I could always be 'on call' if we needed to cancel an outing last minute, and George could have an 'urgent story' come up if he was having trouble sobering up."

Peter doesn't say anything for a few moments, and I wonder if he's condemning me for my cowardice, for not seeking help before it was too late. That's another thing that weighs on me: the possibility that I could've done something if I'd been more open about our problems. Maybe I could've gotten George into rehab or under psychiatric care, and the tragedy of the accident would've been averted.

Of course, the man standing next to me would've killed him regardless, so there's that.

Unable to deal with that thought, I push it away just as Peter asks, "What about his work? How could he continue to function like that? Unless... you said he stopped taking on foreign assignments?"

"Pretty much." Taking a breath to calm the churning in my stomach, I focus on watching the hypnotic swaying of the branches outside. "He traveled a few times after we got married, but mostly, he investigated local stories—like the one about the mafia bribing Chicago police and government officials."

"The one they told you was the reason for his protection."

I nod, unsurprised that he knows. He probably had some kind of parabolic microphones trained on me during my conversation with Agent Ryson. From what I've learned about my stalker in recent weeks, it's entirely possible.

The millions he earns from every hit buys access to all kinds of equipment.

"He must've quit working for the CIA, then," Peter says, and I glance over to see him watching the tree branches too. "Either because he was fired or because he couldn't cope with the aftermath of his fuck-up. That's the only thing that would explain the lack of foreign assignments."

"Right." My head throbs with a nagging tension, and my stomach continues churning and twisting, like my insides are being wound tighter and tighter. My lower back hurts too—a realization that makes me do some quick mental math.

Sure enough, my period is about to start.

We stand by the window for a few moments longer, watching the trees outside, and then I walk over to the medicine cabinet and take two Advils, washing them down with a glass of water.

"What's the matter?" Peter asks, following me with a concerned frown. "Are you sick?"

"It's nothing," I say, not wanting to go into all the details. Then I realize he might find out later today anyway and add, "It's just that time of the month for me."

"Ah." Unlike most men, he doesn't look the least bit uncomfortable with that information. "Does it typically pain you?"

"Unfortunately, yes." As I speak, I feel the cramps getting worse and thank the schedule gods that I'm not on call today. I was going to volunteer at the clinic this afternoon, but I revise that plan in favor of huddling in bed with a heating pad.

"Why aren't you on birth control pills?" Peter asks, following me as I head upstairs. "I haven't seen you take anything all this time, and I believe that usually helps with painful periods."

"An expert on female reproductive health, are we?"

Peter doesn't bat an eye at my sarcasm. "Far from it, but I did get a pill prescription for Tamila because she had bad cramps. I assume you have a reason for not doing the same?"

I sigh, entering the bedroom. "I do. I'm one of those rare women who can't tolerate hormonal birth control. I get migraines and nausea, no matter how small the dosage. Even hormonal IUDs give me headaches, so I have to choose between misery a couple of days a month or misery all the time."

"I see." Peter leans against the doorway as I begin to undress. I can see the heat in his gaze as he watches me strip down to my underwear, and I hope he doesn't get any ideas about joining me in bed. He rarely passes up the chance to fuck me.

Ignoring his staring, I grab my heating pad from the nightstand drawer and curl into a fetal position, hugging it under the blanket as I wait for the Advil to kick in.

I hear a quiet patter of footsteps, and then the bed dips next to me.

No, no, no. Go away. No sex right now. I squeeze my eyes shut, hoping my tormentor gets the hint, but in the next instant, the blanket is turned down, and a rough male hand caresses my naked back.

"Do you want me to get you anything?" His deep, softly accented voice is low and soothing. "Maybe toast or some tea?"

Startled, I roll over onto my back, clutching the heating pad against my stomach. "Um, no, thanks. I'll be fine."

"You sure?" He smooths my hair away from my face. "What about a belly rub?"

I blink at him. "Um…"

"Here." He gently pries the heating pad away from me and places his warm palm on my stomach. "Let's try this." He moves his hand in a circular motion, applying light pressure, and after a couple of minutes, the tight, cramping sensation eases, the heat from his skin and the massaging motion chasing away the worst of the painful tension.

"Better?" he murmurs as I close my eyes in blissful relief, and I nod, my thoughts beginning to drift as drowsiness steals over me.

"It's very nice, thank you," I mumble, and as the soothing massage continues, I sink into a warm fog of sleep.

CHAPTER 42
PETER

I watch Sara sleep for a few minutes; then I quietly get up and leave the bedroom. I could sit by her bedside for hours, doing nothing more than watching her, but I have a phone call with a potential client at noon, and I have to discuss a few logistics with Anton before that.

It takes only a couple of minutes to clean up in the kitchen, and then I'm on my way, slipping out the back door to cut across a neighbor's yard. Ilya's armored SUV is parked on the street two blocks over, and as I walk, I pay attention to everything: the distant barking of a small dog, a squirrel darting across the road, the brand of sneakers on the jogger who just rounded the corner... The hyper-vigilance is as much a part of me now as my lightning-fast reflexes, and both have kept me alive more times than I can count.

Ilya starts the car as I approach, and as soon as I get in, he pulls out, heading down the quiet suburban street at precisely three miles above the speed limit.

He believes that blending in requires acting like a typical civilian, right down to minor traffic infractions.

"Any trouble?" I ask in Russian, and he shakes his shaved head.

"All quiet, like always."

Unlike his twin brother and Anton, Ilya doesn't sound disappointed as he says that. I think he's enjoying our little stint in suburbia, though he'd never admit it out loud. Out of the four of us on the core team, Ilya looks most like the quintessential thug, with his skull tattoos and a jaw thickened by a youthful flirtation with steroids. His twin Yan, on the other hand, could pass for a professor or a banker, with his neatly pressed clothes and brown hair cut in a conservative corporate style. Personality-wise, though, it's Yan who revels in our high-adrenaline lifestyle, while Ilya prefers to focus more on strategy and working behind the scenes.

I suspect if Ilya hadn't followed his brother into the army, he would've ended up as a computer programmer or an accountant.

"Anything from the Americans?" I ask as we stop at a stoplight. Since my guys are fairly busy, I've been using the locals as backup security. Their job is to keep an eye on Sara when she's not with me and alert us of any unusual activity in the neighborhood.

"No. Your girl doesn't deviate much from her routine, but I'm sure you know that."

I nod, scanning the row of neatly manicured lawns as we drive past them on our way to the safe house. Something is bugging me, but I can't place my finger on what it is. Maybe it's just that it's too quiet, with no big jobs on the horizon and minimal progress with locating the North Carolina general who's the last name on my list. The paranoid fucker disappeared along with his family, and he did such a good job of covering his tracks that even the hackers I retained are having trouble finding him.

I might have to go to North Carolina at some point, see what I can shake up in person.

"Tell them I want to review the next few reports myself," I tell Ilya as we pull into the driveway of our safe house. "And tell them to expand the perimeter to twenty blocks, not ten. If anyone so much as sneezes in Sara's neighborhood or around her hospital, I want to know."

"You got it," Ilya says, and I jump out of the car.

Maybe I'm being paranoid, but I can't let anything fuck up what I have with Sara.

I need her too much to risk losing her.

She's lounging on the couch with a heating pad and a tablet when I get home, her slender limbs gracefully arranged and her shiny chestnut hair caught in a messy knot on top of her head. Even dressed in sweatpants and an oversized T-shirt, my little bird looks like she could star in a black-and-white movie, the delicacy of her features accentuated by the loose tendrils of hair waving around her heart-shaped face.

My lungs tighten as she looks up, her soft hazel eyes locking on my face. Each time I see her, I want her, my need for her a clawing hunger in my chest. Over the past three weeks, I've had her so many times the craving should've diminished, but it's only grown, intensifying to an unbearable degree.

I want her, and I want this—the quiet pleasure of sharing her life, of knowing that I can hold her in the middle of the night and see her across the kitchen table in the morning. I want to take care of her when she's sick and bask in her smile when she's well. And sometimes, when my grief wells up, I want to hurt her too—an urge I suppress with all my strength.

She's mine, and I will protect her.

Even from myself.

"How are you feeling?" I ask, approaching the couch. I didn't have a chance to fuck her this morning, and I'm semi-hard just from being near her. However, my lust takes a backseat to my need to make sure she's healthy and well.

Sara won't die from menstrual cramps, but I don't want to see her in any pain.

"Better, thank you," she answers, laying her tablet next to her. It looks like she was watching some music videos on there—something I've seen her do to relax.

"You can keep on doing that," I say, nodding toward the tablet. "I have to make dinner, so don't stop on my behalf."

She makes no move to pick up the tablet, just tilts her head and watches me as I walk to the sink to wash my hands and take out the ingredients for tonight's simple

314

dinner: the chicken breasts I marinated last night and fresh veggies for a salad.

"You know, you never answered my question," she says after a minute. "Why are you really doing this? What do you get out of all this domesticity? Doesn't a man like you have something better to do with your life? I don't know… maybe rappel down the side of a building or blow up something?"

I sigh. She's back on that topic. My ambitious young doctor can't grasp that I just like doing this—for her and for myself. I can't turn back the clock and spend more time with Pasha and Tamila, can't warn my younger self to forego work in favor of what matters because it could all vanish in an instant. I can only focus on the present, and my present is Sara.

"My wife taught me to make a few simple dishes," I say, placing the chicken breasts in the frying pan before starting to chop up the salad. "In her culture, women tended to do all the cooking, but she wasn't big on tradition. She wanted to make sure I could take care of our son if anything happened to her, so to please her, I agreed to learn a few recipes—and found I liked the process of preparing food." A familiar pain tightens my chest at the memories, but I push the grief away, focusing on the sympathetic curiosity in the warm hazel eyes watching me from the couch.

Sometimes, I'm convinced Sara doesn't hate me.

Not all the time, at least.

"So you started cooking for your wife?" she asks when I'm silent for a couple of moments, and I nod, scraping the veggies off the cutting board into a big salad bowl.

"I did, but I didn't learn more than the basics until she was gone," I say, and despite myself, my voice is rough, raw with suppressed agony. "Two months after the massacre, I was walking past a culinary school in Moscow, and on impulse, I walked in and took a cooking class. I don't know why I did it, but when I was done and my *borscht* was simmering on the stove, I felt a tiny bit better. It was something different I could focus on, something tangible and real."

Something that cooled the boiling rage inside me, enabling me to strategize and plan out my vengeance like a recipe, complete with steps and measures I would need to take.

I don't say that last part, because Sara's gaze softens further. I guess my little hobby humanizes me in her eyes. I like that, so I don't tell her that I was in Moscow to kill my former superior, Ivan Polonsky, for participating in the massacre cover-up, or that an hour after the class was over, I slashed his throat in an alley.

His blood looked a lot like borscht that day.

"I guess you never know what you have until you lose it," Sara muses, hugging the heating pad to her, and I feel a flicker of jealousy at the wistfulness in her tone.

I hope she's not thinking of her husband, because as far as I'm concerned, he's no big loss.

That *sookin syn* deserved everything he got and then some.

When the meal is ready, Sara joins me at the table, and we eat while I tell her about some of the cities where I've taken cooking lessons: Istanbul, Johannesburg, Berlin, Paris, Geneva... After describing the cuisines, I share a few stories about temperamental chefs, and Sara laughs, a genuine smile lighting up her face as she listens to me. To avoid spoiling the mood, I leave out all the dark parts—like the fact that Interpol found me in Paris and I had to shoot my way out of the building where the cooking school was located, or that I blew up a target's car in Berlin before going in for my lesson—and we wrap up the meal on a companionable note, with Sara helping me clean up before I shoo her away.

"Go relax," I tell her. "Take a shower and get in bed. I'll be up soon."

Her expression turns wary. "Okay, but just so you know, my period started."

"So what? You think I'm grossed out by a little blood?" I grin at the look on her face. "I'm kidding. I know you're not feeling well. We'll just cuddle, like the good old days."

"Ah, gotcha." An answering smile, genuine and warm, flashes across her face. "In that case, I'll see you up there soon."

She hurries out of the kitchen, and I stand there, unable to breathe, feeling like I just got knifed in the gut.

Fuck, that smile... That smile was everything.

For the first time, I understand why I feel this way around her.

For the first time, I realize how much I love her.

CHAPTER 43
SARA

By Sunday morning, I feel better and decide to go see my parents. I've visited them only once since Peter's return, as I've been busy with my stalker and worried about exposing them to danger. However, I'm now increasingly convinced that Peter wouldn't arbitrarily hurt them. He values family too much to do that to me.

As long as I comply with his demands, my parents should be safe.

My mom is ecstatic when I call her, and we make plans to go out for a sushi lunch. When I inform Peter about that, he nods absentmindedly and types something on his phone.

"What are you writing?" I ask warily.

"Just telling my guys that I'll be in today, after all," he says, putting the phone away. "Why? Did you want me to join you?" His gray eyes gleam as he looks at me.

I laugh. "No, I think the bit where the FBI storm the restaurant to capture one of their most wanted might be a bit of an appetite spoiler."

Peter doesn't smile back, and I realize he's serious.

"You... you'd come out with me in public?"

"Why not?" He lifts his eyebrows coolly. "I met you at Starbucks, didn't I?"

"Well, yeah, but that was before. I mean—never mind." I take a breath. "I guess you're not afraid of being seen in public?"

"I wouldn't parade in front of your local FBI office, but I can go out for an occasional lunch or dinner if the place is scoped out beforehand, and I can make sure there are no cameras."

"Oh." I chew on the inside of my lip as I pick up my bag. "Well, maybe we can go out for dinner later this week..."

"But not today," he says, and I nod, feeling awkward but not knowing what else to do. There's no way I'm introducing George's killer to my parents.

It's bad enough I just offered to go out to dinner with him.

"Okay, then. I'll see you when you get back," he says, and I slip away before he can suggest anything else—like matching tattoos or a beach wedding.

This is total madness, and the craziest part is that it's starting to seem normal.

I'm getting used to having Peter in my life.

———

At lunch, I inform my parents that I decided not to sell the house. I already told them two weeks ago that the lawyers' offer fell through, so they're not particularly surprised to hear about my decision. In fact, they're quite pleased, given that the house is only a twenty-minute drive from them while my new apartment would've been at least forty-five minutes away.

"It's a lovely house," Dad says, pouring himself a little platter of soy sauce. "I think the whole apartment thing was an overreaction. You're young, but years go by fast, and at some point soon, you might want to think about starting a family. You know, get out there and meet a man—"

"Oh, stop it, Chuck," Mom snaps at him. "Sara has plenty of time." Turning toward me, she says in a softer voice, "You take as long as you need, darling. Don't let your dad push you into anything. We *are* glad you're keeping the house, but that doesn't mean we expect you to produce grandkids anytime soon."

"Mom, please." It's all I can do not to roll my eyes like I'm still in high school. My parents are doing the good cop/bad cop thing with me, likely in the hopes of planting the "go out and meet a nice man" suggestion in my mind. "If I'm on the verge of producing grandkids, I promise you and Dad will be the first to know."

Mom gives Dad a beatific smile. "See? She'll go out there when she's ready."

"Right." I busy myself with prying apart my wooden chopsticks. "When I'm ready." Which, given what's happening in my life, might be never. Or at least not until Peter gets bored with me—something that looks increasingly unlikely to happen soon. If anything, I think he's even more fixated on me now, his gray eyes watching me with a peculiar light that sends warm shivers down my spine.

Before I can analyze why that is, the waiter brings out our sushi boat, and my parents *ooh* and *aah* over the artfully arranged fish, sparing me from more of their not-so-subtle machinations. I wish I could tell them the truth, but there's no way I can explain Peter without terrifying them out of their minds.

I'm still not sure how I'm dealing with the whole thing myself.

By the end of the week, my period is over and I'm back in the swing of things, with two on-call shifts early in the week and a three-hour stretch at the clinic on Wednesday on top of my usual office hours. I'm working so much I'm barely home, but Peter doesn't object, though I can sense he's less than pleased with the situation. Despite my period, we've had sex over the last few days—he wasn't lying about his lack of squeamishness—and each time, he's been unusually hungry, his touch unrestrained and borderline rough.

It's as if he's afraid of somehow losing me, as if he hears the ticking of some clock.

On Friday, I spend most of the day in my office, seeing patients, but just as I'm about to head home, I get an urgent message that one of my patients has gone into labor. Suppressing a weary sigh, I hurry to the locker room to scrub up and run into Marsha, who's coming off her shift.

"Hey," she says with a sympathetic grimace. "Just getting started?"

"Looks like it," I say, stuffing my clothes into the locker. "Are you girls going out tonight?"

"Nah. Andy can't make it, and Tonya is busy with that cute bartender. Remember him?"

I pull my hair into a ponytail. "The one from the club we went to?" At Marsha's confirming nod, I ask, "Yeah, why? Did they hook up?"

"You guessed it." Marsha grins. "Anyways, I see you're in a rush, so I'll let you go. Call me if you want to do anything this weekend. Andy is having a barbecue tomorrow night, and I'm sure she'd love for you to come."

"Thank you. I'll call you if I can make it," I say and hurry out of the locker room. I know I won't be calling her, and this time, it's not because I'm afraid for my friends.

As tempting as the barbecue sounds, what I'm most looking forward to this weekend is quiet time at home.

With Peter.

The man I'm finding hard to hate.

———————

Several hours later, I trudge back into the locker room, exhausted. My patient's uterus ruptured, and I had to perform an emergency C-section to save her and the baby. Fortunately, both made it through okay, but I have a splitting headache from hunger and extreme tiredness.

I can't wait to get home, heat up whatever Peter might've prepared for dinner, and, if I'm lucky, get a massage as I'm falling asleep.

"Dr. Cobakis?"

The female voice sounds vaguely familiar, and I spin around, my pulse jumping. Sure enough, I see Karen, the FBI agent/nurse who was with Agent Ryson when I woke up after Peter's attack. Like the last time, she's dressed in nursing scrubs, though I know she doesn't work in this hospital.

She must be trying to blend in.

"Karen?" I try not to betray my nervousness. "What are you doing here?"

She approaches me and stops a couple of feet away. "I wanted to talk to you someplace we wouldn't be spotted, and this seemed as good of an opportunity as any."

I glance around the locker room. She's right: we're the only ones here at this time. "Why?" I turn my attention back to her. "What's wrong?"

"A couple of months ago, you reached out to Agent Ryson," she says quietly. "You said you felt you were being watched. At the time, we dismissed your concerns, but we've since received some new information."

My throat cinches tight. "What... what new information?"

"It has to do with Peter Sokolov, the fugitive who assaulted you in your home."

"Oh?" My voice is an octave too high.

"He was spotted in the area, just a few blocks away from this hospital. A hidden traffic camera caught his face at an angle, and our facial recognition program flagged the photo." She cocks her head to the side. "You wouldn't happen to know anything about it, Dr. Cobakis, would you?"

"I…" My heartbeat is roaring in my ears, my thoughts racing in panicked circles. This is it, the opportunity to get help without Peter knowing I spoke to anyone. The FBI are already aware he's here, and they won't rest until they find him. I can improve the odds of their success, tell them he's most likely at my house, and if they succeed in capturing him and his men, it'll be truly over.

My life will be my own again.

"It's okay, Dr. Cobakis." Karen lays a gentle hand on my arm. "I know this is all very stressful for you, but we'll make sure you're safe. Just please think back to the past few weeks. Any chance someone might've been following you? Have you had any instances recently when you felt like you were being watched?"

All the time—because I am *being watched.* I want to tell her that, but the words won't come; instead, my breathing speeds up until I'm all but hyperventilating.

Peter won't go quietly when the agents come for him; he'll fight, and people will get killed. *He* could get killed. Nausea rises in my throat as I picture his powerful body riddled with bullet holes, his intense metallic eyes dull and faded with death. It should be an image that brings me joy, but I feel sick instead, my ribcage squeezing painfully tight as I try to picture what my life will be like without him in it.

How free—and how alone—I'll be again.

"I… No." I take a step back, shaking my head. I know I'm not thinking clearly, but I can't bring myself to say it. My mouth simply won't form the words. "I haven't noticed anything."

A frown creases Karen's forehead. "Nothing? Are you sure? To the best of our knowledge, you and your deceased husband are his only link to this area."

"Yes, I'm positive." It's as though a stranger is speaking these lies. My headache intensifies until it's a beating drum inside my skull, and I feel like I'm on the verge of throwing up. My thoughts skitter from one alternative to the next, my mind like a rat inside a maze. I don't even know why I'm lying. It's over. One way or another, it's over—because now that they know Peter is in the area, they *will* come for him, no matter what I say. And if they don't succeed in killing or capturing him, he might think that I betrayed him and make good on his threat to take me away, maybe even punish people close to me to teach me a lesson.

I *should* help the FBI.

It's my best chance to be free.

"All right," Karen says when I remain silent. "If you think of anything, here is my number." She hands me a card, and I take it with numb fingers as she says, "We don't want to spook him in case he *is* watching you for whatever reason, so we're not going to take you into protective custody right now. Instead, we'll put a discreet protective detail on you, and if they see anything—and I do mean anything—out of the ordinary, they will act fast to ensure your safety. In the meanwhile, please carry on with your normal activities and rest assured that the man who killed your husband will pay for what he's done."

"Okay. I'll—I'll do that." Hanging on to my composure by a thread, I grab my bag from the open locker and slam it shut, then hurry out of the room.

I'm already next to my car when I realize I'm still wearing my scrubs.

Thanks to Karen's ambush, I forgot to change back into my clothes.

Heavy metal blares from the speakers as I pull out of the parking lot, castigating myself for my stupidity. Even with my headache, the music is somehow soothing, the violent beats more orderly than the mad jumble of my thoughts. I can't believe I didn't confide in Karen and beg for the FBI's help when I had the chance. Now I have no idea what to do, how to act or even where to go. Do I go home with the FBI watching me? And if I do, will they realize that Peter is there, or will the precautions he takes—such as not parking on my driveway—ensure they remain oblivious to his presence? Maybe I should go to my parents' house or a hotel instead, or simply crash somewhere in the hospital. But then what about Peter's men who always follow me around? They'd realize something is wrong, and Peter might come after me, and who knows what could happen then? In general, will the FBI spot my bodyguards, or will they spot the agents first and warn Peter? If I come home, will I find him already gone, having evaded the authorities once again?

How badly did I fuck everything up?

My hands are white-knuckled on the wheel as my mind spins through my conversation with Karen, going over it again and again. God, I had so many opportunities to tell her the truth, to explain the full complexity of the situation and let the experts handle everything. Why didn't I do so? How could I have been so stupid? After I realized I forgot to change, I went back to the locker room, telling myself that if Karen is still there, I would do the right thing, but she was already gone.

She was gone, and I was relieved—because deep inside, I knew I wouldn't do it.

Even with Peter's threat looming over my head, I can't bring myself to hasten the confrontation that could result in his death.

With Metallica screaming in the background, I drive on autopilot, so caught up in my thoughts I don't realize my subconscious already chose my destination. Only when I turn onto my street does it dawn on me where I'm going, and by then, it's too late.

I'm home.

CHAPTER 44
SARA

I'm shaking as I enter the house from the garage, my throat tight with anxiety and my heart pounding in sync with the throbbing in my head. It's well past midnight and all the lights are off, but I can smell the appetizing aromas of whatever Peter made earlier. My stomach rumbles, my body demanding fuel despite the adrenaline shredding my nerves. I'll have to eat something soon, but first, I need to figure out where Peter is and whether he knows what's happening.

"Hungry?"

The familiar deep voice startles me so much I jump, a panicked squeak escaping my throat.

A light comes on, illuminating Peter's figure on the couch in the family room. Despite the comfortable temperature, he's wearing his leather jacket, his tall, powerful body arranged in a casual pose that reminds me of a predator's lazy sprawl.

"Um, yeah." *Oh God, does he know? Why is he sitting here in the dark?* "One of my patients went into labor, and I missed dinner."

"You did?" Peter rises to his feet in a fluid motion. "That's not good. Come, let's feed you before you pass out."

I follow him into the kitchen on unsteady legs. The fact that he's here—and heating up food for me—must mean that his men didn't spot my FBI tail. Does that mean the reverse is true as well? Could the FBI agents assigned to my protective detail have missed whoever Peter has following me?

My hands and feet are icy from stress, and I know I must look like death warmed over as I wash my hands and sit down at the table. I'm hoping Peter will ascribe my paleness to exhaustion rather than the fact that the FBI might storm my house at any moment.

He puts a bowl of hearty vegetable soup and a slice of crusty sourdough bread in front of me, then sits down across the table at his usual place, his face expressionless as he watches me pick up my spoon and dip it into the soup. My hands are trembling slightly—a fact he can't miss, but hopefully chalks up to my tiredness as well. If not—if he suspects something—then things could go south, quickly. He could have me trussed up and on the way to some international hideout faster than my FBI watchdogs could call for reinforcements.

Fuck, why am I taking this kind of risk? Why didn't I just tell Karen everything?

Yet even as I kick myself, I know the answer to that question. It's sitting in front of me, his gray eyes trained on me with an intensity that both chills and warms me inside. I should want to be free of my tormentor, should do everything in my power to have him disappear from my life, but I can't. I'm not insane enough to warn him and risk getting kidnapped, but I can't bring myself to accelerate the moment when justice catches up with him, and he'll have to either run or fight.

It will happen anyway; all I have to do is survive it.

"You work too much," Peter murmurs, tilting his head as he studies me, and I exhale a shaky breath.

Thank God. He *is* ascribing my anxiety to tiredness.

"You should ease up, ptichka, take it easy on occasion," he continues, and I nod, looking down at my bowl to escape the intensity of his gaze.

"Yeah, I guess." I take a bite of the bread and swallow a spoonful of soup, focusing on the savory flavors to quiet the mental clamor in my head. I'm only partially successful, but it's enough to enable me to eat another spoonful and then another.

I'm done with my slice of bread and almost halfway through my bowl by the time I work up the courage to look up again. "Why were you waiting here for me?" I ask, recalling how dark the house was when I walked in. "I thought you'd be in bed or taking a shower or something."

"Because I've barely seen you in recent days, ptichka, and I've missed you." His eyes gleam with that peculiar softness I've been seeing all week.

My stomach flips, a knot forming in my throat. "You… you have?" He's never told me this before; though we both know he's obsessed with me, he's never admitted to any kind of real feelings.

"Hmm-mm. Here, have some more." He pushes another slice of bread toward me. "You still look much too pale."

I pick up the bread and bite into it, looking down again to conceal my expression. The knot in my throat is expanding, my eyes prickling with irrational tears. Why does he have to choose today, of all days, to say these things to me? I need him to be awful to me, not nice. I need to remember that he's a monster, a killer, a man who's done things that would make Ted Bundy blanch.

I need him to jolt me out of the fantasy so I don't miss him when he's gone.

I manage to hold back the tears as I gulp down the rest of the soup while Peter watches me in silence. It's unsettling, the way he can just stare at me without doing anything, as if the mere sight of me fascinates him. I've caught him doing this more than a few times; once, I even woke up to find him looking at me like this.

It's disconcerting and flattering at the same time, like his seemingly endless hunger for me.

When my bowl is empty, I get up to put it in the dishwasher, but Peter takes it out of my hands.

"I've got this," he says softly, dropping a gentle kiss on my forehead. "Go up and start getting ready for bed. I'll be there in a minute."

I nod, blinking to hold back a fresh surge of tears, and go up without objections. He often does this too: freeing me from all chores, no matter how small, when I'm tired. He must realize that putting a bowl in a dishwasher would not strain me, but he still treats me like I'm an invalid instead of a doctor exhausted by long hours.

He babies me and I love it, even though I shouldn't. I should hate everything he does, because none of this is real.

It can't be.

I'm already done with my shower by the time Peter comes upstairs, and he corners me in the bathroom, trapping me against the counter just as I finish brushing my teeth. My towel is wrapped around me, but he pulls it off, dropping it on the floor, and the sight of us in the fogged-up mirror—me pale and completely naked while he's fully dressed in his dark clothes—makes my heart pound with nervous excitement.

He's especially hungry tonight—and more than a little dangerous.

Sure enough, he wraps one big hand around my throat, and though he doesn't squeeze, I feel the darkness behind the thin veil of his control, the threat implicit in the controlling gesture. At the same time, his other hand cups my breast, the rough edge of his thumb rubbing over my taut nipple. His eyes hold mine in the mirror, and I see a strange hunger in the silver depths, lust mixed with possessiveness and that intense something that makes my knees go weak and sends hot chills down my spine.

"Look at you," he breathes in my ear, and I tear my eyes away from his hypnotic gaze to focus on the picture we're presenting: him so big and lethally handsome, and me small and feminine, almost fragile in his dark embrace. "Look at how pretty you are, how sweet and soft and pure. That smooth skin of yours, so thin and delicate, so easily bruised..." He caresses my throat as I swallow, my pulse accelerating even more at his words.

"You know what I wonder sometimes?" he continues softly, and I grip the edge of the counter as his hard fingers pinch my nipple, twisting it with cruel purposefulness. "I wonder if I should put a chain around this pretty neck, lock you to me and throw away the key. Would you cry then, ptichka? Would you rage?" He nips at my earlobe, his white teeth scraping across my skin as his hand moves down from my breast to cup my sex. "Or would you secretly like it?"

I suck in a breath, trembling, so hot I could burst into flames. The picture he's painting is both terrifying and arousing, as darkly erotic as the image in the mirror. With his arms around me, I can smell the leather of his jacket, feel the metallic zipper against my back, and a sense of acute vulnerability washes over me as his fingers part my wet folds and touch my clit, the sharp lash of pleasure exacerbating the feeling of helplessness, of being completely out of control.

"Please." My voice shakes. "Please, Peter..."

"Please what?" His fingers push in and hook inside me, pressing against my G-spot as his teeth graze across my neck again. "Please what, ptichka? Please touch me? Please fuck me? Please go away?"

I squeeze my eyes shut. "Please fuck me." I'm past embarrassment, past denial. It feels like every cell in my body is pulsing with need, burning with the dark craving he awakens in me. Maybe under different circumstances, I'd stay strong, try to hold on to whatever passes for dignity, but I'm too exhausted—and too aware that this might be it.

Tonight might be our last time together.

"Open your eyes," he growls, and I dazedly obey, fighting the drugging pull of pleasure.

Peter's gaze is dark and intense in the mirror, his face taut with violent need. And underneath, I sense that unsettling *something,* that softness I can't quite define.

"Tell me, Sara. Tell me how you want me to fuck you. Do you want it rough"—his fingers thrust viciously into me—"or gentle? Hard"—he grinds the heel of his palm on my sex—"or soft?" Tempering the pressure, he lowers his head to lick my earlobe, his warm breath heating my skin as he rasps into my ear, "Do you want flowers and pretty words, ptichka? Or would you rather have something raw and real, even if society deems it wrong... even if it's not what you've always wanted?"

My breath hisses raggedly through my teeth as his thumb circles my clit, the heat thrumming under my skin making it hard to think. My inner muscles tighten around those rough, invading fingers, and I don't understand what he's asking, what he wants from me. I need more of that pain-edged pleasure, and at the same time, I need relief from the tension winding me tighter and tighter.

"Peter, please…" My heart is racing much too fast. "Oh God, please…"

His grip on my neck tightens as his fingers curl inside me, pressing against my G-spot again. "Tell me, and I'll fuck you." His teeth scrape across my neck, making me shudder from the sensation. "I'll give it to you exactly how you want it, fill your tight little pussy until you're begging for more. Tell me what you need from me, and I'll give it to you, Sara. I'll give you everything and more."

"Hard," I gasp out, my hands slipping off the counter-top edge to grip the steely columns of his jean-clad thighs. My sex clenches around his fingers as I press my pelvis against his hand, desperate for firmer pressure on my clit. I don't know what I'm saying, but I do know what I need. "Fuck me hard, Peter. Please…"

His jaw tightens, and I catch a glimpse of the darkness in the gray shimmer of his eyes. Abruptly, he releases me and sweeps his hand over the countertop, knocking off the toiletries. Spinning me around, he picks me up and sets me down on the cold granite, thighs spread wide. I blink at him, startled, but he's already unzipping his jeans and pulling me forward until my ass nearly hangs off the edge.

"Peter—oh God." I gasp as he spears into me, so thick and hard it feels like he's bruising my insides. He hasn't been this rough since our first time, but I'm so wet today the violent claiming doesn't scare me, the threat of pain only adding to the pleasure. Instead of clamping up, I remain pliant and soft around his cock, and as he sets a hard, driving rhythm, his fingers digging into the soft flesh of my ass, I wrap my legs around his hips and wind my arms around his neck, clinging to him like he's my anchor in a storm. And he might as well be. He fucks me with such fury I feel like a sliver in a hurricane, overwhelmed by his violence, tossed about by the waves of his lust. It's too much, too intense, but the helpless feeling only adds to the tension twisting inside me. With a scream, I come, clenching around him, but he doesn't stop. He keeps going until I come again, and then once more.

It's only when I'm slumped against him, panting and dazed from my third orgasm, that he lets himself go. With one final hard thrust, he comes, his pelvis grinding against mine as a deep groan rumbles up his throat. I feel his cock pulse inside me as I cling to him, trembling, and my sex clenches one last time, squeezing one last shudder of pleasure from my over-sensitized flesh.

Afterward, I'm so out of it I'm barely able to stand as he lifts me off the counter and sets me on my feet. Dimly, I realize I feel unusually wet between my legs—drenched, really—but it's not until Peter steps back and I feel the wetness slide down my thigh that I understand where it's coming from.

"Oh God." My eyes drop to his cock—still semi-hard and glistening with our combined moisture. "Peter, we—"

"Forgot to use a condom? Yes."

He doesn't sound particularly concerned. Instead, as I watch in horrified shock, he casually washes himself, tucks his cock back into his jeans, and zips up the fly. Then he wets a washcloth and gently wipes the semen off my thighs.

"There, all set." He drops the washcloth in the sink, his eyes gleaming as he turns toward me. "Don't worry. You just had your period, so we shouldn't be in the danger zone yet. And I'm clean; I always use condoms and get tested regularly. I assume the same is true for you?"

"Right." I stare back at him, shaken both by the occurrence and his attitude. Theoretically, we should be safe, but the mere fact that it happened, with *him*... My head resumes its painful throbbing, and my exhaustion returns, multiplied tenfold. How could I have been so negligent? With George, I'd always gone out of my way to remind him to use condoms, and during the so-called danger zones, we often skipped intercourse altogether, not wanting to chance the fifteen-percent condom failure rate until we were ready to have a baby. However, with my husband's killer, I haven't been nearly as careful, having sex at all times of the month. And now this...

It's like some sick part of me wants me to be tied to him, to perpetuate this mockery of a relationship.

"We should be fine then," Peter says, stepping closer to me. "Though..." He pauses, staring down at me with a speculative expression.

"Though what?" I ask when he remains silent. My heart is hammering with a dull, fast rhythm. "Though what?"

"Though I wouldn't mind." His words are light, casual, but there's no trace of humor in his voice. "Not with you."

"You—what?" My headache intensifies, my skull feeling like it wants to implode. He can't possibly mean what he's saying. "Why wouldn't you—? That makes no sense!"

"Does it not?" A glimmer of amusement now appears in his eyes. "Why, ptichka?"

"Because... because you're *you*." My voice is choked with disbelief. "You drugged and tortured me before killing my husband and forcing your way into my life. I don't know what you're imagining here, but we're not dating. This is not some kind of love story—"

"No?" His expression hardens, all hints of amusement disappearing. "Then what do you think it is that I feel for you? Why can't I go a single hour without thinking about you, wanting you... fucking *craving* you? You think it's lust that keeps me here, day after day, when the whole world is out for my head and my men are crawling up the walls from boredom?" He steps even closer, and my breathing speeds up as his palms slap against the counter on both sides of me, caging me against the sink. His eyes glitter fiercely as he leans in, his voice roughening. "You think I'm here instead of hunting down the last *ublyudok* on my list because I can't get enough of your tight little pussy?"

My face burns as I stare up at him, the vulgarity of his words intensifying my confusion. I don't know what to say, how to take it all in. He sounds angry, yet what he's saying makes it seem almost as though—

"Yes, I see you understand." His mouth curves in a dark, mocking smile. "It might not be a love story for *you*, ptichka, but as fucked up as it is, that's precisely what this is for me. I started off hating you, but somewhere along the way, you've become the only thing that matters to me, the only person I still care about. And yes, that means I love you, as wrong as that may be. I love you, even though you were *his*... even though you think I'm a monster. I love you more than life itself, Sara, because when I'm with you, I feel more than agony and rage—and I want more than death and vengeance." His chest expands with a deep breath, his expression turning somber as he says quietly, "When I'm with you, ptichka, I'm living."

I'm not aware that I'm crying until his face blurs in front of my eyes. My chest is too tight, my breaths too shallow. I've known that Peter is obsessed with me, but I've never imagined that in his mind, that obsession equals love, that he wants some kind of real future with me... one where we're together as a family.

A future where FBI agents aren't about to storm through the door.

"Don't cry, ptichka." His thumb strokes over my wet cheek, and I see the mocking smile return to his lips. "This doesn't change anything. You can still hate me. Just because I love you, I'm not any less of a monster—and I'm not going to disappear from your life."

But you are. I want to scream out the truth, but I can't. I can't warn him, even though my heart feels like it's tearing apart. I don't love him—I can't—but it hurts as though I do, as though losing him will be the worst thing ever. A choked sob rips from my throat, then another, and then I'm in his arms, clasped securely against his chest as he carries me out of the bathroom.

When he reaches my bed, he sits down, holding me on his lap, and I cry, my face buried against his neck as he strokes my back, slowly, soothingly. He's right; his confession of love shouldn't change anything, but somehow, it makes things worse. It makes me feel like I'm losing something real… like I'm betraying him and *us*.

How can a monster hold me so tenderly? How can a psychopath love?

My skull feels like it's being sawed open from the inside, my headache worsened by my crying, and I push at Peter's chest, twisting out of his embrace—only to fall onto the bed, whimpering as I clutch my temples.

He leans over me, concern darkening his features. "What's the matter, ptichka?" he asks, stroking my arm, and I manage to mutter something about a headache before squeezing my eyes shut. What I'm feeling is more along the lines of a migraine, but I'm in too much pain to explain.

The bed dips as he rises to his feet, and I hear footsteps as he walks out of the room. A couple of minutes later, he returns with Advil and a glass of water. I pry open my swollen eyelids long enough to swallow the medicine, and then I close my eyes again, waiting for the violent drumbeat in my skull to quiet to a manageable roar.

I expect him to leave then, or to get in bed with me, or whatever he was planning to do, but instead, I hear the bathroom door open, and a minute later, a cool, wet towel covers my eyes and forehead, bringing with it a welcome sliver of relief.

Once again, he's taking care of me, giving me comfort when I need it most.

The tears return, trickling out from under the towel as he tucks the blanket around me and sits on the edge of the bed, his hand slipping under my neck to massage the tense muscles in my nape. It's torture of a different kind, this tender care of his. It soothes my headache but intensifies the searing pain in my chest. I've been fooling myself when I called what we have a sick fantasy. It might be sick, but it's real, and when he's gone, I *will* miss him, just like I missed him when he went to Mexico. It's not love I feel for him—love can't be this dark, this illogical and insane—but it *is* something.

Something other than hate, something deep and disturbingly addictive.

A dog barks in the distance, and I hear a car door slam. It's most likely my neighbors on the next block over, but my heart still jumps, my stomach churning as I picture a SWAT team busting through my door and gunning down Peter at my bedside. It plays like a movie in my mind: the black-clad figures rushing in, the bullets tearing through the bedsheets, the pillows, his chest, his skull...

Bile surges up my throat, my head all but exploding with agony.

Oh God, I can't do it.

I can't stay quiet and let it happen.

"Peter..." My voice trembles as I ball my hands under the blanket. I know I will regret this in a thousand different ways, but I can't stop the words from spilling out. "You've been spotted. They're coming for you."

His hand on my nape stills mid-stroke, then resumes its gentle massage.

"I know, ptichka," he murmurs, and I feel his lips brush against my wet cheek as something cold and hard pricks my neck. "I know they are."

Lethargy rushes through my veins, and with strange relief, I realize that this is it.

He knew about the FBI all along.

He knew, and I'll never be free again.

CHAPTER 45
PETER

"Hurry," Anton hisses from the passenger-side front window as I approach the SUV, carrying Sara's blanket-wrapped body against my chest. "Did you not get any of my messages? They're less than ten blocks out."

I tighten my grip on my human bundle. "I couldn't leave until I learned what I needed."

"What's that?" Yan asks, opening the back door from the inside. He scoots over, and I climb in, being careful not to bump Sara's head as I bring her into the car.

It's bad enough she had a headache when I drugged her.

Ignoring Yan's question, I settle Sara's unconscious figure between us and shut the door before catching Ilya's gaze in the rearview mirror. "To the airport. Make it fast."

"On it," Ilya mutters, slamming on the gas, and we torpedo forward, zooming down the quiet suburban street.

"What did you need to learn?" Yan persists, glancing at Sara's face—the only part of her not wrapped in the blanket. With her thick lashes fanning out over pale cheeks, she looks like a sleeping Disney princess, and I don't blame my teammate for the flicker of interest on his face.

I don't blame him, but I still want to kill him.

"Something to do with her?" he continues, oblivious, then looks up at my face and blanches.

"Yes." My voice is jagged ice. "Something to do with her."

He nods, wisely looking away, and I wrap my arm around Sara's shoulders, arranging her comfortably against me. In the distance, I hear sirens, accompanied by the roar of helicopter blades, but despite the approaching danger, I feel calm and content.

No, more than content—happy.

Sara warned me.

She chose me, when she had every reason not to. She might not love me yet, but she doesn't hate me, and as I hold her tight, breathing in the delicate fragrance of her hair, I'm certain that one day, she *will* love me—that one day I'll have all of her.

She warned me—she chose to be mine—and now she'll stay that way.

I love her, and I'm going to keep her.

No matter what it takes.

Thank you for reading! If you would consider leaving a review, it would be greatly appreciated. Peter & Sara's story continues in *Obsession Mine*. If you'd like to be notified when it's out, please sign up for my new release email list at http://annazaires.com/.

If you enjoyed *Tormentor Mine*, you might like the following books:

- *The Twist Me Trilogy* – Julian & Nora's story, where Peter appears as a secondary character and gets his list
- *The Capture Me Trilogy* – Lucas & Yulia's story
- *The Mia & Korum Trilogy* – A dark sci-fi romance
- *The Krinar Captive* – A standalone sci-fi romance

Collaborations with my husband, Dima Zales:

- *Mind Machines* – An action-packed technothriller
- *The Mind Dimensions Series* – Urban fantasy

- *The Last Humans Trilogy* – Dystopian/post-apocalyptic science fiction
- *The Sorcery Code* – Epic fantasy

Additionally, if you like audiobooks, please visit my website to check out this series and our other books in audio.

And now please turn the page for a little taste of *Twist Me*, *Capture Me*, and *The Krinar Captive*.

EXCERPT FROM
Twist Me

Author's Note: *Twist Me* is a dark erotic trilogy about Nora and Julian Esguerra. All three books are now available.

———————

Kidnapped. Taken to a private island.

I never thought this could happen to me. I never imagined one chance meeting on the eve of my eighteenth birthday could change my life so completely.

Now I belong to him. To Julian. To a man who is as ruthless as he is beautiful—a man whose touch makes me burn. A man whose tenderness I find more devastating than his cruelty.

My captor is an enigma. I don't know who he is or why he took me. There is a darkness inside him—a darkness that scares me even as it draws me in.

My name is Nora Leston, and this is my story.

———————

It's evening now. With every minute that passes, I'm starting to get more and more anxious at the thought of seeing my captor again.

The novel that I've been reading can no longer hold my interest. I put it down and walk in circles around the room.

I am dressed in the clothes Beth had given me earlier. It's not what I would've chosen to wear, but it's better than a bathrobe. A sexy pair of white lacy panties and a matching bra for underwear. A pretty blue sundress that buttons in the front. Everything fits me suspiciously well. Has he been stalking me for a while? Learning everything about me, including my clothing size?

The thought makes me sick.

I am trying not to think about what's to come, but it's impossible. I don't know why I'm so sure he'll come to me tonight. It's possible he has an entire harem of women stashed away on this island, and he visits each one only once a week, like sultans used to do.

Yet somehow I know he'll be here soon. Last night had simply whetted his appetite. I know he's not done with me, not by a long shot.

Finally, the door opens.

He walks in like he owns the place. Which, of course, he does.

I am again struck by his masculine beauty. He could've been a model or a movie star, with a face like his. If there was any fairness in the world, he would've been short or had some other imperfection to offset that face.

But he doesn't. His body is tall and muscular, perfectly proportioned. I remember what it feels like to have him inside me, and I feel an unwelcome jolt of arousal.

He's again wearing jeans and a T-shirt. A gray one this time. He seems to favor simple clothing, and he's smart to do so. His looks don't need any enhancement.

He smiles at me. It's his fallen angel smile—dark and seductive at the same time. "Hello, Nora."

I don't know what to say to him, so I blurt out the first thing that pops into my head. "How long are you going to keep me here?"

He cocks his head slightly to the side. "Here in the room? Or on the island?"

"Both."

"Beth will show you around tomorrow, take you swimming if you'd like," he says, approaching me. "You won't be locked in, unless you do something foolish."

"Such as?" I ask, my heart pounding in my chest as he stops next to me and lifts his hand to stroke my hair.

"Trying to harm Beth or yourself." His voice is soft, his gaze hypnotic as he looks down at me. The way he's touching my hair is oddly relaxing.

I blink, trying to break his spell. "And what about on the island? How long will you keep me here?"

His hand caresses my face, curves around my cheek. I catch myself leaning into his touch, like a cat getting petted, and I immediately stiffen.

His lips curl into a knowing smile. The bastard knows the effect he has on me. "A long time, I hope," he says.

For some reason, I'm not surprised. He wouldn't have bothered bringing me all the way here if he just wanted to fuck me a few times. I'm terrified, but I'm not surprised.

I gather my courage and ask the next logical question. "Why did you kidnap me?"

The smile leaves his face. He doesn't answer, just looks at me with an inscrutable blue gaze.

I begin to shake. "Are you going to kill me?"

"No, Nora, I won't kill you."

His denial reassures me, although he could obviously be lying.

"Are you going to sell me?" I can barely get the words out. "Like to be a prostitute or something?"

"No," he says softly. "Never. You're mine and mine alone."

I feel a tiny bit calmer, but there is one more thing I have to know. "Are you going to hurt me?"

For a moment, he doesn't answer again. Something dark briefly flashes in his eyes. "Probably," he says quietly.

And then he leans down and kisses me, his warm lips soft and gentle on mine.

For a second, I stand there frozen, unresponsive. I believe him. I know he's telling the truth when he says he'll hurt me. There's something in him that scares me—that has scared me from the very beginning.

He's nothing like the boys I've gone on dates with. He's capable of anything.

And I'm completely at his mercy.

I think about trying to fight him again. That would be the normal thing to do in my situation. The brave thing to do.

And yet I don't do it.

I can feel the darkness inside him. There's something wrong with him. His outer beauty hides something monstrous underneath.

I don't want to unleash that darkness. I don't know what will happen if I do.

So I stand still in his embrace and let him kiss me. And when he picks me up again and takes me to bed, I don't try to resist in any way.

Instead, I close my eyes and give in to the sensations.

All three books in the *Twist Me* trilogy are now available. Please visit my website at http://annazaires.com to learn more and to sign up for my new release email list.

EXCERPT FROM CAPTURE ME

Author's Note: *Capture Me* is a dark romance trilogy featuring Lucas & Yulia. It parallels some of the events in the *Twist Me* trilogy. All three books are now available.

She fears him from the first moment she sees him.

Yulia Tzakova is no stranger to dangerous men. She grew up with them. She survived them. But when she meets Lucas Kent, she knows the hard ex-soldier may be the most dangerous of them all.

One night—that's all it should be. A chance to make up for a failed assignment and get information on Kent's arms dealer boss. When his plane goes down, it should be the end.

Instead, it's just the beginning.

He wants her from the first moment he sees her.

Lucas Kent has always liked leggy blondes, and Yulia Tzakova is as beautiful as they come. The Russian interpreter might've tried to seduce his boss, but she ends up in Lucas's bed—and he has every intention of seeing her there again.

Then his plane goes down, and he learns the truth.

She betrayed him.

Now she will pay.

He steps into my apartment as soon as the door swings open. No hesitation, no greeting—he just comes in.

Startled, I step back, the short, narrow hallway suddenly stiflingly small. I'd somehow forgotten how big he is, how broad his shoulders are. I'm tall for a woman—tall enough to fake being a model if an assignment calls for it—but he towers a full head above me. With the heavy down jacket he's wearing, he takes up almost the entire hallway.

Still not saying a word, he closes the door behind him and advances toward me. Instinctively, I back away, feeling like cornered prey.

"Hello, Yulia," he murmurs, stopping when we're out of the hallway. His pale gaze is locked on my face. "I wasn't expecting to see you like this."

I swallow, my pulse racing. "I just took a bath." I want to seem calm and confident, but he's got me completely off-balance. "I wasn't expecting visitors."

"No, I can see that." A faint smile appears on his lips, softening the hard line of his mouth. "Yet you let me in. Why?"

"Because I didn't want to continue talking through the door." I take a steadying breath. "Can I offer you some tea?" It's a stupid thing to say, given what he's here for, but I need a few moments to compose myself.

He raises his eyebrows. "Tea? No, thanks."

"Then can I take your jacket?" I can't seem to stop playing the hostess, using politeness to cover my anxiety. "It looks quite warm."

Amusement flickers in his wintry gaze. "Sure." He takes off his down jacket and hands it to me. He's left wearing a black sweater and dark jeans tucked into black winter boots. The jeans hug his legs, revealing muscular thighs and powerful calves, and on his belt, I see a gun sitting in a holster.

Irrationally, my breathing quickens at the sight, and it takes a concerted effort to keep my hands from shaking as I take the jacket and walk over to hang it in my tiny closet. It's not a surprise that he's armed—it would be a shock if he wasn't—but the gun is a stark reminder of who Lucas Kent is.

What he is.

It's no big deal, I tell myself, trying to calm my frayed nerves. I'm used to dangerous men. I was raised among them. This man is not that different. I'll sleep with him, get whatever information I can, and then he'll be out of my life.

Yes, that's it. The sooner I can get it done, the sooner all of this will be over.

Closing the closet door, I paste a practiced smile on my face and turn back to face him, finally ready to resume the role of confident seductress.

Except he's already next to me, having crossed the room without making a sound.

My pulse jumps again, my newfound composure fleeing. He's close enough that I can see the gray striations in his pale blue eyes, close enough that he can touch me.

And a second later, he does touch me.

Lifting his hand, he runs the back of his knuckles over my jaw.

I stare up at him, confused by my body's instant response. My skin warms and my nipples tighten, my breath coming faster. It doesn't make sense for this hard, ruthless stranger to turn me on. His boss is more handsome, more striking, yet it's Kent my body's reacting to. All he's touched thus far is my face. It should be nothing, yet it's intimate somehow.

Intimate and disturbing.

I swallow again. "Mr. Kent—Lucas—are you sure I can't offer you something to drink? Maybe some coffee or—" My words end in a breathless gasp as he reaches for the tie of my robe and tugs on it, as casually as one would unwrap a package.

"No." He watches as the robe falls open, revealing my naked body underneath. "No coffee."

All three books in the *Capture Me* trilogy are now available. If you'd like to find out more, please visit my website at http://annazaires.com.

EXCERPT FROM THE KRINAR CAPTIVE

Author's Note: *The Krinar Captive* is a full-length, stand-alone scifi romance that takes place approximately five years before *The Krinar Chronicles* trilogy.

Emily Ross never expected to survive her deadly fall in the Costa Rican jungle, and she certainly never thought she'd wake up in a strangely futuristic dwelling, held captive by the most beautiful man she'd ever seen. A man who seems to be more than human…

Zaron is on Earth to facilitate the Krinar invasion—and to forget the terrible tragedy that ripped apart his life. Yet when he finds the broken body of a human girl, everything changes. For the first time in years, he feels something more than rage and grief, and Emily is the reason for that.

Letting her go would compromise his mission, but keeping her could destroy him all over again.

———————

I don't want to die. I don't want to die. Please, please, please, I don't want to die.

The words kept repeating in her mind, a hopeless prayer that would never be heard. Her fingers slipped another inch on the rough wooden board, her nails breaking as she tried to maintain her grip.

Emily Ross was hanging by her fingernails—literally—off a broken old bridge. Hundreds of feet below, water rushed over the rocks, the mountain stream full from recent rains.

Those rains were partially responsible for her current predicament. If the wood on the bridge had been dry, she might not have slipped, twisting her foot in the process. And she certainly wouldn't have fallen onto the rail that had broken under her weight.

It was only a last-minute desperate grab that had prevented Emily from plummeting to her death below. As she was falling, her right hand had caught a small protrusion on the side of the bridge, leaving her dangling in the air hundreds of feet above the hard rocks.

I don't want to die. I don't want to die. Please, please, please, I don't want to die.

It wasn't fair. It wasn't supposed to happen this way. This was her vacation, her regain-sanity time. How could she die now? She hadn't even begun living yet.

Images of the last two years slid through Emily's brain, like the PowerPoint presentations she'd spent so many hours making. Every late night, every weekend spent in the office—it had all been for nothing. She'd lost her job during the layoffs, and now she was about to lose her life.

No, no!

Emily's legs flailed, her nails digging deeper into the wood. Her other arm reached up, stretching toward the bridge. This wouldn't happen to her. She wouldn't let it. She had worked too hard to let a stupid jungle bridge defeat her.

Blood ran down her arm as the rough wood tore the skin off her fingers, but she ignored the pain. Her only hope of survival lay in trying to grab onto the side of the bridge with her other hand, so she could pull herself up. There was no one around to rescue her, no one to save her if she didn't save herself.

The possibility that she might die alone in the rainforest had not occurred to Emily when she'd embarked on this trip. She was used to hiking, used to camping. And even after the hell of the past two years, she was still in good shape, strong and fit from running and playing sports all through high school and college. Costa Rica was considered a safe destination, with a low crime rate and tourist-friendly population. It was inexpensive too—an important factor for her rapidly dwindling savings account.

She'd booked this trip *before*. Before the market had fallen again, before another round of layoffs that had cost thousands of Wall Street workers their jobs. Before Emily went to work on Monday, bleary-eyed from working all weekend, only to leave the office the same day with all her possessions in a small cardboard box.

Before her four-year relationship had fallen apart.

Her first vacation in two years, and she was going to die.

No, don't think that way. It won't happen.

But Emily knew she was lying to herself. She could feel her fingers slipping farther, her right arm and shoulder burning from the strain of supporting the weight of her entire body. Her left hand was inches away from reaching the side of the bridge, but those inches could've easily been miles. She couldn't get a strong enough grip to lift herself up with one arm.

Do it, Emily! Don't think, just do it!

Gathering all her strength, she swung her legs in the air, using the momentum to bring her body higher for a fraction of a second. Her left hand grabbed onto the protruding board, clutched at it... and the fragile piece of wood snapped, startling her into a terrified scream.

Emily's last thought before her body hit the rocks was the hope that her death would be instant.

———

The smell of jungle vegetation, rich and pungent, teased Zaron's nostrils. He inhaled deeply, letting the humid air fill his lungs. It was clean here, in this tiny corner of Earth, almost as unpolluted as on his home planet.

He needed this now. Needed the fresh air, the isolation. For the past six months, he'd tried to run from his thoughts, to exist only in the moment, but he'd failed. Even blood and sex were not enough for him anymore. He could distract himself while fucking, but the pain always came back afterwards, as strong as ever.

Finally, it had gotten to be too much. The dirt, the crowds, the stink of humanity. When he wasn't lost in a fog of ecstasy, he was disgusted, his senses overwhelmed from spending so much time in human cities. It was better here, where he could breathe without inhaling poison, where he could smell life instead of chemicals. In a few years, everything would be different, and he might try living in a human city again, but not yet.

Not until they were fully settled here.

That was Zaron's job: to oversee the settlements. He had been doing research on Earth fauna and flora for decades, and when the Council requested his assistance with the upcoming colonization, he hadn't hesitated. Anything was better than being home, where memories of Larita's presence were everywhere.

There were no memories here. For all of its similarities to Krina, this planet was strange and exotic. Seven billion *Homo sapiens* on Earth—an unthinkable number—and they were multiplying at a dizzying pace. With their short lifespans and the resulting lack of long-term thinking, they were consuming their planet's resources with utter disregard for the future. In some ways, they reminded him of *Schistocerca gregaria*—a species of locusts he'd studied several years ago.

Of course, humans were more intelligent than insects. A few individuals, like Einstein, were even Krinar-like in some aspects of their thinking. It wasn't particularly surprising to Zaron; he had always thought this might be the intent of the Elders' grand experiment.

Walking through the Costa Rican forest, he found himself thinking about the task at hand. This part of the planet was promising; it was easy to picture edible plants from Krina thriving here. He had done extensive tests on the soil, and he had some ideas on how to make it even more hospitable to Krinar flora.

All around him, the forest was lush and green, filled with the fragrance of blooming heliconias and the sounds of rustling leaves and native birds. In the distance, he could hear the cry of an *Alouatta palliata*, a howler monkey native to Costa Rica, and something else.

Frowning, Zaron listened closer, but the sound didn't repeat.

Curious, he headed in that direction, his hunting instincts on alert. For a second, the sound had reminded him of a woman's scream.

Moving through the thick jungle vegetation with ease, Zaron put on a burst of speed, leaping over a small creek and the bushes that stood in his way. Out here, away from human eyes, he could move like a Krinar without worrying about exposure. Within a couple of minutes, he was close enough to pick up the scent. Sharp and coppery, it made his mouth water and his cock stir.

It was blood.

Human blood.

Reaching his destination, Zaron stopped, staring at the sight in front of him.

In front of him was a river, a mountain stream swollen from recent rains. And on the large black rocks in the middle, beneath an old wooden bridge spanning the gorge, was a body.

A broken, twisted body of a human girl.

The Krinar Captive is now available. Please visit my website at http://annazaires.com to learn more and to sign up for my new release email list.

ABOUT THE AUTHOR

Anna Zaires is a *New York Times, USA Today,* and #1 international bestselling author of sci-fi romance and contemporary dark erotic romance. She fell in love with books at the age of five, when her grandmother taught her to read. Since then, she has always lived partially in a fantasy world where the only limits were those of her imagination. Currently residing in Florida, Anna is happily married to Dima Zales (a science fiction and fantasy author) and closely collaborates with him on all their works.

To learn more, please visit http://annazaires.com.